JAMAICAN DRAW

By Marilinne Cooper

Dedicated to Celeste Andries, "Aunt C,"
who opened her Jamaican heart and home
to me in the 1970s and 80s

PREFACE

In the early 1980s, the island of Jamaica was still in the early stages of becoming a mass market tourist destination. In those last years before the internet began connecting the planet into one worldwide web of cultural fusion, it was still possible to journey around this roiling island nation and find people and places of pure Caribbean character and unspoiled natural beauty. It was a country I learned to love for its spirited personality and welcoming warmth, despite the pervasive poverty and unstable political and economic climate.

Twenty-five years ago, I decided to write a mystery story set against this lively, pulsing backdrop, melding the tropical temperament of traditional Jamaican values and villages with the country-changing revolution brought on by the roots and reggae movement. I wanted to bring together the dark mystery and steamy passion I had experienced during my visits and create a tempestuous tale that traveled from one side of the island to the other. When I began to reread and edit the manuscript a quarter-of-a-century later, I realized that, beneath its coming-of-age story, it captures a time and place worth remembering and sharing.

If nothing else, it can be enjoyed as a good beach read or as a diverting escape on a cold winter's night.

CHAPTER ONE

Every time the minibus stopped, the air inside became suffocating, hot and still. The dust from the road drifted through the open windows, settling on the sticky arms and legs of the passengers, most of whom were familiar with the route as well as the routine. They patiently tolerated the afternoon heat as the driver's helper unloaded baskets and parcels for departing travelers and took their crumpled bills and change. The school children, who packed their tiny bodies into the aisle between the seats, always seemed to slip away without paying.

Carson closed his eyes as drops of sweat continued their endless journey down his face. Wedged between two enormous Jamaican women, there was no possibility of his moving a muscle until one of them got off the bus. In his mind he could almost hear the sucking sound of damp shoulders pulling apart, and he sighed with the anticipation of it. He vowed that the next time he traveled to Savannah-La-Mar to paint the vegetable market ladies, he would bide his time and wait until sundown to catch a big bus back to Negril.

The driver seemed to have disappeared. Carson craned his neck to look out the open side door as the man emerged from a little roadside store carrying an open bottle of Red Stripe beer. Draining half of it, he swung back into his seat, started the engine and called for his helper. Without looking behind, he put the bus in gear and pulled slowly out into the road.

Instantly the long-legged teenage boy was back at his station. He pulled the sliding door half shut and squatting in the open doorway he called, "NE-gril! NE-gril!" in case anyone in town had not realized where the bus was headed.

Carson found it hard to believe that at least seven passengers had disembarked at the last stop, not to mention the school children. The bus seemed just as crowded as before. Looking around to see if there were any telltale empty spaces, he noticed now that he was not the only white person on board. Squashed into a corner of the last row of seats, with her face turned towards the open window, was a woman with extraordinarily bright red hair that seemed to dominate her appearance. The long, curly locks were clipped up with a barrette high on her head; he imagined how heavy it must feel in the afternoon heat.

As he watched, the Jamaican woman next to her made a quick comment in the thick native patois which he still found incomprehensible. He was amazed to see the red-haired woman laugh and reply in the same intonations. He thought perhaps she too was Jamaican, but her next statement was in broad American English and dispelled any notion that she might be West Indian. Probably just another tourist with a good ear for the local lingo.

He was surprised again when the bus stopped a mile or so before reaching Negril to discharge her and her companion. He watched as they slung bags over their shoulders, lifted baskets of food to their heads and began a slow, swaying walk up a dusty road leading into the countryside. Carson was fascinated; the woman's pale skin was lightly tanned in a healthy way, not fried to a leathery brown like most of the sunbathers on the beach. The sturdiness of her body seemed to belie the softness of her features and skin. She looked like a French peasant woman or an Irish milkmaid...

The sudden jerk of the bus starting up jolted him back to his stifling reality. Maybe he would look her up one day and do some sketches. He was sure any child on that road could point out where the red-haired lady lived.

Putting her out of his mind, he thought ahead to the steamy bakery in the shopping plaza where he would pick up a loaf of freshly baked bread and a couple of callaloo patties to munch on during the mile long walk up the beach to Mango Grove.

Another mile down the road, the bus stopped at its final destination - Negril. Peeling himself from the plastic seat, he crawled out and finally stretched his lean body to its full length of six foot, four inches. From the back of the bus he retrieved his backpack and paint box. His long legs took him quickly across the roundabout to where the road from Sav-La-Mar met the road to Montego Bay. He neatly avoided most of the hustlers and drug dealers who hung around this busy street area, which was the closest thing Negril had to a town square.

The atmosphere was so very different from Sav-La-Mar, particularly the way the people dressed. Nowhere else in Jamaica did women walk down a street or into a shop wearing only a skimpy bikini and flip-flops. In fact, he noticed that most of the native women wore only dresses, never pants, and absolutely no shorts. Of course, no place else in Jamaica had a seven-mile-long beach either, which accounted for the touristy but relaxed air of Negril. He'd heard stories from the diehards who came back year after year about the way it had been ten years earlier, back in the seventies, before the rapid growth of hotels and other attractions that now lined the beach and the cliffs.

"Seven miles of unspoiled white sand," George would say. "Only two or three hotels and a handful of cottages. Just the little Wharf Club Grocery and some local woman selling vegetables next to it in an open acre of beaten dirt with baby goats and pigs scrounging for garbage. Hell, there wasn't even a public telephone in town! You had to take the bus twenty miles to Sav to make your goddam return plane reservations. Nothin' up the West End but two or three restaurants and Rick's Café. It's just not like it used to be. Hell, any old jerk can come here now in 1986 and have a vacation. Used to be it was work to get here and hard work to live here. We were travelers, not tourists -"

"George, shut up!" Emma would always cut him off. "I'm sick of your stories of the good old days in Negril. If you hadn't told everyone in Manhattan about how wonderful this place was, it might still be a well kept secret. You can feel personally responsible for the decline of Negril if you want to, but I happen to still enjoy myself when come here and so do our children. Next year why don't you stay home?"

Carson laughed to himself at the mental image of George and Emma, two aging hippies from New York City, sitting in their beach chairs in the sun, arguing the pros and cons of economic development in third world countries while their children played Frisbee in the waves. They'd been spending winters at Mango Grove for over a decade, supposedly they'd even given Miss Faye and Mr. Wilford several thousand dollars so they could build cottages and get their little business rolling. George and Emma ran some sort of art gallery and import business that they could leave every winter for months at a time and Carson had a sneaking suspicion what some of their import business probably included.

As he walked up the beach toward home, he savored all the elements assaulting his senses; the soft lapping of the warm sea water at his feet, the spiciness of the callaloo patty still on his tongue, the beauty of the long bay with its clean white sands and clear turquoise waters. It reminded him of all the things he loved about this turbulent island. He never felt ambivalent about Jamaica; one moment he could be deeply in love with the country, the next he could feel pure hatred and anger. But the intensity of everything here was precisely what attracted him.

Unfortunately, Jamaican culture had not had the same effect on Molly. Molly had not been very happy since she joined him here three weeks ago. Carson liked the scene at Mango Grove. He relished the relaxed atmosphere that Miss Faye and Mr. Wilford had created with the help of their yearly regular visitors. He enjoyed the young Jamaican men who strolled through the yard and stopped to chat in the doorways of the little wooden guest cottages which had been randomly built in the shade of the ancient mango trees. He appreciated the way people took care of you once they trusted you. When he stepped inside the gate, he felt protected.

Molly, on the other hand, never felt safe. She didn't trust any of the men or boys who hung around. "It's not their fault that they're poor and unemployed and hungry," she had said. "But it means that our money looks awfully good to them, and would look even better if it were in their own pockets." And it was true that her watch had disappeared on her first day there.

She didn't trust them sexually either. She would never venture any farther than the bathroom alone at night and she never felt comfortable swimming topless on the beach the way so many other young women did in Negril. "They're always watching me, Carson. Everywhere I go, someone's eyes are always on me."

Much of the time Carson felt the same way himself. There did always seem to be someone standing in a doorway or squatting in the shade of a bush with nothing to do but watch who went by. He told Molly not to worry, that no one would hurt her. He never mentioned how he had been questioned as to whether she was his woman.

"She is your property, mon," he had been assured. "We don't steal what another mon control."

Molly would go through the roof if she knew he had made it clear that she was indeed his property. But he had only done it for her own safety.

Molly didn't like the way the rooms were arranged either. Each little cottage was divided into two separate guest quarters with their own doors. Unfortunately, the dividing wall stopped about two feet short of the ceiling, with a thin latticework covering the remaining area. Most Jamaican houses were built this way to let the air circulate more freely from room to room. Unfortunately, it was not only the air that moved between the two living spaces. All noises and lights had to be shared, like it or not. Every creak of an iron bed, any whispered endearment between lovers, each midnight cigarette or three a.m. homecoming was mutually experienced by the neighbors on the other side of the wall.

She would lie in bed quietly cursing when their neighbor, Alex, and his girlfriend, Fawn, would come home in the middle of the night, fight, and make up, and then have sex with the lights on. At these times Carson would quietly stroke her hair and try to comfort her by telling her how many poor Jamaican families had even less privacy than this. That, if they were Jamaicans, they would probably be sharing their bed with two children and their room with at least four other family members. Molly, of course, did not find his reasoning comforting at all.

When Carson had chosen Jamaica as the place he wanted to spend the winter, he had assumed Molly would just want to come along. They had been inseparable since college, now two years behind them, and had never really thought about the future without each other. But now Molly's inability to figure out what she wanted to do with her life seemed to be causing them to slowly drift apart.

Carson had taken a few years off to travel and sort himself out before he had gone to college. Even though he had studied Elementary Ed and had planned a career as an art teacher, all he really wanted to do was paint. The previous fall he had sold a couple of his paintings for more than he'd ever believed anyone would pay for the work of an unknown artist. On an impulse he bought a round trip ticket to Montego Bay and made plans to stay away for four months. Although he had lived most of his life in Florida, he found that the bright tropical colors and sultry island lifestyle attracted him much more than the pinks and aquas of Miami ever could.

Molly had never been as focused as Carson had. She had gone directly from high school to college, where she'd met Carson. He had become her focal point. She took liberal arts classes and didn't really know what she wanted to do when she graduated. She ended up just following Carson to Jacksonville and getting a waitress job in a natural food restaurant. She had been so in love with Carson at the time that nothing else had really mattered.

Strangers often mistook them for brother and sister. They had the same sun-bleached, straight blond hair and golden brown skin, but that was where the similarity ended. For all of Carson's towering leanness, Molly was barely over five feet tall; while his brown eyes were flecked with wild amber, hers were almond-shaped and the color of the Caribbean Sea. But it was their playful interaction, so comfortable and careless, that made them seem like siblings, and which had kept their relationship so easygoing - up to the point that Carson had decided to go to Jamaica.

Molly hadn't really wanted to go and for the first time had asserted her right to say so. She decided to stay on in their apartment and join Carson after Christmas when she could take a month's vacation from her job.

As soon as she was alone, she began to see how empty her life was when it stood on its own. Her dissatisfaction with her job and herself grew, and by the time she arrived in Negril she was more insecure and unsettled that she'd ever been in her life. She and Carson began to disagree on almost everything, and instead of being the inseparable twosome, they started spending more and more time apart.

As he approached Mango Grove, Carson thought about their relationship. He didn't understand why Molly should suddenly feel she needed so much space to herself, or why she now needed to do something meaningful with her life. They'd argued before he'd left for Sav-La-Mar that morning; he'd wanted her to come with him, but she hadn't wanted to wait around all day in a hot town while he painted. Instead, she planned to walk up to the West End; she wanted to see the Negril lighthouse on the cliffs. She had heard it was peaceful and beautiful there.

"Pssst! Carson!"

He looked around. A short, muscular Jamaican with wild dreadlocks, wearing only sunglasses and red bathing trunks, was gesturing to him from a pile of coconut husks at the edge of the sand.

"How do you know me, mon?" Carson stopped a few feet from him.

"Jazmo tell me you might want to buy some good ganja."

Carson laughed and shook his head and started walking again.

"Not me, mon. Jazmo told you wrong."

"Is cool. Must mean some other somebody."

He did not let trivial hustling of that sort bother him. If he did, he would never be able to stay in Jamaica.

Inside the gate at Mango Grove, he could see two young Americans with backpacks getting off the bus from the airport. He did not need to see their luggage to know they were "fresh". Their pale white skin said it all.

He could hear their voices as he got closer. They were engaged in a loud discussion with Alex and by the stance of their bodies, Carson thought that there seemed to be quite a bit of tension between them. Alex was a hefty fellow with a Mediterranean complexion and a few unruly wisps of hair that were always a little greasy. Every winter he ran a glass-bottomed boat business on the beach and stayed at Mango Grove. At the moment, he did not have a pleasant expression on his face.

"Everybody is always looking for Fawn," he was snarling. "Every Jamaican claims to be her relative or her closest friend. Why should I believe your story, man?"

One of the newcomers started visibly forward with his fists clenched. Although he was tall and slim, he had a cherubic face displaying a Boticelli-like beauty framed in soft, dark curls. His friend quickly grabbed his arm.

"Well, when you see her," he said after visibly gaining control of himself, "tell her Robinson Dubois is staying at Paradise Park and will be back tonight." Then he hoisted his pack onto his back and headed off in the direction of the campground he had mentioned.

His friend hurried after him. Carson heard him say, "Jesus, Rob, you didn't have to get so hyped up at that jerk," and then the rest of their conversation went down the beach with them.

From the look on Alex's face, Carson didn't think this would be just another peaceful evening on the beach at Mango Grove.

His uneasy feeling became even greater when he unlocked the door to his room and discovered that all of Molly's things were gone. There was a note propped up on his pillow.

"Dear Carson, A single room opened up today on the other side of the Grove and I told Miss Faye I wanted it for a few days. I really need some space to myself right now. You understand, don't you? Besides, I'm tired of listening to you know who and could use some real sleep. See you tonight at the dance. Love, Molly."

He threw the note on the floor and stretched out on the cool sheet. He was suddenly too exhausted even for a swim. Closing his eyes, he slept.

"Hey! Carson!"

The voice came through the window next to Carson's right ear, just loud enough to wake him. When he opened his eyes, the room was in complete darkness. For a moment he could not get his bearings as to what time of day or night it was.

"Who's there?" Picking up his head, he peered out into the shadows.

"Jazmo. Miss Faye send me to find out if you want her to set up one plate of food fah you. She closin' up de kitchen now."

"Yeah, sure. I'm starved. Thanks."

"Alright den. Soon come wit' it, mon." Jazmo's steps retreated into the night.

Carson sat up and stretched. He reached above his head, grasping the string that turned on the single light bulb that was screwed into the ceiling. His alarm clock said it was almost eight o'clock. He'd been asleep for hours.

Slinging a towel over his shoulder, he stepped out of the doorway and headed for the outdoor showers. The night air was refreshing but cool, and once inside the corrugated tin walls of the shower, he slipped off his shorts and stepped quickly under the warm water.

Taking a nighttime shower was one of the things he enjoyed most in Jamaica. He loved how the moonlight reflected off the large elephant ear palm leaves that hung over the shower walls and how warm the water felt after sitting in the pipes all day, baking in the hot sun. By morning the water would be quite cool again, but during the day the sun would shine down into the stalls, warming the bathers as well.

He returned to his room, a towel wrapped around his waist, wet hair dripping down his back. Jazmo was waiting in the doorway with a plate of "steam" fish and rice. While Carson sat on the doorstep devouring his supper, Jazmo squatted on the ground next to him, smoking a large spliff and making conversation.

"Big dance tonight at Tree House, eh? Are you going?"

"Might as well, I took a long enough nap." Dances and concerts in Negril didn't usually start until after eleven, finishing up at three or four in the morning. Most of the time, Carson could not even stay awake until they started.

"Yes, mon. Your woman is gone now?"

"No, she's just moved out." Carson picked at a bone in his fish.

"Yes, I know this. So now she is not your woman, right?" There was something about the way he pronounced the word "wooo-monn" that sounded almost sinister to Carson.

"I don't know anymore," he replied finally. I think she probably still is, but she is just taking a vacation from me right now." Putting the plate down on the floor behind him, he looked up and grinned. "Why? You want to cruise chicks with me at the dance tonight, Jazmo?"

Jazmo could not keep from laughing and the smoke he'd been holding in his lungs billowed out around his head. "No, mon. I'm cool. I need to keep an eye on my sister. She is trouble, dat one."

"Fawn?" Carson forgot at times that Jazmo and Fawn were related. Their statuses at Mango Grove were so different. Jazmo lived in a ramshackle hut behind the kitchen which he had built for himself. In exchange for his squatter's rights, he helped out around the yard in a handyman capacity. He also made a little money by hiring himself out as a guide to tourists who did not feel confident traveling about alone, but Carson knew that his real income came from his ganja patch up in the hills.

"Of course, Fawn," Jazmo was answering. "Men will be fighting about Fawn tonight."

She was really Jazmo's half-sister. They had different fathers, same mother, but that was the way of so many Jamaican families that no talked about "half-sisters" or "stepfathers." Jazmo's skin was a dark, rich black; Fawn's was a pale coffee color. Although they had spent their early childhood together in Kingston, as they grew older they also grew apart. Jazmo spent most of his time on the street corners, while Fawn was quickly recognized as the beauty she was growing up to be. Her high grades in school matched with her natural sophistication and attractiveness soon won her several beauty contests and a scholarship to a university in the U.S.

When she finally returned to Jamaica, it was as a high paid fashion model on a location shoot for Vogue, after which she received dozens of offers for jobs. Eventually her working and school visas ran out and she was forced to return home to reapply for another one. Government papers could take months to come through, so while she waited she did a few commercials for JBC-TV and then settled in Negril for the winter at the urging of Jazmo.

Carson had seen the looks on the faces of men and women alike when Fawn appeared on the beach. Her leopard print bikini blended in with the color of her skin so that the spots seemed to be just a natural extension of the animal sensuality she exuded. Her hair and makeup were professionally perfected to enhance her subtle seductiveness.

It was hard to understand what a woman like Fawn was doing hanging around with a man as surly and unpleasant as Alex. Carson had not wasted much time trying to figure it out, but he did know that Alex was extremely protective of Fawn and tried to keep all the beach riff-raff out of her life.

"What men will be fighting?" Carson stood up. Crossing the small room, he began rummaging through dresser drawers for some clothes to wear.

"You know one man named Robinson Dubois?"

Carson frowned. The name was familiar. Then he remembered. "I saw him this afternoon talking to Alex. Who is he?"

"Fawn went to university with him. He was her boyfriend there for some years. Him still love her so much, mon! I can see it in his eyes when he ask for where she gone. Alex – well, Alex is not happy to see him."

Yes, Carson knew that much already. Alex had a violent temper, even when it came to Fawn. The thin wall between their rooms could attest to that.

"You see how him act towards just any mon on de beach," Jazmo continued. If someone bother his woman, he swat them down like a fly. But this one – he is not just another pesty insect, mon. No, sir." He picked up the plate that Carson had left in the doorway. "This finish now?"

"What? Oh, sure. Thanks for bringing that over, Jazmo." Carson had been looking for a particular T-shirt which he now suspected Molly of taking with her.

"Then I carry it back." Jazmo turned to leave and then stopped in the doorway, giving a low whistle. "Come, mon, and look on this pretty sight."

Carson joined him in the doorway. Across the yard, a light had gone on in another room where the curtains had not been drawn. The window was like a screen at a drive-in movie theatre; they could see the two women inside getting undressed and moving about the room half naked.

"I bet you do this every night, don't you, Jazmo?" Carson said to humor him.

"No, mon. Dis is not MY doorway. You should have to pay more for a room wit a view, you know." Jazmo laughed at his own joke never taking his eyes off the window. Eva and Irena, the two German girls who occupied the room, were sitting on one of the beds, sharing a cigarette and chattering away in their own language. Eva was rubbing sunburn ointment on Irena's bare back while they talked and then went on to rub some of the lotion into her own burnt breasts.

"Dat one is for me tonight," Jazmo said softly almost to himself.

Carson went back inside and left Jazmo to his harmless voyeurism. He had little doubt that Jazmo would get what he wanted from Eva this evening. In the two weeks since they'd arrived, the two German girls had become notorious for their topless sunbathing and their promiscuous interest in sex with Jamaican men. They were on a never-ending search for the "Big Bamboo" as it was jokingly referred to in Negril. He had even seen Alex leaving their room at dawn one morning, but that was not a fact he had shared with anyone except Molly. She was outraged and disgusted, of course, and it did nothing to raise her already low opinion of Alex.

Thinking about Molly made Carson angry and sad. Slipping on a faded Hawaiian shirt without bothering to button it, he stuffed his wallet into a back pocket and left the room abruptly. Locking the door, he hung the key on its string around his neck and then he strode off into the darkness in the direction of the beach.

He didn't care what Molly was doing. He was going to have a good time tonight.

CHAPTER TWO

Carson had no idea what time it was getting to be and, even though the question ran through his mind, he knew he didn't care. After several beers and a few puffs of strong ganja, he didn't really care about anything except the pulsing beat of the music and the way it made him want to dance.

He had spent the band's first set with Jazmo and the two German girls, Eva and Irena. But after they had danced together several times, he could sense Irena beginning to come on to him and he found himself desperately scanning the crowd for any sign of Molly.

He finally saw her sitting lonely and forlorn on a bench at the back of the crowd, so familiar with her French-braided hair and sunburned nose. She wore a gauzy flowered skirt covered and a tiny red knit camisole that accentuated her petite figure. He used her as an excuse to break out of the uncomfortable situation with Irena.

But when he finally made his way to her through the dancing bodies, he realized her loneliness had been an illusion. She wasn't by herself at all, but part of a group from Mango Grove that included George and Emma, Fawn, a construction worker from Texas named Dallas, and a couple of other young men whom he quickly recognized as Robinson Dubois and his friend.

It was easy to look casual as he strolled forward to join them. Molly was deeply engrossed in a conversation with George and did not even look up as he approached.

"There's a lighthouse on the exact opposite end of Jamaica from Negril, you know," George was saying. "The easternmost tip, Morant Point it's called.

I've never been there, it's really off the beaten track. However, I have been to the one in Port Royal, right by the Kingston Airport."

Molly finally noticed that Carson had joined them. "Hi, Carson. George was just telling me about other lighthouses on the island. I really liked the one I visited today. I can't imagine the others can be any more special. How was your trip to Sav-La-Mar? Did you get some good drawings at the market?"

Molly seemed excessively bright and chatty. It was her party personality, Carson had seen it before, and the empty banana daiquiri glass in her hand spoke for itself. He loved her when she loosened up like this. As he bent down to kiss her lightly on the lips, he pried the glass out of her fingers.

"My day was fine," he replied. "Let me get you another."

"But I've already had three-"

"Then four will make you feel even better." As he turned towards the bar, he caught a glimpse of Alex out in the dance area with Eva. He wondered what had happened to Jazmo's hot plans for the evening.

When he returned, Fawn was just slipping off with Robinson Dubois, her arm in his. They were deep in earnest conversation, unaware of Alex's volatile presence as they passed by in full view.

"What's the story with Fawn and that guy?" Carson asked quietly as he sat down next to Molly. George and Emma had disappeared, leaving Molly sitting with Dallas and Robinson's friend. Dallas was in his usual stoned stupor, his chin resting on his chest, his huge belly showing between his shirt and pants, the tattoos on his biceps in repose.

"Robinson? I guess they went to college together in New Hampshire somewhere. He seems like a nice guy. He and Henley are camping out at Paradise Park." She nodded to indicate that Henley was the young man with the shock of short brown hair that seemed to stand on end, the one who he'd seen with

Robinson before. "I don't understand why Fawn would leave him for someone as sleazy as Alex." Molly shook her head and downed half her drink.

"Well, you don't know what might have gone down between Fawn and that guy. Maybe they weren't even lovers."

Molly raised her eyebrows and gave him a "don't be ridiculous" look. Before the conversation could go any further, Henley leaned over and invited her to dance with him. "Sure," she replied, and without even a backward glance at Carson, she disappeared into the throng of dancers.

Carson sat there, inwardly fuming. She was definitely declaring her independence from him and he couldn't figure out why. He thought they had a great relationship.

He drank his beer and aimlessly watched the crowd. Suddenly there was a lot of shouting. Even though Carson was an eyewitness to what happened next, he was never really sure who had started it. People stopped dancing and moved away, giving the four people who were punching and pulling at each other lots of space to do it in.

When he finally focused in on the tableau, he saw Alex sitting on top of Robinson with Eva and Fawn trying to pull him off while they both shouted at each other. Eva seemed to be yelling German obscenities and Fawn was letting loose a stream of Jamaican patois. Robinson appeared to have the beginnings of a shiner and Alex had several long scratches on his face.

To add to the confusion, Henley pushed through the crowd and was soon down on his knees next to Robinson's head. It sounded like he was alternately comforting him and scolding him before he shifted his attention to Alex.

"Get off of my friend, you bastard," he said clearly, getting to his feet.

"What, are you in this with him?" Alex's large hands were instantly off of Robinson's throat and his fists were up and ready in Henley's direction. "I suppose he let you in on a piece of the action, huh?" Upon hearing that remark, Robinson, his upper body now free, landed a punch in Alex's stomach, which set the girls to shrieking again. At this point, several large Jamaicans, some of whom worked at the Tree House, and some who were just bystanders, descended on the five and separated them.

"We cahn't have violence here, you know," one of them said. "You will have to leave now."

"You can't do this to me, man," Alex protested as he was escorted to the exit. "I'm a business owner here, you can't treat me this way."

"Come back when you can behave, blood clot!" shouted a loose-jointed man with long matted dreadlocks. "We want peace here in Jamaica! Go back to your own country and be foo-foo!" He continued ranting until he too was thrown out.

Jazmo had stopped them from evicting Fawn; he also changed the ugly tone of things by announcing in a loud tone of voice just who she was. Because she was a national heroine of sorts, several people immediately crowded around her and the evening tenuously resumed its festivity.

A light touch on his arm gave Carson a start. It was Molly, looking tired and scared. "Would you walk me home?" she asked in a tiny voice.

"Of course," he replied. Leaving his unfinished beer on the bench, he put his arm around her shoulders. "Beach or road?"

"Beach."

As they walked silently towards the dark stretch of shoreline, the loud music began to fade into the background. It was so late that most other places were closed for the night, the tourists asleep in their cottages and hotel rooms. The warm surf lapped softly at their feet and they walked in their usual positions, Carson in the water and Molly on the sand. Because of his long legs, even the occasional small wave breaking on the shore did not get his shorts wet.

He could tell Molly was upset so he didn't press her to talk. When they finally arrived at Mango Grove, he automatically led her to his door and she did not protest. "You want to stay here with me tonight?" he asked softly, drawing her in close to his chest.

"I don't know, I am paying for that other room," she murmured as she held him tightly with her small arms.

"So what? It's only money." Carson took the key from around his neck and unlocked the door.

"Well, maybe just for a little while," she said, following him in and sitting on the bed.

"It'll be morning soon anyhow." He unbuttoned his shirt and hung it up.

"So what?" Falling back on the pillows, she closed her eyes.

"So if you stay for a little while, you'll be staying all night." He looked at her lying there, the nipples on her small breasts showing hard through the thin shirt. He was ready to make love to her but he could tell that she was already drifting away into banana daiquiri dreamland.

"You don't make any sense, Carson," she mumbled, barely moving her mouth. And then her breathing changed and she was asleep.

He carefully removed her skirt and underpants, but taking her shirt off while she slept was too complicated. Pulling the sheet up, he crawled in beside her.

He had only been asleep for a few minutes when loud voices out in the yard awoke him. He was about to get up and ask whoever it was to be quiet, when the shouting became even louder and angrier. By then he recognized the voices, Jazmo and Fawn, and after the evening's events Carson didn't dare speak up for fear of becoming involved.

His sleepy brain was having trouble understanding the fast paced words that were being slung back and forth in heavy Jamaican vernacular. The gist of it seemed to be Jazmo calling Fawn every kind of imaginable word that meant "whore" and Fawn defending herself by calling him a hypocritical liar.

"Never should have invited you come here. You gone back Kingston where your wicked kine belong!"

"De pot call de kettle black! You ganja seller will end up in jail for sure. Your badness show big in dis nice place!"

"Is not ganja what cause de trouble tonight. Is your fucking cunt is -" A loud crack cut him off as Fawn's hand slapped him across the face.

"And don't you dare to strike me back," she said quietly, switching to the perfectly modulated British accent of well-bred Jamaicans. "Or you will have not just your sister but all of Jamaica fighting against you." The door of the adjoining room slammed shut, shaking the little building.

"Bumba clot!" Jazmo shouted, kicking the door and stumbling off in the darkness to his shack. Carson had not quite figured out what that dreaded expression meant, but he knew it was a terrible thing to call anyone, especially your sister.

A few moments later he heard Fawn softly crying into a pillow. Then silence. Rolling over, he threw an arm around Molly's waist and floated back into sleep only to be abruptly awakened a few minutes later by the door to the other room slamming again and the light that suddenly spilled over the wall.

"So there you are, you bitch! Didn't expect to find you here." Something slammed against the wall – a shoe, a body, a chair. Carson groaned and tried to cover Molly's ears, but it was too late. Her green eyes had already blinked open and her lips were becoming thin with anger.

"Alex, what are you doing? Get away from me!" The sound of cloth ripping made Molly sit bolt upright in bed. "Stop it! I haven't done anything wrong! You don't own me! You're drunk and disgusting. Why don't you just go to sleep and leave me alone?"

"I'll leave you alone when I'm done showing you whose woman you are!" The sound of Alex's pants falling to the floor was followed by the sound of the bedsprings sighing under his heavy weight.

"No, Alex, get off of me! I don't want to! You're hurting me!"

Molly didn't wait to hear anymore. She was out of bed and out of the door, oblivious to the fact that she all she had on was a shirt. Carson started to go after her, but by the time he reached the doorway with her skirt in his hand, she was back. Wrenching it from his grasp, she pulled it on and grumbled, "I'll see you in the morning."

Carson watched her disappear into the darkness. He couldn't blame her for leaving. He stood there listening to the rhythmic creaking of the bedsprings and the occasional sob that escaped from Fawn. It was a miserable and personal exhibition for anyone to hear.

He saw the light go on across the way in the German girls' room. He didn't know who they had with them, but from the sound of the raucous laughter he suspected it might be Dallas.

It was just one of those Negril nights when everything seemed raw and immoral and unfriendly. When you had to wait for the quiet, rosy glow of dawn to make it all right again. The darkness was full of moving shadows and whispers, and he had the distinct feeling that there was someone out there watching him. A dog barked somewhere nearby.

Wearily, Carson lay back down and waited for sleep to overtake him again.

"Miss Faye! Miss Faye! Come quick!"

Once more Carson was rudely awakened by the sound of shouting in the yard. The room was full of light; the alrm clock said seven.

"Miss Faye! Miss Faye!" The voice belonged to Neville, Miss Faye's eight- year-old grandson. "Hurry! Down by de beach! Hurry!"

Carson sat up and looked out the window by his head. His few hours of rest had left him feeling more tired than if he hadn't slept at all. Leaning against the window frame, he watched Neville drag his grandmother by the hand towards the gate that led to the beach. They stopped just inside the fence and looked down at the ground.

"Lord have mercy!" Miss Faye exclaimed, dropping to her knees to look at something. "Neville, run get Mr. Alex, quick, boy!"

Carson saw the top of the child's head flash by just below his window and then heard the banging on Alex's door. "Mr. Alex, wake up! Miss Faye say you must come! Something happen to Fawn. Something bad."

There was no response and Neville banged on the door again, repeating his urgent message. Finally there was a grunt as Alex found his way to the door. "What are you raving about at this time of morning?" he growled.

"Fawn, she down by de gate. Miss Faye say you must come. Fawn not moving, man. She just lie there, still."

A chill went up the back of Carson's neck and he shivered. Wide awake now, he quickly pulled on a pair of shorts and followed Alex and Neville across the grass still wet with dew.

"Oh, my god, who did this?" Alex went down on the ground next to the sprawling form of Fawn's body. "WHO DID THIS?"

Despite the genuine grief and despair in Alex's voice, Carson had a hard time dismissing the memory of Alex's angry words just a few hours before. But his thought process ended as he reached the body and his eyes took in the ugly reality.

Fawn was wearing a thin white cotton robe, tied loosely around her waist. It had fallen open well above the thigh to expose one long, coffee-colored leg. The dozens of tiny braids in her expensively dressed hair lay spread out on the ground around her head, the brightly colored beads at the end of each braid catching the first rays of the morning sun as it came through the mango trees. Her neck was a mass of red bruises and the expression on her face was strained and contorted. There were marks in the dirt near her hands; it looked as though she had dragged her long red fingernails across the ground before finally letting go.

Carson's artistic eye for detail quickly took in the whole picture. The sandy ground definitely showed signs of a struggle and the proximity to the fence and gate opened up several questions. Fawn's attire indicated she had probably been headed to the bathroom which was the opposite direction of the beach.

His thoughts were interrupted by an anguished cry from behind him. Jazmo stood a short distance away, wearing only a pair of brightly colored briefs, toothbrush in hand, his eyes bulging in disbelief.

"I knew it mean trouble," he said in a hoarse voice, edging forward. "But dis is more den trouble, man. Dis is murder. Murder!" He shouted the last word as if it were a battle cry and then flung himself down in the dirt next to his sister. He held her lifeless hand and moaned softly, rocking back and forth.

"Jazmo, you mustn't touch her before police come!" Miss Faye warned him in a low voice. "You fingerprints on her now. Neville, go quickly and tell Mr. Wilford to call police station."

Carson felt helpless as he watched the two grieving men and yet he could not keep himself from remembering the harsh words they had both had with Fawn only hours before. Who could have been angry enough to do such a thing – or did anger have nothing to do with this? He turned from the scene and leaned against the gate, looking out at the beach and the sea.

Early risers were already moving about. Fishermen. Joggers. A father walked by with a baby in a backpack. A man swept seaweed off the sand in front of a small hotel. Life went on for these people, peacefully ignorant of the crime on the other side of the fence. He longed to join them but he knew he could not be peaceful or ignorant this morning.

A light tap on the shoulder startled him. "Coffee ready." Miss Faye's daughter, Mayrene, was standing behind him holding out a fresh cup of coffee sweetened with canned condensed milk. She tried hard not to look at the dead body as she ran back to the kitchen.

A few sips of the steaming hot liquid seemed to clear his head. Molly. He had to find Molly and make sure she was all right. He flew across the yard to the tiny cottage surrounded by a thick croton hedge.

Peeking through the louvered window, he could see her sleeping on the single bed across the room. He waited until he was sure he could see her chest rising and falling with each breath before he relaxed his vigil and moved around the building to sit on the cinder block which served as a doorstep. Leaning back against the door, he finished the rest of his coffee and closed his eyes. It was going to be a long day.

CHAPTER THREE

By mid-morning the police had come and gone, leaving behind a false sense that nothing much had changed and that life would go on in its usual way at Mango Grove. Everyone staying there knew that things would no longer be the same, but it was too soon to know exactly in what way they would be different.

Carson sat on a wooden bench by the edge of the sand. His sketchbook was lying idly at his side; his mind throbbed and he felt dazed as he stared blankly out to sea. He could not stop the continuous reel of the morning's events as they replayed in his mind.

The police had questioned everybody at Mango Grove, rapping on doors and waking up the late night party-goers, many of whom had just barely gone to bed. Several people had recounted the fight they had seen taking place at the Tree House and their stories cast an ugly light on Alex's innocent grief. An extensive questioning of Alex seemed to reveal very little – after coming home, he had passed out very quickly, not to be roused until Neville awoke him at dawn.

Molly's sleepy eyes had met Carson's as Alex was making his loud declaration of innocence, but Carson had shaken his head ever so slightly in response. Her eyes became angry and questioning as she set her mouth in a grim line and crossed her arms over her chest.

He was uncomfortable knowing so much about Alex's personal relationship with Fawn and he didn't know how much of it needed to be revealed at this important moment. He really believed that Alex had been in a dead and drunken sleep after his sexual foray with Fawn. But it was also true that Carson himself had been out so soundly that he had not heard Fawn get up and leave for the bathroom in the pre-dawn hours, had not heard the door creak or drag across the floor.

He was glad Molly had already been asleep when Jazmo had brought Fawn home and he hoped he had been the only one who had heard their argument. Unfortunately, it turned out that they had also passed by George and Emma's window and Emma, not yet asleep, had heard their angry voices. She hesitated before relating this to the police and rightly so. In the end it was Jazmo they took away to the station for further questioning, an angry Jazmo, fighting every step of the way to the police Land Rover. He was tossed unceremoniously into the back and the door was locked behind him.

George was furious at the way Jazmo had been treated. He paced back and forth in the sand by the open dining pavilion where they had all been assembled. "It's only because he's a poor Jamaican," he fumed. "Even if they suspected a white tourist they would probably never lock him up, they'd just deport him. It's the unfair bureaucracy of this third world country. I've known Jazmo for years – he wouldn't hurt a flea. He's a gentle guy and he loved his sister."

When the police left, he got dressed and followed them, walking the two miles to the Negril police station, hoping to bail Jazmo out. Carson didn't know much about the judicial system of the country, but he had a feeling it was a futile attempt.

Emma felt miserable and wished she hadn't said anything. Now she was busy consoling her very distressed children, Mickey and Hanalei, who didn't understand what had happened or why nobody wanted to talk to them about it.

Alex, of course, had lashed out some angry words about Robinson Dubois and his friend Henley. He advised the police to check out their stories as to where they had been around 5 a.m. A few of the red-jacketed officers had dutifully tromped up the beach to Paradise Park while the others removed the body and roped off the area where the murder had been committed.

Still dressed in her clothes from the night before, Molly had stormed off down the beach, but Carson had quickly caught up with her. He put his arm around her but she shook it off, moving away from him. Her face was red and her eyes were full of tears.

"How could you?" she accused him, stopping finally and turning her body away, holding a hand under her running nose. "How could you let that slimy Alex get away with what he did?"

"Now hold on a second, Molly, you don't have any proof that Alex did anything. All you heard was what we've heard every night from the other side of that wall – Alex banging away at her-"

"But he was forcing her! He hurt her! He's disgusting! I hate him!" People ambling down by the water's edge turned to look at her as she shouted so vehemently.

"But what you didn't hear was how fast they both went to sleep. Don't forget, you left."

Molly was silent for a moment, biting her lip and wiping her eyes with the back of her hand. "I did think I heard someone out in the bushes by the showers," she admitted finally. "It could have been a dog or it could have been someone waiting for Fawn." She shivered suddenly. "Carson, I don't want to stay in Negril anymore. I'm scared. I want to go home."

Carson held her close for a minute and said nothing. He didn't blame her, he felt almost the same way. "Nobody's out to kill you," he said eventually, looking down at her tear-stained face. "But if you feel like you want to go home, don't let me stop you." Putting his arm around her shoulders, he guided her back in the direction of Mango Grove. "Go have a shower and get cleaned up. You'll feel better and then we can talk about it some more."

But after Molly had washed, she put on her jade green bikini and headed up the beach alone, her head down, watching her own feet wade through the clear green water. Carson was left sitting there on the bench under the drooping leaves of an old royal palm, watching the beach scene in front of Mango Grove take shape for the day.

Although there were people sunbathing to the right and left of him, the patch of sand directly in front of Mango Grove was fairly empty today, the pallor of Fawn's death still hanging over most of the guests. He watched Mickey and Hana as they tried cut the top off a water coconut with a small machete, much to the amusement of Neville, who sat off to one side waiting for them to call for his expert assistance.

Mickey was thirteen and Hana was twelve but, in the usual way of puberty, Hana was two or three inches taller than her older brother and had already developed the long-limbed, round-breasted figure of a young adolescent. They had been named after two favorite destinations of their well- traveled parents - the Greek island of Mikonos and the little town of Hanalei on the north coast of Kauai in the Hawaiian Islands.

Having spent several winters of their life in Negril, the two were perfectly at ease spending days on the beach, living in nothing but bathing suits. Carson didn't quite understand how they managed to spend so many weeks out of school each winter, but somehow the family pulled it off.

The only other occupants of the immediate vicinity were Eva and Irena, stretched out on their beach towels, soaking up the sun in full bare-breasted glory. Eyes closed, they were oblivious to the uncomfortable stares and drooling leers they elicited from passersby.

They were not the only topless sunbathers on the beach; it was just that they were such big women, the kind with large thighs and thick waists and muscular arms and hands, not to mention their close-to-enormous breasts. Most women with bodies like that did not expose so much of them in public, let alone so flagrantly. Carson thought it was kind of nice that it was okay to do that sort of thing here. He had grown used to seeing their display of well-oiled skin over the past several days and it did not disturb him anymore.

"Mmm-mmm! A sight for sore eyes, ain't it?" Dallas had straddled the bench next to him and was boldly feasting his eyes on the two German girls. "I'll tell you, Carson, last night those two gave me one of the finest nights in the sack I've ever experienced. Mmm-mmm!" He smacked his lips again.

Carson looked at the man sitting next to him with distaste and then burst out laughing. There was something about Dallas. His stringy mouse-colored hair grew long around his bald pate and the effect was accentuated by a sun visor emblazoned in red with the legend, "This Bud's for You." He had a marijuana leaf tattooed on one arm and an eagle on the other and around his navel was a wreath of thorny roses which was generally in prominent view as it hung over the waistband of his cut-off jeans. He was a gung-ho All-American redneck who loved getting high and consequently he was best buddies with many of the Jamaican hustlers on the beach.

"I'm telling you, man, you should let those girls show you the secrets of Deutschland. The two of them are really something!"

"You had them both at once?" Carson's curiosity got the better of him and the question slipped out.

"You betcha. It wasn't planned that way, I guess Eva had been expecting Alex to show up, I guess they had set up something after they got thrown out of the dance. He went back to his room to get

35

something and then never came back, and well, she joined in with us like a wildcat in heat!"

Despite the erotic images that were dancing in his mind, Carson had to laugh again at Dallas's unabashed enthusiasm.

"Yeah, she was mad as a hornet," Dallas continued. "I guess she's had the hots for Alex for some time now, but never had the opportunity to get him away from Fawn." His tone of voice changed. "Guess she can have him now if she wants."

Carson frowned at the implications of what Dallas was saying. He looked at Eva's large strong hands as they lay limp on the towel on either side of her. It didn't seem possible but –

He shook his head to clear the image. He wasn't a private detective, he was an artist. He didn't have to spend all day thinking about who might have murdered Fawn. He just needed to stay out of the way if anyone was thinking about doing it again.

Dallas pulled out a cigarette out of a pack of Craven A's and lit one up. "Yeah, old Jazmo and I were supposed to take a little trip up to the hills today," he went on. "He was gonna show me a real pretty ganja plantation he has. Guess that trip is postponed for a while."

From a little cook shack about fifty yards down the beach, Carson could hear the familiar strains of a Bob Marley tune. It seemed that everywhere you went in Jamaica there was always music – if you stood still you could hear the distinctive bass line particular to reggae coming from somewhere. He liked to think of it as the heartbeat of the island, deep, dark and pulsing. But today he was feeling irritable and it just bothered him.

The sunlight reflected off the brilliant red-gold hair of a woman walking by, holding the hands of two small Jamaican children. With a start, Carson realized it was the same woman he had seen the previous afternoon on the bus trip from Sav-La-Mar.

Before he even realized what he was doing, he had picked up his sketchbook and was following her down the beach towards town.

Molly had wandered a good distance up the beach, deep in her own thoughts, paying no attention to the beauty of the morning or the heat of the sun as it beat down on her already bronzed shoulders and back. She was still angry with Carson and although she had thought a walk would help her let off steam, it only seemed to intensify her feelings.

She had never put it into words before, not even in her head, but she was beginning to realize what bothered her about Carson. He was a great visual artist, a superb observer of detail, but that's all he was – an observer. He always sat on the edge of things, watching what was going on, forming pictures in his brain that would later materialize into images on paper. But he never got involved; he wouldn't stick his neck out or jump into the thick of a situation.

She didn't know whether he was right or wrong about not telling somebody the argument between Alex and Fawn. She thought that if you knew something like that, something important and incriminating, that you were supposed to speak up. Alex's abusive behavior scared her and she did not want to hang around Mango Grove much longer if he was staying on.

"Molly!"

Startled, she looked up to see who could possibly be calling her name. Shading her eyes, she saw Henley sitting in the sand with an open bottle of Red Stripe between his legs and a paperback open to the first page. His "fresh" white skin was already beginning to show signs of burning although it was not even noon yet. He was wearing vintage-style black sunglasses, brightly patterned swimming trunks and the goofy, euphoric look of somebody spending their first day in warm, eighty-five degree sun after leaving the brutal winter weather of New England. He motioned for her to come over.

"Hey, how you doin'?" he asked, patting the sand next to him and gesturing for her to sit down. "Pretty heavy what happened this morning, huh?" It hadn't seemed to have affected his mood, however. "Must be kind of depressing down at Mango Grove. Rob's back at the tent just kind of moping around." He indicated the direction of the campsite with this thumb.

Molly hadn't realized that she'd walked as far as Paradise Park. Through the trees she could see the bright reds, blues and oranges of the nylon tents. It was a romantic idea, camping out on the beach in Jamaica, and before she had come here it might have appealed to her. But now all she could think of was how vulnerable she would feel with only a thin piece of water-repellent cloth separating her from the dark night of Negril and its potential murderers.

"Gee, you've really got a great tan," Henley was saying, comparing his leg to hers. "You been here all winter?"

"No, I'm from Florida," she explained. "Seems like I've always had a tan." She laughed, but just a little. "How's Robinson doing? He must be pretty upset."

"Upset is too mild a word for it. Suicidal would be more appropriate. Actually, I ought to check up on him. Why don't you come along? He would probably appreciate some female sympathy."

She tried to decline, she wanted to say that she was in no mood to show compassion for anyone else. But Henley was already heading for the campground, expecting her to follow him, and she decided that she was being foolish and selfish.

Robinson was as bad off as Henley had described him. He was laying half in and half out of the tent, his head on an inflatable plastic pillow on the ground outside of the unzipped open flaps, his feet on the air mattress inside. He was staring sightlessly at the sky and trees above him, and he was completely naked.

"Rob, put some clothes on, we have company!" Henley called out to him as if he wasn't a mere three feet away. In the short twenty-four hours that she had known them and seen them interacting, Molly could already appreciate the deep friendship these two seem to have.

Robinson slowly turned his head until his bloodshot eyes focused in on them. One eye was puffy and purple around the edges from Alex's well-aimed punch the night before. "Oh, hi," he said in a dull voice. "How's the water, Henley?" He made no effort to get up.

"It's great! You should come down to the beach for a swim." Seeing that Robinson had no intention of moving, Henley reached inside the opening of the tent and threw a T-shirt over his lower half.

Something about the grief in Rob's face touched Molly. She sat down next to him and picked up his hand in her own. "I guess this must be pretty awful for you," she said. "You and Fawn must have been pretty close."

Rob's hand gripped Molly's tightly. "I was in love with her," he replied, closing his eyes at the pain of the memory. "We had such a great thing together – I don't know what she needed this Alex guy for. He seems like such a jerk. He's probably the one who killed her. The fucking police come here and question me like I'm some kind of criminal..." He choked on the words and a few tears ran from the corners of his eyes.

Henley stood off to one side, eating a peeled banana and trying to look nonchalant, as though he hadn't calculated exactly the effect that Molly's presence would have on his friend.

"They questioned all of us," she said softly. "It would only make sense that they would talk to you too."

Robinson sat up and wiped his eyes. "I'm sorry." He seemed to be apologizing in a sort of general way for his appearance and his behavior.

"Tell me what happened, would you? I've only heard about it from the police."

It wasn't easy for Molly to objectively discuss the events surrounding Fawn's murder, but she took a deep breath and tried anyway. His sorrowful brown eyes never left her face as she described what Fawn was wearing and where her body had been found, how Jazmo had been taken to jail and how George had gone after him. She found herself going on to tell him her own problems and how she had decided to leave the island as soon as possible and why.

"You shouldn't judge all of Jamaica by Negril alone," Robinson said to her, finally emerging from his funk. "The rest of the country isn't like this place. Last time I was here, I traveled to the eastern part of the island and it was very different. The people were friendlier and not so tourist-oriented, and the countryside was really beautiful. Supposedly Negril was more like that before it got so built up."

"So what are you saying – that I shouldn't leave Jamaica, just leave Negril?" It was a new thought and she tasted the words as she spoke them.

"Yeah, that's what I'm saying. Port Antonio – that's where you should go. You'd love Port Antonio. It's more like the rest of the West Indies are, I've been told. I've never been to any other island so I don't really know. Probably I ought to go with you. It would do me good to get away from here for a few days."

Rummaging around in the tent, he managed to pull on a pair of shorts and then stood up. "Actually," he continued, "while I was lying here this morning, I was thinking that I'd like to get in touch with Fawn's mother and find out when the funeral is going to be, and then Henley and I would take the bus down to Kingston for a few days." He looked at Henley questioningly.

"Kingston? What are you, insane?" Henley stared at him in alarm. "I mean, I know you're crazed with grief but even a crazy white man should know better than to show his white ass in Kingston!"

Molly watched as Rob and Henley faced each other and held a silent and steady gaze. Finally Robinson said, "Well, I'm going to Kingston. Henley can do what he wants," and turned away.

"Have you ever been to Kingston?" Molly asked hesitantly, not sure whether or not she should continue the conversation.

"Once, last year. Faye took me to her mother's house when we came down here on spring break together. And I'm still here to tell about it," he added with a meaningful glance at Henley.

"All right, all right. It would be an adventure. I'll go with you. So much for a relaxing vacation on the beach." He tossed the banana peel into the air. "I guess I'll hang up my sunglasses."

"We could meet you in Port Antonio next week some time," Robinson said to Molly. "If you're into it, that is."

"I am, I guess. I don't know, I hadn't really thought about it yet." The idea was beginning to appeal to her more and more. "Will I really like it better? Can you promise that?"

"Hell, yeah! Where's our map of Jamaica, Hen? Let's take the map and Molly out to lunch somewhere and show her what we're talking about."

Molly spent the rest of the day with them, having more fun than she'd had since she'd stepped off the airport minibus at Mango Grove. The three of them had an easygoing affinity, but mostly what she liked was how these two made things happen for themselves. They were the kind of guys who could enjoy their own company anytime anywhere. They told funny jokes and did ridiculous things and they were a refreshing change from Carson.

By the end of the day she felt good about herself for the first time in weeks. Robinson had convinced her to leave the next day for Montego Bay and then travel along the north coast via Ocho Rios all the way to Port Antonio and he assured her that she would not be raped or murdered along the way.

Henley had praised her privately for helping him lift Robinson out of his grief, although several times during the course of the day he had experienced, as was to be expected, deep relapses of depression and anger.

They walked her back to Mango Grove at sunset, planning to have breakfast together the next morning before she departed. When they left her at the gate, she watched them disappear down the beach in the fading daylight. She liked these guys – they were good, wholesome company and they didn't seem to want more than friendship from her.

As she headed back to her cottage, she wondered where Carson was and how he would take to her plans

CHAPTER FOUR

Carson had no problem keeping the woman with the brilliant hair in his view. With his lengthy strides he had trouble not overtaking her as she matched her steps to the pace of the two children. He had to keep finding reasons to stop and rest. He checked out some baskets that an old woman was selling beneath a palm tree; he bought a bottle of freshly squeezed orange juice and then sat down to drink it.

He followed her across the bridge over the Negril River. Once he was hidden in the crowd of people making their way through the center of town, it was easier to really study her. She was wearing a bright African print sarong over a shiny black one-piece swimsuit. Her hair was so long that it completely covered her bare back and he wondered how she kept from sitting on it.

When the trio crossed the street and headed towards the shopping center, Carson trailed about ten feet behind them, unnoticed. He walked idly up and down the aisles of the supermarket with a plastic grocery basket over his arm, pretending to be interested in neatly stacked jars of Grace guava jelly and mango chutney. He checked the difference in price between Blue Mountain Coffee and Salada brand, he read the ingredients on a can of Milo, and he actually put a colorful box of Breeze laundry detergent in his basket. As he rounded the corner by the bread, he bumped into the three of them looking through the blue and white boxes of Cremo milk, trying to find one that wasn't frozen solid.

"Excuse me," he mumbled. She nodded and smiled at him and then turned back to the task at hand. He felt foolish, and quickly walked, crimson-faced, to the check-out counter. He didn't know why he was doing this.

Leaving the supermarket, he crossed to the bakery and bought a cup of coffee. He drank it at an outside table, watching the human traffic move through the shopping center. There was a line of tourists waiting to trade their foreign currency in for Jamaican dollars at the Exchange. People were buying T-shirts, postcards and records, it was all just the same old thing. A thin, ancient Jamaican man with long, gray dreadlocks creeping out of his red, gold and black tam tried to sell Carson some hand-painted wooden buttons that said things like "Roots" and "Irie." He wondered if the man was a true Rastafarian; he looked too old to have been swept up in the recent Rasta mania that had attracted so many of the young men in Negril.

His thoughts were interrupted when the red-haired woman suddenly came into view as she and the children emerged from the grocery store. Tossing the half-filled cup of coffee into a nearby trashcan, he was off and following her again before he even realized what he was doing.

They were headed towards the West End this time. When they stopped at the post office, Carson sat on the wall outside and did a quick sketch of a man changing the flat tire of a motorcycle across the road. He glanced up just as the woman came out of the post office and thought he saw the flicker of a frown cross her face when she saw him sitting there. He continued working on his sketch until she was a good distance up the road. Then, ripping it out of the book, he went over to the man who was repairing his motorbike and handed him the picture.

"Thought you might like it," he called over his shoulder to the fellow who stood staring at it in surprise and delight. Once again his long legs carried him quickly to within a few hundred feet of the threesome he was tailing. The next time they stopped it was at a little sand beach just past the Negril Yacht Club, the only such beach on the west end of Negril, where the coral cliffs began to grow higher and higher as the road wound toward the lighthouse.

No one knew how the Yacht Club had earned its name because there was never a yacht in sight. The rocky reef on which the thatched roof establishment was perched made it even more of a joke because no sailor in his right mind would try to anchor a boat anywhere near the place. Carson knew there was a good view of the little beach from one of the seaside tables, so he ordered a beer and sat with his sketchbook open, watching the peaceful little scene in the sand.

Sometimes his sketch pad was all that kept him from feeling like a voyeur. But as he whiled away the afternoon, drawing what he observed, he began to feel closer and closer to the beautiful woman, and he knew he would have to overcome his shy nature and figure out a way to meet her.

There was an outdoor shower at the far end of the Yacht Club where it met the little sand beach. When it was time to leave, she packed up all their things and brought the children over to the shower to rinse off. Carson knew it was now or never. While she was rinsing the sand off the little girl's back, he motioned to the boy who stood dripping and shivering in his towel off to one side.

"Come here," he called. "I want to show you something." The three beers he'd had made him feel bolder than usual. He picked out a couple of his better sketches from the afternoon. Carson had been nowhere near close enough to have seen the details he had drawn, but still he had zoomed in like a telephoto lens, embellishing his outlines from memory and imagination.

The boy's eyes widened in amazement as Carson showed him the pictures. "It us!" he cried in delight. "You one artist man?"

Carson laughed. "Yes," he said. "Now dry off your hands and take these pictures over to her, what's her name?"

"The white woman, she Gwen. You give these to her?"

Carson showed the boy how to hold the drawings carefully by the edges. Then he leaned back in his chair to watch Gwen's reaction. She was rinsing the sand and sea water out of her long, glorious hair and the boy waited impatiently until she was done. Then he ran up and held the pictures in front of her face, speaking very fast and excitedly to her.

She looked up at Carson and then back at the sketches. Carson could feel his palms getting sweaty and he tried to look nonchalant and relaxed. He toyed with his last empty Red Stripe bottle as though there was still beer left in it. The next time she looked from the drawings to him, he smiled and waved and then he lost his courage. He had begun to put his things away in his backpack when suddenly she was standing there, looking down at him.

"These are very good," she said laying the two pictures on the table. The black and white drawings were like shadows of the vibrant and colorful being standing next to him.

"Pen and ink doesn't do you justice," he heard himself saying. "I've been watching you all day."

"I know," she replied, sitting down on the other side of the table, holding a pile of wet towels and clothing in her lap. "Why?"

Her large brown eyes met his own and held them for a moment. His fear and embarrassment drifted away. He was not wrong, he knew there was something special happening here.

"Because I'm fascinated by you." Carson leaned forward in his chair and studied her face closely. Everything about her was round and soft, yet strong at the same time. "You're not like the rest of the Americans here."

46

She laughed. "That's because I'm not a tourist. Can I buy you another beer?"

He was flustered because he'd been about to ask her the same thing and she beat him to it. "No, no," she assured him. "I owe you for these pictures. Roy," she said, pulling the little boy towards her. "Run and tell the bartender that we want one Red Stripe, one Heineken and what for you two? Ting?" Carson knew Ting was a popular grapefruit soda drink, but he'd never tried it. Digging in a large straw bag, Gwen came up with a Jamaican twenty dollar bill. The two children ran off in delight towards the bar.

"So, if you're not a tourist here, what are you?" he asked.

"I don't know, just a visitor, I guess. A friend of a family up in Mt. Airy. I've spent several winters with them. When I first came here, there weren't many places to stay in Negril and families in towns nearby would rent rooms to travelers. Someone directed me up to Mt. Airy and I've never stayed anywhere else. Aunt Belle takes care of me and I take care of her. It's very different from what you think you are seeing of the 'real" Jamaica."

Carson took in more about her than just her words as she talked. He was immediately aware that she was a good bit older than him, but that did not lessen his attraction to her. Everything about her was exactly the opposite of Molly – her self-assurance, her easy-going and relaxed way of dealing with Jamaican culture, her womanly figure and face. He tried not to get caught up in the reasons he might be looking for someone as unlike Molly as possible. He wanted to just enjoy this new friendship, not psychoanalyze it.

"Thanks, Gwen," he said when the children returned carrying the drinks for them. "I'm Carson Corrigan by the way."

"You're welcome, Carson," she replied warmly. "Here's to you and your artistic talent." She clicked her beer against his. "Do you do this for a living?"

"Not exactly." Carson started to tell her about the two paintings he had sold that had made his trip possible, but he was so anxious to find out more about her that he cut the story short. He tried not to sound like a freshman boy with a crush on a senior girl, but that was how he felt. "Let's talk about you," he said quickly.

"What do you want to know?"

"I don't know. Why did you leave the other beach and come down to this little one today?" He wanted to know everything about her so it made sense to start with the present.

"I like this beach. There usually aren't any other people on it and besides, this morning I heard about a murder at Mango Grove and I didn't feel like hanging around after that."

The events of the early part of the day came sweeping back over Carson. He had successfully pushed them from his mind by filling it full of images of Gwen. But he was surprised she knew about the murder; he thought it had been well covered up.

"How did you hear about it?" he asked.

"All the Jamaicans are talking about it. A friend of mine who sells banana bread on the beach told me. I guess it was a woman who's pretty famous on Jamaican TV. Fawn something." She sipped her beer and looked at the ocean.

"She was staying next door to me at Mango Grove. It was pretty awful." He looked meaningfully at the kids. Tell me about Mt. Airy," he said, changing the subject. "Tell me about the REAL Jamaica."

At the end of the afternoon, he walked them to the roundabout where they would wait to catch a minibus up to Mt. Airy. There were not very many buses which would take them there, up the back road up to Negril Spots on the other side of Sheffield, but Gwen seemed to know just which one she was looking for. After they had boarded an ancient, battered blue minibus, Carson walked slowly back to Mango Grove, along the road, feeling both excited and peaceful at the same time.

After spending two or three hours focusing on nothing but Gwen, he felt an exhilaration he had not felt in a long time. He had made plans to go up to Mt. Airy under the pretext of wanting to paint some of the people she had described to him. It wasn't totally untrue – he did want to paint them, but what he really wanted was to paint her, to fill his mind and his paper with nothing but her.

He had been curious how she had been able to spend so many winters in Jamaica, but apparently she had arranged her life in such a way that she could do so. She was the director of a summer theater camp in upstate New York, the kind of place wealthy people paid thousands of dollars to send their budding actors and actresses to learn how to paint scenery, memorize lines and strut their stuff on stage. It was Gwen's camp – she was the one who saw the profit from it at the end of every summer. It had been her grandfather's farm, and when he had died, she and a few friends had converted the barn into a theater, built some cabins, and then she had hired them to be the counselors. A few of them would stay in her farmhouse each winter rent free in exchange for maintaining the place and she would spend the coldest months of the year living in her little room off the side of Aunt Belle's house in Mt. Airy.

Carson started guiltily as a slim girl walking by in a bikini reminded him of the scene with Molly that morning. She had gone off up the beach and instead of following her to see if she was okay, he had run off in the other direction, chasing another woman.

Before he had time to wallow in his guilt, he was stopped abruptly by a police officer at the entrance to Mango Grove.

"That one is okay. That one is Carson, the Mango Grove artist man." Mr. Wilford's voice came from behind the tall, imposing uniformed guard. "We are getting a little police protection," he explained, coming forward to greet Carson. "Not to worry."

Carson nodded, but still deep in his own thoughts, he did not stop to chat with Wilford. He found the door to his room unlocked and slightly ajar. Pushing it open slowly, he saw that Molly was inside, sitting in the one chair, going through her purse. A large Jamaican basket with a lid was between her legs on the floor.

"Hi," he said expressionlessly. "What are you doing?"

"Going through my stuff. I'm off to Port Antonio tomorrow and I wanted to leave some of my clothes and important things here. You know, my airline ticket, my birth certificate, a few traveler's checks. It doesn't make sense to rent my own room while I'm gone, so I thought you wouldn't mind keeping this basket here for me. You don't, do you?"

"No, but –" Carson shook his head in bewilderment. "What are you talking about? Port Antonio? I thought you wanted to go home."

As she began telling him about her day, Carson sank down in the doorway and only listened with half an ear. He did not know why he should feel so depressed; perhaps he was just coming down off the high of his afternoon. But he knew that it was more than that. He and Molly were really going off in their own directions and it was definitely the end of something in his life. He wasn't sure if their relationship was over, but he knew it wouldn't be the same after this.

"Are you listening to me?" Molly asked in irritation.

"Yes, I'm listening," he snapped back. "Where the hell is Port Antonio, anyway?"

"It's about as far as you can get from Negril and still be on the island of Jamaica," she replied. "Will you put my ticket in a safe place? I have to fly back a week from Thursday, so I'll have to be here before then. Robinson and Henley have to fly back the same day, it turns out, so we'll all be back a few days before that."

"Has Jazmo come back yet?" Carson asked, trying to break the train of her endless chatter.

"Jazmo?" All the seriousness of the reason she was traveling away from Mango Grove crept in on her as she remembered why Jazmo was not around. "I haven't seen him, no."

Carson stood up. "Well, I'm going to find George and ask him what went down at the police station this morning. Just leave that stuff on the bed. I'll put it away."

"Carson, will you come to breakfast with us tomorrow before I go?"

He felt as though he barely knew this girl he'd lived with for two years. "Of course, I'll go with you."

He turned to leave.

"Carson, are you mad at me?"

"No, I'm not mad at you," he answered without turning to meet her eyes. "I'm just tired." He headed off in the twilight for George and Emma's cabin.

CHAPTER FIVE

The sky was unusually gray by the time Molly was seated on a minibus bound for Lucea, a large town halfway between Negril and Montego Bay. During the time Molly had spent in Negril, there had been little more than tropical afternoon rain showers and this change in the weather was a bit unsettling.

Traffic was light on a Sunday morning and the bus passengers consisted mostly of women and children carefully dressed in their best clothes and headed for some unnamed church down the road. Molly felt rather self-conscious of her bare legs and arms, as well as her naked midriff peeking out between her shorts and halter top. She wished now that she'd worn a skirt instead.

Large drops of rain were falling from the sky as she switched buses at the square in Lucea. She hadn't imagined rain in her fantasy of easy traveling along the coast of Jamaica to Port Antonio, and she began to get a little nervous as she realized how much of the trip would not be as she had planned. The lush countryside looked almost foreboding in the unusual darkness of the day. She saw people on their way to church holding palm leaves or large pieces of cardboard over their heads as protection from the rain. A few luckier ones had real umbrellas.

She had not really thought about where the bus trip would end once they got to Montego Bay. She was still sitting on the bus alone after the other passengers had departed, when the driver looked in the open door and said, "Dis is de end of de line, my lady."

"Oh." She looked around. She was in a large park of some sort in the center of downtown Montego Bay. "What place is this?"

"It called de "Parade'." He got her bag out of the back of the bus. "Where are you going – airport?"

"No, Port Antonio." She fished in her luggage for a small traveling rain jacket. It only went down to her hips, but it was better than nothing.

"Port Antonio? Ay! Such a long way! There is no bus that goes all the way to there from here that I know of. You must switch and switch."

Molly's heart sank. "Well, where can I get a bus that heads in that direction?"

"You can catch one bus to Ocho Rios easy, mon." He proceeded to give her directions but she could barely understand his quick Jamaican accent. He pointed down the street as he talked and she caught the words "post office" and something about the "water's edge." She nodded miserably, pretending she understood, not wanting to give in already to the overwhelming fear that she could not pull this trip off alone.

She headed down a street that looked unwelcoming and dingy in the rainy Sunday morning light. All the shops had barred gates pulled across their doors or wooden shutters that were closed to keep out looters. A woman selling fruit stood under an overhanging eave; several people were clustered beside her, out of the rain, just standing and watching the weather. Molly could imagine how the street must look on a busy morning, with assorted and colorful wares piled up outside the open doors and people shouting, hustling and hanging out on the street corners.

After a half hour of walking, she was damp and tired and knew she must be headed in the wrong direction. She had not come to any water and had seen nothing resembling a post office. She asked a young girl where she could get a bus to Ocho Rios, but the girl only stared at her and giggled before running off. She asked an older woman the same question and the woman scolded her as she answered.

"You headed in the wrong direction, dearie. It back the other way, the other side of the Parade."

Her tears mixed with the raindrops on her face as she switched her suitcase from one aching arm to the other and headed back the way she had come.

Fifteen minutes later, she sat down on the steps of a closed office building and cried her eyes out. When she finally looked up, she saw that across the street there was some kind of sleazy establishment that had actually opened up on a Sunday morning. She realized bleakly that it was probably afternoon by now. Its bamboo walls were painted red and covered with posters of half-naked women inviting patrons to come in and enjoy the evening entertainment. Loud, distorted reggae music blasted from somewhere inside.

Several men stood in the open doorway, drinking Red Stripe beers and watching her. I must be an unusual sight for them, she thought numbly, trying to stay objective about her situation. A white face joined the black ones that were staring at her.

"Ya lost ya way, girlie?" someone called to her.

She didn't know how to answer – she didn't even know if she should respond. Was it more dangerous to trust a large unknown group of men or to be lost indefinitely in Montego Bay? She watched the water drip off the ends of her soaking braids, her light hair dark in its wetness.

"She look like one lost little child," another voice remarked. "We can help you, you know." The rising and falling inflections of his musical Jamaican tones sounded appealing to her even in the midst of the unsavory scene. "Where you are from?"

"She reminds me of someone I know in Negril." The flat American voice sounded familiar. Molly looked up sharply and peered through the downpour at the white face in the doorway.

"White pussy all look alike to me," commented another and there was raucous laughter in agreement.

She flushed at the lewd remark and stood up to leave. As she grabbed her suitcase and headed blindly into the rain, she heard the American say, "Hey, I do know her!" There was the crunch of running feet on the road behind her. "Molly, wait!"

At the sound of her name, Molly turned in amazement. But her spirits dropped immediately as she recognized the heavy, dark-haired man who stood in the road behind her. Alex. It was beyond her comprehension what he was doing in a seedy bar in Montego Bay on a Sunday afternoon, although the setting certainly suited him.

"What are you doing here?" She was surprised to see true concern on the face of this man whom she considered so despicable. "Where's Carson? Why are you alone?"

The smell of rum on his breath washed over her as he questioned her, and that, combined with his chauvinistic attitude, brought back her disgust. None of it was his business, but because he was the only familiar face in a strange place, and because she felt so desperate, she answered him.

"I'm on my way to Port Antonio. Carson is back in Negril. Do you have any idea where I can get the bus to Ocho Rios?" Her voice came out in a monotone as she tried not to disclose her feelings about her own problems, or about how she felt towards him.

"You are?" He seemed to be appraising her in a new light. Then he grabbed her firmly by the arm and, despite her obvious stiffening at his touch, began guiding her back towards the bar. "Come in out of the rain and we'll see what we can work out."

Although she was reluctant to go anywhere with him, there was something comforting about the way he easily took charge of her situation. He led her through the dark interior of the beer joint and sat her down at a rickety table against the back wall, away from the crowd of men around the bar. "Let me get you something to drink," he offered as she sat gingerly on the edge of a bench. "What would you like – a Red Stripe? A rum and coke?"

"A cup of coffee, actually," she admitted, realizing how damp she felt. "Can you get something like that here?"

"My friend Carlo, the bartender, can fix it, I'm sure. Why don't you take off your wet raincoat and relax?" He left her and went to talk to the lean, sour-faced man behind the bar.

Molly was reluctant to remove her jacket because of the skimpiness of her clothes underneath. Now that she was out of tourist territory, she felt half-naked in her beachfront attire. So she sat uncomfortably the way she was and watched Alex.

The ugly irony of meeting up with him made her want to laugh and cry at the same time. This man was one of the main reasons she had left Mango Grove. He was the one who, only yesterday morning, she had immediately suspected of killing his own girlfriend. And here he was, in all his pompous masculinity, gallantly rescuing her from her dilemma, and she was actually feeling gratitude to someone she often thought of as a pig.

"He's heating some water in the back. It'll take a few minutes." Alex sat down in a chair across from her. "Now, tell me, how did you end up all the way out here?"

She explained the morning's events to him and when she had finished, posed his own question back to him. "What about you? Why aren't you back in Negril?"

"Glass bottom boats don't run on rainy days." He laughed to himself. "I was planning to head into Kingston tomorrow morning to see Fawn's mother and find out about funeral arrangements. Since it was raining, I left a day early and took the scenic route. Figured to visit my friend Carlo here and then go over to Ocho Rios to spend the night. It's an easy drive from there to Kingston in the morning."

There was a long pause during which time Molly knew they were both thinking the same thing. Travelling to Ocho Rios with Alex would have been at the top of her list of ways she did not want to spend her day if she hadn't just spent two hours beating the streets of Montego Bay in the rain.

"I'll see if the coffee is ready," Alex said abruptly, breaking the silence.

While she waited for him to return, Molly tried to convince herself that a murderer would not want to go to the funeral of someone he had just killed. He would hide out, lay low, hit the trail, all those cliché activities. And Carson had assured her that it was highly unlikely Alex had left his room that night after he had come back from the dance and passed out. But even so, she still did not totally trust him.

She watched how easily he bantered with the Jamaicans gathered at the bar, answering their quick patois remarks with his own American ones. He certainly knew this country and its ways a lot better than she did. It would probably be a safe and comfortable ride to Ocho Rios. By the time he returned carrying a plastic mug of instant coffee and a can of sweetened condensed milk, she had made up her mind.

"How are you travelling?" she asked as she stirred the thick yellow liquid into her coffee.

"I have my car." He indicated a burgundy Toyota with a smashed right front fender which was parked outside the door. "Would you like a ride as far as Ocho? There's plenty of room and you're welcome to come. I'd enjoy your female companionship."

Don't push your luck, Alex, she thought to herself. Aloud she answered pleasantly, "Thank you.

I was just about to ask if you wouldn't mind my coming along."

"So what's the story, you and Carson having a fight? I thought you two were inseparable. He's quite an artist, that old man of yours. He did a great watercolor of Fawn on the beach once, I got it hanging in my room back at Mango Grove." A frown crossed his face as he thought of Fawn. Sitting back in his chair, an aura of anger surrounded him.

Molly felt angry also. She had struck out on this adventure on her own and already she was in Carson's shadow again, discussing his great talent. She remembered the day Carson had painted that picture of Fawn. The foreground had been all earth tones, Fawn's perfect cocoa curves against the sand, the background a carnival of bright colors and abstract shapes of other people on the beach. It had been one of his best, he could have sold it for sure, but he'd thought it appropriate to give it away to Alex and Fawn in a gesture of neighborliness.

"Were you close with Fawn's family?" she asked, steering the subject away from Carson.

He shook his head. "Never met them. I got their address out of her things. Thought they ought to meet me, see who Fawn spent the last days of her life with."

"How long were you two together?" she asked curiously, thinking about Robinson and his grieving love for the same woman.

"About four months. Ever since she came to Negril. But she was so special, man, you know? She was so perfect..." His expression softened a little as he thought of her.

Molly was surprised at the short length of their relationship, but she knew that tropical environments could intensify feelings of lust and love. From the personal events she had been forced to listen to each night, she was aware of how intense their sex life had been anyway.

"She was too perfect." Alex stood up suddenly and crossed to the bar. He returned a few minutes later with a fresh half pint of white overproof rum. He took a large swig from the bottle before setting it down hard on the table. She wasn't like a lot of other women," he went on after the fire of the rum had put a rosy color into his olive complexion. "She was so sweet and undemanding. She would do whatever I wanted."

Molly knew he meant in bed and she didn't want to hear about it. "Is there a ladies room here?" she asked, standing up so suddenly she nearly upset the little table.

"There's a john outside around back. There's no separate place for ladies though. Not very many ladies come here." He laughed and lifted the rum to his lips again.

It was a filthy little outhouse with a door that didn't shut completely and no toilet paper, but Molly knew she had no choice. Walking back around the side of the building, she was confronted with the smashed fender of Alex's car and realized that she needed to get him on the road before he had much more to drink.

"Are you ready to leave?" she asked immediately upon rejoining him.

"What's your rush?" he replied thickly. The bottle was half empty already. "It's a shitty day and I haven't spent an afternoon with Carlo in a long time."

"Well, I can't hang around." She was not going to wait until Alex had finished his bottle of rum. Being mugged on the streets of Montego Bay was more appealing than being in the same car with him any drunker than he was already. She picked up her suitcase and headed for the door.

"Which way to the airport?" she asked a man sitting on a broken pinball machine. If she got to the airport she could find a way to Ocho Rios, she was sure of that.

"You are not traveling with him?" He indicated Alex with a nod of his head.

"He won't be fit to travel by the time he's finished drinking," she said in disgust. "I value my life."

"Smart woman." The way he said "woman" – deep in his throat, stretching out the two syllables into "wooo-monn" – seemed to come out of the mysterious heart of ancient Africa and it reminded Molly of where she was and why she wanted to travel with Alex. "You should drive him, you know."

She stopped to consider this new idea, but the thought of driving on the left side of the road in a strange country terrified her. "Do you think a man like him would even let a woman drive?" They looked at Alex who sat studying the now nearly empty bottle in his hand.

"You will find a way. You know what he likes." She looked at him sharply and he shrugged. "Woman know how to make man listen."

Molly squared her shoulders determinedly and walked back over to Alex. But then at the last minute she chickened out. "Alex," she said timidly. "I'd like to get going now. How about you?"

"I told you, sweetheart. I'll leave when I'm ready and I ain't ready yet." Their eyes met for an instant – his dark and resentful, hers pale and uncertain.

"Fine. I'll see you then. Have a good time at the funeral." She knew it was a totally inappropriate and obnoxious thing to say, but she couldn't help herself. She went back to the fellow on the pinball machine by the door. "Where can I get a cab to the airport?" she asked again.

"Go down de end of de road, you will see one large green color Chevy parked in front of a pink-pink house on a corner lot. The man who own it drive taxi, but him home now for Sunday dinner. Tell him Ivan send you and he will give you transport."

"Thanks, Ivan." Pulling up the hood of her jacket, she headed out into the drizzle again.

Before she had gone halfway to the corner, she heard the sound of a car engine starting up behind her. A minute later there was Alex, rolling down the window of his beat-up Toyota. "All right, get in," he said impatiently.

"You mean it?"

"I've got a friend who works in a little place in Discovery Bay that I'd like to stop and see. It's right on the way so we might as well get going."

Molly sighed with relief as she opened the door on the passenger side and tossed her suitcase over the back of the seat.

The rain had stopped by the time they reached Falmouth, a small city about twenty-five miles north of Montego Bay. Alex's driving was passable and he made the time go by quickly as he pointed out various spots of scenic beauty or of interesting cultural value. Molly was still on edge because of her own feelings and suspicions about her traveling companion. Every time she found herself laughing at something funny he said, she would see his strong hands as they clutched the steering wheel, the black hairs that grew on his knuckles and thick short fingers, and then she would remember the bruises on Fern's neck and grow instantly sober.

She wondered what Carson would say if he knew she was speeding along the North Coast highway with the man she used to spend hours cursing about in the middle of the night. She smiled to herself, remembering how Carson had talked Dallas out of going with her this morning as she had waited for a minibus at the gate to Mango Grove.

Dallas had been all psyched to go up into the hills with Jazmo for a few days. But Jazmo still had not returned from the police station and Dallas was getting restless. He seemed very anxious to get away from Mango Grove for a while. When he realized that Carson was not going with Molly, he started coming on to her in no uncertain terms. He told her how he wanted to see some more of Jamaica before he had to go back to building high-rise apartment complexes in Texas, and how much fun they could have exploring the ganja fields of the island together. If she could just wait until he packed his bag...

Laughing, Carson had suggested maybe he shouldn't talk about his plans in front of the cop who was stationed at the gate. Dallas had immediately become paranoid when he realized how intently the guard was listening to him, and he quickly hurried off.

"It's pretty up here, isn't it?" Alex's voice broke into her thoughts. "Much prettier than the Negril area, but I like the action down there better."

He was right, Molly realized, looking around. On one side of the road the sea was crashing against the coral reef in all its aquamarine glory; on the other, the lush green countryside rose sharply into hills that rose again into mountains. A hedge of brilliant rose-colored bougainvillea ran along the roadside, alternating with red hibiscus and delicate lantana. Here and there a small two room house could be seen perched on the side of a hill, its open patch of yard dotted with banana trees, goats and chickens.

By the time they pulled up outside of Aunt Mandy's Roadside House, she had learned almost as much about Alex as she had about Jamaica. Somehow, while he was telling her about the ghost in the Rose Hall Great House and pointing out the place where Columbus had landed in Discovery Bay in 1494, she also found out that he had been born and raised in Brooklyn. He had become close friends with several Jamaicans who had relocated there and had come back to their homeland with them to set up some kind of money-making venture which had eventually led to his glass bottom boat tours in

Negril. His full name was Alexander Xavier Santorelli and he could speak fluent Italian if the occasion should arise, which it never did in Jamaica.

"Do you think I could get something to eat here?" As she climbed out of the car, she realized that she hadn't eaten all day.

"Hell, yes. They have great food here. Lock your door." Molly obeyed and then, stiff from the long ride, she stretched her arms and rolled her neck a little. Alex checked her out with the critical eye of a man who spent a lot of time looking at women. When he caught her angry gaze, he said, "You're too damn thin. Let's get some of Aunt Mandy's food to fatten you up."

She followed him into the building which, from the outside anyway, seemed somewhat more respectable than the last place they had been. It was nicely painted a pale pink with red trim and red shutters, and someone had meticulously planted poinsettias next to the well-swept steps leading up to the front door.

It took her eyes a moment to adjust from the daylight to the darkness of the barroom. Black lights on the ceiling gave everything an eerie purple hue. A horseshoe-shaped bar in the center of the room was surrounded by barstools with seats of extremely worn leather. There were some dayglow posters on the walls featuring a naked black woman tangling with wild jungle animals, the same look of extreme rapture on her face in each pose. In one she had a python wrapped around her body, its head rearing up between her voluptuous cartoon breasts, in another she was riding on the back of a leopard, and in the third she was on all fours with a tiger riding her.

When Molly could finally tear her eyes from these bizarre pornographic pictures, Alex had disappeared. There was no one else around and she had the feeling the place was not really open for business yet. A colorful curtain of plastic beads hung in the doorway to the back room and she cautiously poked her head through it and looked around. It led to a little dining room and through another doorway she could see into a kitchen. There she could see Alex with the front of his body pressed against the back of a tall, very dark woman, his hands running up and down her thighs, his tongue licking her ear lobe.

Guiltily, Molly pulled her head back through the curtain, but the quickness of her movement set the little plastic beads clicking against one another. Seconds later the woman appeared. She put a plastic placemat, a napkin and a fork on the bar in front of one of the stools, and with a sullen expression on her face, she muttered, "Dinner soon ready."

Molly sat down obediently at the place setting and watched the woman with fascination as she fiddled with the dial of a radio. She had enormous hips which she had somehow managed to pour into a tight pair of shiny red satin jeans that covered her huge buttocks like a second skin. It was hard not to stare at her enormous behind because the sheen of the material caught every glimmer of light. Molly could imagine the bar full of men whose eyes never left that rear end as it moved behind the bar. The large bottom half of her body contrasted sharply with the smallness of her shoulders and the pert little breasts showing through her ribbed T-shirt. Viewing her face last, Molly realized the bartender was much younger than the sway of her hips led one to believe. She was probably only sixteen or seventeen, and she tried to disguise her age with heavy eye shadow and red lipstick the same color as her pants.

The red pants disappeared through the bead curtain and returned a moment later carrying a plate of steaming food. Before Molly could thank her she was gone again.

There was rice and red peas and some kind of meat in a yellow curry sauce. From the musky, unfamiliar smell of it, Molly suspected it was goat but she was too hungry to care. As she ate, she thought about why Alex had wanted to stop here to visit his "friend;" she was almost certain they were screwing somewhere in the building right now. Any feelings of good faith she had gained towards him in the last few hours were quickly replaced by her innate disgust for a man who could stop for a quick fuck on the way to his beloved girlfriend's funeral.

By the time she had cleaned her plate, Alex had rejoined her at the bar with a big grin on his face. "Let me buy you a drink, baby" he said, slapping her on the back. "Cherry! We need some service out here!"

Cherry reappeared a moment later, still adjusting her clothing and hair. "What you need?" she asked, turning her back to them as she straightened the bottles of liquor behind the cash register.

"Rum and coke for me. What'll you have, Molly?"

"A Heineken, I guess." Molly was beginning to feel a little uptight and she thought a beer might help her relax. As Cherry fixed their drinks, Molly noticed the corner of a Jamaican twenty dollar bill sticking out of the front pocket of her satin jeans. The equivalent of four U.S. dollars. She wondered if that was all Alex had paid her.

Miserable, she stared down into her beer and wished she had never left Negril. Or better yet, Jacksonville.

It was dusk by the time they departed from Aunt Mandy's Roadside House and by then the place had filled up with regulars. Molly felt ashamed to be seen leaving with Alex, afraid that people would think she was his girlfriend. Not that it mattered what these strangers thought. Mostly she was worried about what the night might bring.

Alex had picked up the Sunday edition of the Daily Gleaner as they were leaving. The newspaper lay there on the seat between them, the black headlines on the front page screaming, "FAWN FARREL MURDERED IN NEGRIL." The full length picture from one of her more recent fashion poses was a constant reminder to both of them just what it was they were running away from.

Alex started rambling on again about what a special woman Fawn had been, but after the behavior Molly had witnessed that afternoon she did not want to hear it. She closed her eyes and exhaustion overcame her.

She awoke with a start when the car stopped moving. "Where are we?" she asked sitting up, but Alex was already out of the car and moving to speak to a woman standing in a lighted doorway.

Looking around she could make out two long, low whitewashed buildings which sat at right angles to each other. A few cars were parked in front of each building and she could hear some reggae music playing loudly not too far away. A baby was crying, a dog was barking and she thought she could hear the crashing of ocean waves nearby. She wished desperately that she had not fallen asleep and that she had seen what route they'd taken to get here.

"We're in luck," Alex said when he returned to the car. "She had one room left." He started up the motor and pulled the car up to a dark door at the end of one of the buildings.

"Where are we?" Molly asked again, the quaver in her voice revealing a little too much of her fear and uncertainty.

"Just a small hotel on the edge of Ocho Rios. Nothing fancy."

Molly shut her eyes and prayed for a quick instant that there would be two twin beds in this "nothing fancy" room. She watched Alex unlock the door and flick the wall switch on and her heart sank. There was one not-too-large double bed in the middle of the black and white tiled floor. It was covered with a mustard-colored acrylic blanket, the pillowcases had tiny purple violets on them and one had neat little lime green patch stitched on one corner.

She leaned against the doorway and willed herself not to cry as she watched Alex inspect the room. Besides the bed, there was a green vinyl easy chair with electrical tape holding the cracked seat together, a small table and shaggy pink bathroom rug on the floor. Alex sat down hard on the bed and bounced up and down a few times.

"A little saggy but it'll do," he announced. "Come on in, you look exhausted."

"Where's the bathroom?" she asked weakly.

"Down the other end. Last door." He spread the newspaper out on the bed and began reading it, paying no attention to her obvious unwillingness to share the room and the bed with him.

As she walked slowly down the sidewalk to the bathroom, she told herself that she would live through the night, that nothing was going to happen to her, that she could sleep in the car if she had to.

But in her mind she kept hearing the creaking of bed springs through a thin wooden wall and the protests of a female voice.

CHAPTER SIX

Carson did not experience the emptiness he expected to feel after Molly rode off in the bus to Lucea. He was so full of anticipation for his impending visit to see Gwen in Mt. Airy that he could think of nothing else. But not wanting to appear overanxious, he decided would not even consider leaving for Mt. Airy until noon.

In an aimless attempt to make the hours go by quickly, he wandered over to George and Emma's cabin and knocked on the door. "Yeah, come on in, Carson," George called.

Hana, Mickey, Emma and George were all sprawled on the bed playing poker with Jamaican ten cent pieces. "Hard to amuse the kids on a rainy day," Emma replied grinning, but Carson noticed that her pile of coins was the largest.

"Wanna play?" Mickey invited.

"No, thanks. I don't gamble." He sat down on a straight-back chair piled high with towels which had been brought in before the storm.

"Oh, come on, Carson, they're only worth about two cents each!" Hana laughed and threw down her cards. "I've got a shitty hand. I fold."

"What's the latest on Jazmo?" Carson asked.

"Nothing." George's mood became gloomy. "I guess because it's a weekend they can't let him out on bail or question him or anything. We have to wait until Monday morning to even talk to anybody in charge."

"Yeah, they won't even feed him," added Hana. "Mom's putting together some food and we're gonna take it down there later. They would just let him starve if nobody cared."

"Yeah, it's like totally medieval. I wonder if they keep him in a dungeon too, all chained up to the wall." Mickey's adolescent imaginings seemed almost right in this instance.

"George, who do you think did it?" Carson asked.

"That's a loaded question, Carson. I have no idea who even had a reason to want her dead." He and Emma exchanged meaningful looks across the room.

"We've actually discussed this quite a lot," Emma admitted. "I tend to think it was just some sex-crazed madman off the beach who lost control at the sight of a Jamaican sex goddess in her bathrobe and when she rejected his interests he went wild and strangled her."

"I, on the other hand, think it was totally premeditated," George said. "I think it was someone who had a vengeance for Fawn in particular. Prostitutes are killed by sex maniacs. Famous people usually aren't."

"I think you guys are all working under sexist delusions."

"What?!" Four pairs of eyes turned to stare at little Hana as she cleared the cards off the bed and began shuffling them again. She sat cross-legged, her dark eyes and curls and oversized white T-shirt making her look as innocent as teenager at a slumber party.

"I mean, I don't know why you think it had to be a man who killed her. It could have been a woman, you know."

There was a stunned silence in the close cabin. The air, already heavy with humidity, was now charged with curiosity as well. "What do mean, dear?" Emma asked gently after a minute.

"Well, you know, I've felt that way a few times. Like Fawn was so perfect and beautiful, and I'm so little and flat and ugly, and how it's just not fair that some people get all the beauty and other people get nothing. Maybe some girl was just so jealous she couldn't stand it anymore."

"You're nuts," said Mickey, laughing at her. "Girls aren't strong enough to strangle people. Come on, you goon. Try and strangle me, I dare you!"

"You chauvinist pig!" Hana flung the deck of cards at him. Still taunting her, he dashed through the door into their connecting bedroom. She ran after him, calling him names and pummeling him on the back with her fists.

"It's an interesting theory," George said as he got up to shut the door after them, blocking out the shrieks of anger that alternated with laughter. "But he's right about most women not being strong enough."

"That's bullshit!" Emma burst out emphatically. "Have you ever watched Miss Faye and her sisters and daughters on wash day? I mean, have you ever tried to wash a bed sheet by hand in a washtub and then wring it out? Have you, George Goldberg?"

"She's right, George," agreed Carson. "A big Jamaican woman could easily have squeezed the life out of Fawn." But it was a pair of well-oiled and very tanned white hands he was seeing in his mind as he spoke.

When he left George and Emma, they were still discussing how probable or improbable it was that a woman could possibly have murdered Fawn. Stopping at the kitchen to see if there was any coffee left from breakfast, he found Miss Faye peeling yams and muttering to herself.

"De all leave me, Carson, my dear boy," she said when she became aware of his presence. "My rooms dey all stand empty with no one to fill dem."

"Who left?" he asked puzzled.

"Your lady friend gone, Mr. Alex him gone for some days-"

"Alex left?"

70

"Yes, aye. And me can't rent him room because he keep so many tings in it even when him not residing. De police dey take Jazmo from me and dat man with de pictures on him-"

"Dallas."

"Yes, him, he want to go away too. It de murder drive dem all from Mango Grove. I knew dat girl would be trouble from de moment she set foot on me ground. All her fancy hair and frocks and face, her half-naked body on de beach..." Miss Faye began mumbling again as she dumped the yams into a large kettle on the gas range.

"Miss Faye, where did Alex go?" Carson peeked into the coffee pot but there were only wet grinds left in the bottom of it.

"Him say him gone Kingston for funeral, but me never trust de man, you know. All de time him sayin' him love-love dat girl so much. Me see him off with dem bad Germany girls and sometimes even de ones on de beach who ax for money! Him give me plenty money to stay here and him bring me nice tings so I can't complain, but..."

Her language began to lapse more and more into patois, as if she were talking to herself again, and Carson slipped quietly away.

He decided to walk up the beach for a cup of coffee, but the rain was coming down much harder now so he stopped off at his room to pick up his poncho. Across the yard he could see Eva and Irena sitting in their open doorway, smoking cigarettes and glaring gruesomely at the weather. He wondered what they would do with a rainy day in paradise – did they read or knit or just drink beer? He realized that because of the language barrier, he knew very little about them personally, whether they had jobs back in Germany or if they were wealthy heiresses spending their inheritances.

As he watched, Eva detached herself from the doorway and moved out into the rain, crossing the yard towards him. "Oh, God, what does she want with me?" he groaned softly to himself.

She was wearing a thin pink polyester robe that hid nothing once it began absorbing the large raindrops falling from the sky. Something about the wet cloth clinging to the swells of her tanned skin sent a tingling sensation through his body that he was embarrassed to admit he felt. He could not make her stand in the rain and as she obviously wanted to speak to him, he motioned for her to step into his room. He stood uncomfortably, a few feet from the door, as she wiped her bare feet on the mat before stepping inside.

"You have seen Alex?" she asked immediately and Carson breathed an almost audible sigh of relief that she was not interested in anything to do with him.

"No, Miss Faye says he went to Kingston for Fawn's funeral and the he'll be gone a few days."

"Kingston? What is 'funeral'?"

"For Fawn. When people die, you know, a service, a burial, you go to church..." He couldn't figure out any other way to explain it, but as soon as he mentioned Fawn's name again, she seemed to comprehend what he was saying and her eyes lit up with anger.

Letting loose a string of German expletives, she stamped her wet foot and crossed her arms angrily over her wet chest. "Danke schoen," she muttered, and then dashed out into the rain again, the jiggling of her large buttocks showing clearly beneath the sheer, wet robe as she ran back to her own cabin.

Carson was not the only one who appreciated the spectacle of Eva sprinting across the yard. He heard a door slam shut not far away and before long there was Dallas knocking on the wall next to the open door of the girls' room. "Anybody home?" he called jokingly, and he did not wait for an invitation to enter.

72

Seconds later the door shut behind him and the drapes were closed. Carson laughed to himself – now he knew what they did for excitement on a rainy day. He also knew that if the right person were with him, he would be doing the same thing.

Instead he walked up to the T-Water Hotel for a cup of coffee. There he met Robinson and Henley. They each had their feet up on chairs as they read paperback novels and nursed beers, despite the fact that it was only ten thirty in the morning.

"It's a bummer spending a rainy day in a tent," Henley said, as Carson pulled a chair up to join them. "We're on vacation, so why not start early?" He indicated the beer in his hand.

"Molly find a bus okay?" Robinson asked.

Even though the age difference was only a few years, Carson felt infinitely older than these two guys. He had sat quietly through breakfast with them and Molly, watching how Molly had warmed to Henley's bad jokes and Robinson's winning smile. They seemed like silly college kids, but Molly seemed to enjoy them. Carson had noticed more than once that she and Robinson had exchanged glances that seemed to hold some sort of promise.

He swallowed. "Yeah, fine. She got a bus as far as Lucea, anyway."

"Well, if everything goes right we should be having a great time with her in Port Antonio in a few days." Robinson had an odd, dreamy look in his eyes and Henley, sensing trouble, quickly changed the subject.

"You going to the concert up at Kaiser's tonight?" he asked Carson. "I hear Yellowman gives a great show."

"I don't know. I don't think so. I'm headed up to the hills to visit a friend," he replied slowly. He had not even thought as far as night time. His anticipation seemed to have him living from moment to moment until he could see Gwen again.

He ended up walking the entire distance from Negril to Mt. Airy. Although it took him over an hour and it was uphill all the way, he did not mind as much as he might have on another day. The air was warm and humid, but there was no scorching sun beating down on his head. The rain seemed to come in fast outbursts as though every so often someone were emptying a large pan of dish water out of the sky. He went barefoot much of the way as the road was full of potholes and puddles. He'd already destroyed one pair of sandals since he'd come to Jamaica. It was an incredibly rough roadbed – in places the road seemed to be built right on rock ledge. He was amazed that any bus or car could make its way to Mt. Airy in one piece.

His art supplies were carefully packed in a plastic bag inside his backpack, which was under his rain poncho so that they were more or less inaccessible to him. There were images all around him begging to be painted, but he did not stop.

Occasionally some ragged children would join him in splashing through the puddles. One small boy who walked along with him for a while was pulling a crude homemade toy. Carson was fascinated and stooped down to inspect it. It looked like a train. The engine was made out of a Cremo milk carton with cardboard wheels on twigs pushed through for axles. Behind it were flat cars, also made of cardboard, with buttons for wheels.

"A train?" he asked the boy.

"Cane truck," was the nearly whispered reply. Carson recognized it now. He had seen the big tractors on the road between Negril and Sav-LaMar pulling three or four open wagons loaded with freshly cut cane. He was so impressed with the little toy that he did not get caught up in the depression that such obvious poverty usually brought on him.

Later, when he thought back to that first walk into the village, what stood out most in his memory was the "Mt. Airy All Age School." The biggest building in town, it hung over the main street on a steep hillside, as large and imposing as a Victorian schoolmarm. A long, ancient wooden structure, it had lots of windows with old-fashioned shutters that were hinged at the top and held open at the bottom with a stick. There was a big, grassy schoolyard shaded by an enormous cottonwood tree.

Another indelible image was the big old tank with the warning painted in bold, but now very faded letters on its side: BOIL ALL YOUR DRINKING WATER. It didn't look like it got much use these days, but he knew it was only in the last twenty years or so that "the pipe" had reached small villages like this one.

He felt as though he had travelled to another country, it was such a different Jamaica from the touristy one in Negril. The distance was short enough to be covered on foot, no more than four miles, and yet he did not see another white face in all those that watched him from the windows and doorways.

He wasn't really surprised when the first person he asked knew exactly who Gwen was and where she lived. Probably the smallest child in town could have given him explicit directions. He turned off by a public water tap and headed up a dirt track to a small group of houses overlooking the main road next to a flat area that appeared to be a garden or grazing area for animals.

"Miss Gwen, Miss Gwen! Artist man come!" He recognized Roy, the small boy from the beach, as he streaked by into one of the houses off to his left.

Gwen appeared around the side of the house, a welcoming grin on her face. Her bright hair was in a braid down her back and she wore a patched apron over a vintage blue and white print dress that must have come from a secondhand store. Her hands were covered with flour and as she brushed a stray hair from her face, she left a white streak across her cheek. She looked perfect.

"Hi, Carson!" Her greeting was so warm that suddenly his legs felt weak and watery, as if he might just wash right back down the hill into the little gutter next to the path. "I'm in the middle of making dumplings in the kitchen out back. Come 'round and keep me company."

He'd envisioned sweeping her off her feet and ravishing her in a big squeaky bed. Instead he followed her to the little ramshackle kitchen behind the house and sat on a stool that was missing a leg while she shaped the dough into rough balls and then dropped them into a simmering chicken stew that was cooking over an open fire on a ledge inside the building. The walls and ceiling showed evidence of having caught fire at least once and Carson knew that was why Jamaican kitchens were always in a separate building from the main house.

"Did you have to walk the whole way? I thought you might on a Sunday. Well, I'm glad you came, anyway." She chatted on and Carson was amazed by how much more relaxed she seemed here in these primitive surroundings than she had at the Yacht Club.

The afternoon passed in a pleasant daze. The exhilaration he was feeling gave everything a special dreamlike quality – he felt as though he'd stepped back in time. They ate Sunday dinner at a little table covered with a shiny blue oilcloth patterned in giant red flowers. There were only three chairs so the children sat on the steps to eat and Aunt Belle joined Carson and Gwen at the table.

While the girl helped Gwen clean up, Carson and Aunt Belle sat in rocking chairs on the porch and Carson made a detailed sketch of her beautifully wrinkled face and bright eyes surrounded by a fuzzy white halo of hair. She told him stories of her childhood, growing up in Mt. Airy, and he fell in love with her tinkling laugh as she recalled humorous anecdotes from the early part of the century.

Aunt Belle and her grandchildren lived in the two rooms off the porch – one being the combination kitchen/sitting room, the other being the bedroom where they all three slept in a double bed that dwarfed the tiny space containing it. Gwen's room was actually an addition to the house, which she herself had paid to have built. When Gwen was not there, Aunt Belle could rent it out and keep the meager income for herself. ("Rooms in Mt. Airy don't fetch much, you know.")

As it began to get dark, Aunt Belle rose with great effort and moved about the house, lighting the kerosene lamps and coming back onto the porch with a smoking mosquito coil which she placed on the floor between them.

"A blinkie in de house," Aunt Belle said suddenly. Putting his sketch pad away, Carson looked up to see what she was talking about. A lightning bug was flying around in the softly lit room. "It mean a stranger coming to visit me tonight. And see – it true! You are here already!" She laughed merrily and Carson couldn't help `but join in.

"You two seem to be getting along," commented Gwen as she joined them on the porch.

"She's great. I'm in love with this woman!" Carson laughed again, taking one of Aunt Belle's gnarled hands in his own. "I want to do a painting of you in the daytime on this porch, Aunt Belle. Will you pose for me?"

"What? Me? No, sir. You don't want my ugly mug in your picture." She hid her face with her free hand and laughed again. "It one nice boy you bring us, Gwen. Me gone inside now. De night air, it chill dese old bones."

After Aunt Belle departed, Carson felt suddenly uncomfortable and not sure what to do next. He did not relish the idea of walking back to Negril alone in the dark, but he was not sure how Gwen felt about him spending the night.

"You haven't seen my room yet," she said before he had time to think about it anymore. She took him by the hand and led him off the porch and around the side of the house to her little addition.

It was an airy room with two large louvered windows. The double bed was covered with a bright Indian print bedspread and there was an old dresser, a wooden desk and chair, as well as a striped collapsible beach chair. The room was lit by an oil lamp, but Carson saw that she also had a battery-powered reading lamp near the head of the bed. Tacked to the wall over the desk was one of the pictures he had done of Gwen at the beach.

"Phew! I'm exhausted!" Gwen flopped across the bed. "Sunday dinner is always such a big deal – it wipes me out."

Her long braid was stretched out on the bedspread next to her head. Carson knelt down on the floor beside the bed and pulled off the rubber band that held the thick braid together. He gently separated the glistening strands of hair and spread them out across the pillow next to her.

"You have such beautiful hair," he said quietly, holding up one amber curl to examine it in the lamplight.

She sighed and sat up, the wavy tresses cloaking her back. "Yeah, lots of men have been in love with my hair."

The lamp was behind her, making it appear as a golden red halo around her head, but her face was in shadow and he could not read her expression. He leaned forward from his kneeling position on the floor and kissed her bare knee. "But it's still beautiful," he whispered, and then kissed her other knee, thrilled by the shiver he felt run through the leg that was pressing against his chest.

"Carson, stop. Let's talk a little." She grabbed his head with both of her hands, forcing his lips away from the path they were taking up her inner thigh, making him look up at her.

"I don't want to talk." He felt as though he was about to explode with desire. The strength behind the passion with which his mouth found hers knocked her down on the bed again, his body pressed on top of hers. She did not respond with all the energy he knew she was feeling, some part of her was resisting him. Finally he rolled over and lay next to her, his face nestled into her neck and said, "Okay, what's wrong?"

She got up slowly and walked across the room to sit in the beach chair facing him. "I've just been through this so many times," she replied at last. "Don't forget – I've been coming here for ten years. I know how a tropical island affects northerners and how magical these friendly people and their simple lifestyle can appear. It's not that what we're feeling isn't real, but I've had enough of these romances to know that they don't hold up away from this time and this place and ...and I just don't need that anymore."

"How can you say that? I've never felt this strongly about anyone before!"

"Not even about your girlfriend, Molly?"

"I don't even know where Molly is. She left this morning to go travelling." He hadn't even thought about Molly once since he'd left Negril and in his present emotional condition, it angered him to remember her rejection of him. "She's done with me. She moved out and then she left for Port Antonio. There's no question that our relationship is over. And no, I never felt this way about her! I don't think she's capable of feeling this strongly. I mean, she's just a girl – you're a woman!"

He had blurted it out in a fit of emotion, but it definitely was the crux of the issue. He didn't know how much older Gwen was than him, but he suspected there was a good ten years between them. She had probably been through dozens of lovestruck men, all swept off their feet by her strength and beauty. Molly had always been like his little sister, following him around, doing whatever he did, growing up with him. But he couldn't ever remember feeling a burning attraction like this for her.

Gwen laughed softly. "Carson, you've only known me for one day. How can you think we're ready for such intimacy?"

He moved across the room to where she sat. Taking her by the hands, he pulled her out of the chair. The flickering lamplight was reflected in his eyes as they gazed deeply into hers, flames that were only a small indication of the fire that was burning inside.

"Because I want to know you that way. I want to know you every way, everywhere. I want to prove to you that I'm not just another tropical romance, that what I'm feeling for you is something special." His words all sounded like trite clichés and made him feel even more desperate. Running his fingertips lightly up the soft, sensitive skin on the inside of her arm, he whispered, "Let's just explore each other and see what we can find out. Okay? If you don't want to make love, we won't."

Closing her eyes, she gave into the electricity that his slender fingers created as they moved sensually over her body. Leading her back to the bed, he said, "Lay down on your belly and I'll give you a massage."

"How about if I give you one first?" she suggested, placing her hands on his shoulders and beginning to work the tight muscles of his neck with her strong hands.

"No, you're the tired one." Carson stilled her hands with his own and stopped her protesting mouth with a hungry kiss. "I want you to relax."

Gwen stretched out across the bed and, lifting her glorious hair out of the way, he began gently kneading the muscles of her back. The thin fabric of the ancient dress seemed about to disintegrate and at one place beneath her shoulder blade the old threads suddenly gave way beneath his probing fingers. As he touched the warm flesh beneath, both of them gasped, realizing what had happened.

"I'm sorry-" he began, but she cut him off.

"Never mind. It's just a dear old dress that has seen better days." He watched as she slowly undid the buttons down the front and then, with one simple movement, slipped it over her head. She wore nothing underneath but a pair of underpants. As she carefully folded the dress and put it aside, he filled himself with the beauty of her body.

He could not help but compare her with Molly – he had not been with any other woman in years. He marveled at the round shape of her large breasts with their dark, erect nipples so different from Molly's tiny pink ones. The soft curve of her belly fascinated him with its contrast to Molly's concave one. When he finally lifted his eyes to meet her own, they were alive with a light he had not seen in them before. Then she lay back down again, leaving him with a view of her naked back. Where her swimsuit had covered it, there was a white space like a continent surrounded by the dark ocean of tan on her shoulders, arms and legs.

"These too," he said, gently pulling down her underpants. Her buttocks appeared creamy white in the soft glow of the kerosene lamp. Lightly running his fingers over the tiny scars on both sides of her hips, he asked, "What are these from?"

"Stretch marks," she replied, her voice muffled by the pillow on which her face lay.

"From what? Did you used to be fat?" His question rang of such innocence that despite herself, Gwen laughed.

"No, Carson. I had a baby once." She picked up her head and turned to see his reaction. He was sitting back on his heels, a stunned expression on his face.

"Oh." He ran his fingers through his own shoulder-length, straw-colored hair, pushing it off his forehead in a nervous gesture. "When was that?"

She lay down and closed her eyes again. "I was seventeen," she sighed, a pained look crossing her relaxed features. "I was still in high school. I had to drop out for a few months in the spring, I gave birth in August and was back in school for the fall semester as though it had never happened."

"But what happened to the baby?" Carson had stretched out next to her, his face propped up on one hand, while he began rubbing her back again with other.

"I had to give it away. That's what you did in those days. You never even got to see it. I know it was a boy, though, because I heard the nurses talking after the birth."

"You didn't consider abortion?"

"An abortion was barely an option back then – they weren't even legalized yet. Adoption was the only answer, at least in the eyes of my upper-middle class parents." Suddenly she rolled over and threw her arms around him, hugging him close to her. "So somewhere in the world is an eighteen year old boy who doesn't know who his real mother is or that he's my son."

"Do you think about it much?" he asked softly as he felt the wetness on his neck from her tears.

"Hardly ever. It was so long ago. It hurts to think about it and I've done a lot of good living since then." Then, as quickly as her tears had come, they were gone and she was laughing. "Carson, this is obscene! You still have all your clothes on and I'm stark naked. Is this some kind of fantasy of yours?"

"Well, that's easy to fix." As he pulled his T-shirt over his head, she ran her fingers down his smooth brown chest and over his lean torso. She began to unbutton his shorts and then stopped, all too aware of the swelling hardness that seemed about to explode out of his pants. "What's the matter?" he teased. "Afraid we might set the bed on fire?"

It was nearly dawn by the time they actually made love. By then Carson knew every inch of her body, from her freckled toes to the mole behind her left ear. Long after the wick of the oil lamp had sputtered out, and there were no sounds other than the occasional crowing of a confused rooster or the barking of the dogs from one yard to another, there were still small sighs of delight and moans of desire coming from the addition to Aunt Belle's house.

He fell asleep afterwards with his head nestled between her breasts, one hand resting in the moistness between her legs. Still in the same position, he was awakened a few hours later by the loud braying of an unwilling donkey being dragged up the road and to the crunch of feet on the path next to the window. Morning sunlight was filtering through the curtains, the pattern of the louvered windows casting their shadow across the bed.

He lay there, motionless, savoring the happiness he felt waking up in this perfect place with this special woman. Then he became aware of her soft white breast next to his face and, with the slightest of movements, he was able to reach the large nipple with his tongue and lips. She whimpered and stirred a little in her sleep. He moved his mouth to her other breast, aware of the sweat dripping down his cheek from where it had rested against her skin as he slept. She made a moaning noise deep in her throat, but still she did not seem fully awake. The fingers that had been reposing in her crotch came alive now and suddenly her eyelids fluttered open.

"I was dreaming you were making love to me," she said, starting to rise. Then she sighed happily and sank back onto the pillow. "I guess I wasn't dreaming." Running her fingers through his soft hair, she closed her eyes and let herself drift away on his caresses until he brought her to heights of pleasure that made her grasp his head and arch her back and bury her face in the pillow so that the children in the yard would not hear her screams.

It was noon before they finally dressed and opened the door, an unheard of time for rising in Mt. Airy. The heat of the midday sun was oppressive, but as Carson sat in the shade of Aunt Belle's porch drinking Grace instant coffee sweetened with canned milk, he could think only of how beautiful Mt. Airy looked in the sunshine. Everything was fresh and green from the rain, and the houses and people were colorful patches against the brilliant landscape.

Aunt Belle came of her house and gave Carson a reproving look. "You keep my girl from her clothes washing. How de clothes gone dry by dark now?" But behind her stern expression there was a twinkle in her pale brown eyes that made him burst out laughing.

"It was she who kept me, Aunt Belle, from getting started on my portrait of you." He thought about spending the afternoon painting her, but the exhaustion he felt in his limbs counteracted any inclinations towards working. "Tomorrow morning. Okay?"

He left Mt. Airy a few hours later and almost immediately caught a ride in a very beat-up Morris Minor all the way into the Negril roundabout. As he walked up the beach, all he could think of was a cool shower, a swim, a change of clothes and possibly a nap. He was totally oblivious to everyone he passed, unaware of the excited buzzing of conversation between tourists, or of the angry, fearful shouts that seemed to be passing between the Jamaicans.

As he reached the gate to Mango Grove, George came running up to him and grabbed his arm. "Where you been, man? The police were starting to get suspicious when you didn't show up today after being gone all night."

"What do you mean? I can't spend a night out if I want to?" Carson's euphoric haze was quickly disappearing. He tried to shake George's hand off his arm, but George grasped it even tighter and moved his tanned face closer to Carson's own.

"You mean you didn't hear about the prostitute? I thought everyone in Negril knew already."

"What prostitute? What are you talking about? I wasn't in Negril last night."

George shook his head, his gray curls bobbing lightly. "A prostitute was murdered last night on the beach. She was just a young kid, maybe sixteen, you've seen her, I'm sure. Tiny little thing, always wears a fringed denim skirt?"

Carson leaned again the gate. "Jesus! Sure, who doesn't know her? Baby Bomba, isn't that what she calls herself? God, why would anyone want to kill her?"

"Well, you know, things like this happen to hookers in New York all the time. Some deranged lowlife guy who's mad at all women for something his mother did to him takes it out on some poor girl he doesn't know. But thing about this one is-" George paused for effect, making sure he had Carson's attention. "She was strangled, the same way that Fawn was."

CHAPTER SEVEN

The second murder in the space of a just a few days had cast an atmosphere of fear and depression over most of Negril. Many tourists made plans to leave a few days early for home or decided to spend the rest of their vacation elsewhere on the island.

"What they don't realize," George said that night as they sat around the tables in Miss Faye's open air dining area, "is that both of the women killed were Jamaicans. That, if this is the pattern of some serial killer, the white foreigners have nothing to worry about."

"But you can't say that for sure," argued Emma. "You really can't prove that the two murders are even connected."

George rolled his eyes and looked at Carson, who shrugged and deferred to Emma.

"I mean, really, the second murder happened a mile up the beach from the first, not to a famous fashion model and TV personality but to a sixteen year old girl who had a reputation of performing any sexual act for forty Jamaican dollars."

"How do you know how much she charged?" George demanded.

"George, you know she's right." Carson shut him up with his quiet agreement. "You can't tell me you haven't been approached at night on the beach by numerous girls and women offering the same low price for happiness."

"The reason the amount sticks in my mind is because simple arithmetic will tell you that it comes to about eight dollars in American money. It's absolutely pitiful that sleazy college kids can get away with paying this small amount to-"

"To get V.D. and other sexually transmitted diseases?" George finished her sentence. "We're straying from the point here. The reason, my dear Emma, that I think these two deaths might be related is because we have been coming here for ten years and nothing like this has ever happened before. Now in just three days two innocent women have been murdered and you're trying to tell me it was a coincidence?"

Emma glared at him. Before the argument could go any further, a dark figure materialized out of the shadows of the yard and joined them in the dining area. Carson was visibly surprised and jumped out of his chair to welcome the newcomer. "Jazmo, my man! When did they let you out?"

From his appearance, it was obvious that Jazmo's vacation in jail had not been a pleasant one. One eye was black and swollen, there was a large bruise on his jaw, and he held his right arm limply cradled in the left. He winced as Carson clapped him unthinkingly on the back, and when he sat down in the offered chair, he grimaced visibly with pain.

"Oh, yeah, I forgot to tell you the good news." George's tone was black and cynical. "After they found Baby Bomba, they let Jazmo go because they realized he couldn't have strangled her from behind bars and the police seem to think these murders are connected." He looked meaningfully at Emma. "I'm sure they didn't say they were sorry." George refilled his glass from the pitcher of banana daiquiris on the table and then topped off everyone's glasses all around.

Carson's stomach churned as he thought about what Jazmo must have endured in those few days to end up in this condition. "Why did they do this to you?" he asked.

"Why do you think, mon? They try to make me admit to de murdah of me sistah, but you cahn't make a dog to fly, you what I am saying? It is bad

87

enough fah me that me sistah dead and dey want to make me say is me who do it? Dey jus' lookin' fah someone to pin it on, so de damn tourists will tink de place safe if dey lock me up. Bumba clots, all of dem!"

With his good arm, Jazmo pulled a pint of white rum from somewhere on his body and took a good long swig of it. His bloodshot eyes along with a pervading alcoholic odor made it evident that he had already been drinking for several hours.

Carson closed his eyes. He was tired and the tension in the air was not conducive to relaxation. He wished he was back in Mt. Airy with Gwen, but they had both agreed to a night apart to catch up on sleep.

"Carson's falling asleep," Emma commented with a giggle.

"Hmm? No, I'm not." He sat up straight and opened his eyes. They were all staring at him. "So, Jazmo. You been to a doctor yet?"

"About dis arm, you mean? Tomorrow, mon. Tomorrow me gone down Kingston way fah funeral. I will see a doctah dere. Me can't wait hours in Sav, you know. One hundred people wait all day to see one doctah dere. Me cahn't do it, mon. De pain will have to wait." In his drunken irate state, Jazmo was slipping back and forth from his Jamaican dialect to the more proper speech patterns he used with Americans.

Voices outside of the dimly lit dining area made them all sit up in their seats. Everyone seemed to be on edge. Mango Grove was not the relaxed place it had been a week before.

"Oh, good. They're still awake. And Jazmo is here! We're all set, man." Robinson and Henley came through the open doorway. They were barefoot and sunburned, their feet and the bottom half of their legs covered with wet sand. Henley wore a woven straw visor, his spiky hair sticking up through the top if it; the earphones of his Walkman were around his neck, the cord running down to his waist. Robinson carried his map of Jamaica and a bottle of milky white soursop juice. Carson's tired digestive muscles rumbled at the sight of it. He'd never developed a taste for the excessively sweet, thick juice squeezed from the pulpy soursop fruit, although it was considered a delicacy by many.

"What's happening, man?" Henley pulled up a chair next to Carson and straddled it backwards. "Didn't see you at the concert last night. D'ja poop out early?"

"Not exactly." Once again he was struck by the overwhelming youth of these two.

"It was really great," Henley went on enthusiastically, not waiting for Carson to continue. "It lasted till like three in the morning and by then were so high we couldn't sleep anyway. And boy, were the prostitutes thick on the way home! We could've gotten laid twenty times if we were into it."

"As a matter of fact, that's when they think Baby Bomba was murdered," George interjected. "They think it was by someone returning from the Yellowman concert."

"Yeah, it's creepy, isn't it?" Henley's continual chatter began to make Carson suspect that perhaps it was chemically induced. Robinson had not said a word. He was calmly spreading out his map on the next table. "Makes you wonder why it was her out of all those hookers," Henley continued. "I mean, they seem to be thicker at that time of night then at say, eleven or twelve. You'd think they'd be worn out by then. But I guess they sleep during the day and-"

"The reason we came by," Robinson said loudly, cutting him off. "Was to ask Jazmo how to get to the funeral once we get to Kingston."

"You are going to Fawn's funeral?" A light came into Jazmo's red eyes.

89

"Yes, sir! We were very close, she and I. We were-were good friends in college." There was a respectful pause among them all for a second.

"Yes, mon! I know dis fact. But it is dangerous for white men to travel dat part of Kingston alone." Jazmo shook his head at the idea.

"I'm not afraid. Besides, I don't feel like I have a choice." Robinson's voice made his intentions clear.

"I think you're right, Jazmo," Henley said, picking up his babbling monologue where he left off. "I mean, if what's happening in Negril is any indication of the violence of Kingston, which I've always heard is a really wild place, then we would be fools to think we could leave there alive or with our shirts still on at any rate. I heard this story about this guy who had the pocket of his vest slashed right off because-"

"Henley – enough, okay?" Robinson turned back to Jazmo. "Would you look at this map with me, anyway?"

"How will you be traveling, mon? You have car?"

"No. We'll be taking a minibus in the morning. I want you to show me where we are going in Kingston." Robinson flipped over the map to the reverse side where there was a large street map of Kingston.

Carson pushed back his chair and stood up, stretching. "I'm exhausted. Guess I'll turn in."

"Where did you spend last night, anyway?" George asked him curiously.

Carson grinned. "In Mt. Airy," he replied, unable to keep wipe the grin off his lips.

"He looks like he's in love, don't you think?" Emma laughed.

Carson's exit was cut off as Dallas's large frame filled the doorway. "You seen Jazmo?" he demanded loudly. "Oh, there he is Jazmo, man, we headed for the hills tomorrow or what?"

Jazmo looked up from the map. "Me gone Kingston tomorrow. Me cahn't be bothered wit your business."

Dallas's face was already flushed, but as he began sputtering angrily, it grew even redder. Henley saved the moment by turning to him and saying blithely, "Hey, you were at that Yellowman concert , weren't you? Wasn't that a gas? Didn't I see you up front with a couple of black chicks?"

Dallas stared at him for a moment without comprehending. Then he seemed to recognize Henley, and he answered suspiciously, "Yeah, I was there. So what?"

Carson had a feeling that Dallas must have been cross-examined by the police at some point during the day concerning the most recent strangling. But he was too tired to deal with these guys and their scene any longer. He slipped out past Dallas and headed for his room with nothing on his mind but sleep.

As he sat on the edge of the bed, undressing, a pair of Molly's sandals beneath the bed caught his eye. But strangely enough, he felt no guilt. She was probably in Port Antonio by now, waiting for her new young boyfriends to show up after they were done in Kingston. He wondered which one she was interested in. Maybe both. No, if there was one thing Molly was not, it was kinky.

Well, he wasn't worried. He pulled the string on the light bulb and climbed beneath the cool sheet. Molly would come back to get her airline ticket, they would have a little talk, she would leave, and then he could enjoy the rest of the winter with Gwen. It all seemed so simple.

He was up early enough the next morning to see the results of what had transpired after he'd gone to bed. Dallas was drinking coffee outside the kitchen, his duffel bag propped up against a nearby palm tree. Henley and Robinson came trooping in from the beach with their backpacks and joined him. They seemed to have exchanged personalities from the previous evening, Henley was subdued and quiet, while Robinson paced nervously waiting for Jazmo to show up.

"We decided it made sense for us all to go together," he explained to Carson. "Dallas said he would go along so that he and Jazmo could make their excursion on the way home. With Jazmo as our guide in Kingston, we should have nothing to worry about."

Carson wasn't so sure of that, but he kept his thoughts to himself. He avoided meeting Robinson's eyes as he remarked casually, "And then you two will head up to Port Antonio to meet Molly?"

"That's the plan. Any messages for her?"

Carson could not keep himself from turning sharply to meet Rob's gaze. Perhaps it was just his current frame of mind, but he had the feeling that behind Robinson's innocent warm brown eyes, there lurked some deep pent-up passion.

"Just tell her I hope she's having a good time." He headed for the beach with his coffee mug. On the way he passed Jazmo lugging a battered cardboard suitcase through the yard with his good arm. "Good luck!" he called to him.

Jazmo nodded sullenly; he didn't seem to be in very high spirits.

The beach was beautiful and quiet in the early light of day. The sun had not yet risen above the tops of the palm trees so the sand was still cool and shaded, not yet appealing to sun worshipers. He saw a fisherman paddling towards shore in a dugout canoe and thought perhaps he should buy some fresh fish to take up to Mt. Airy for dinner.

Heading back to his room for some money, he realized how quiet it would be around Mango Grove for the next several days. There was no one in residence besides George and his family other than the German girls, and they were scheduled to leave by the end of the week. Miss Faye had rented Molly's single room to a young French Canadian woman. Her English left much to be desired and she spent most of her time hanging out with some other French-speaking Canadians from Montreal whom she had met.

Miss Faye was probably sobbing and moaning about everyone leaving again, although it was hard for Carson to understand why. She was still getting rent money from Alex and Dallas and himself, even if none of them were around.

He got a good deal on some red snapper from a fisherman who said the restaurants were not buying as much as usual. Apparently the second murder was having a profound effect on the tourist business in Negril. Many people had left the day before and more had plans to leave today.

Carson put the fish in Miss Faye's refrigerator, made some light conversation with Mayrene as she washed dishes, and then started back to his room. He could see Robinson and Henley still standing by the gate waiting for a bus to take them in the direction of Sav-La-Mar where they would pick up another bus for Kingston. There were two figures hidden by the hibiscus hedge which he assumed were Jazmo and Dallas.

There was something strange about this foursome, something he couldn't quite identify. He felt sure that one of them could not be trusted, but he didn't know which one it was. He shuddered to think who might be trying to leave the scene of two crimes, but he knew that he was as influenced as anyone by the drama of movies and television. These were just regular human beings, three vacationers and one happy-go-lucky Jamaican hustler; they were not hardened criminals.

As he packed, the absence of sound from the room next to his made him pause for a moment and think about Alex. Now there was a suspicious character; he had disappeared after Fawn's murder and not been seen or heard from since. He wondered what corner of the island Alex was raising hell on now.

With a few changes of clothes in his backpack, carrying his paintbox in one hand and the bag of fish in the other, Carson left Mango Grove behind him and headed back to Mt. Airy.

Murders and Mango Grove were the farthest thing from his mind later that night as he sat cross-legged at the foot of the bed, sketching Gwen stretched out naked across the soft pillows. Her head rested peacefully on one arm, her shimmering hair covered her shoulders and the top part of her body, one breast showing itself seductively between the long strands.

"Still comfortable in that position?" Carson asked her, as he rapidly colored the drawing in shades of amber and gold.

"Mmm, I could fall asleep. If you want me to stay awake, you'd better talk to me."

"Talk to you? I'm not much of one for long-winded monologues. Why don't you talk to me, Lady Guenevere? Isn't that what your name is short for?"

The bed shook with her laughter. "Sorry to ruin your fantasy about me, Sir Lancelot, but it's short for Gwendolyn. I always hated it. Sounds like the name of some walking, talking oversized baby doll."

"Well, can you imagine what it was like being in kindergarten with a name like Carson? My nickname was Kit, like Kit Carson, and I never shook that one until I got to college."

"Who was Kit Carson anyway?" she asked sleepily. "I always heard of him but never knew who he was."

"Some old cowboy. There!" He felt good about the drawing as he held it up and surveyed it. He hadn't felt this inspired in months. After spending the afternoon doing a colorful portrait of Aunt Belle on her porch, he had spent the evening involved in this sensual picture of the woman with whom he was falling in love. He felt as if he could go on this way forever, drawing Jamaican life in Mt. Airy by day, and this beautiful lady by night. "You can move now."

She rolled over on her back and sat up. "Ouch! My arm's asleep." She rubbed it vigorously as she tried to peek at the picture he was surveying. "Let me see it, Picasso."

He turned it around so she could look it over. "My God!" she breathed. "It's so...so..."

"So what?" He unfolded his long legs from their cramped, crossed position and stretched them out on either side of her.

"So sexual! You make me look like a Victorian prostitute!"

Carson hooted with laughter.

"Like one of those pictures on the wall over the bar in a Wild West saloon, you know what I mean."

Carson got off the bed, slightly offended. "Well, great. We'll put it up in some bar in the wild West End of Negril then." He began putting his pastels away.

"Oh, come on, Carson." She came up behind him, kissing the small of his bare back as she put her arms around his waist. "It just kind of surprised me that's all. I was just lying there feeling like the exhausted washerwoman I was today and you saw me as this- this- golden sex goddess!"

"Well, what's wrong with that?"

"How would you like it if someone drew a picture like this of you?"

They were silent for a moment, feeling the closeness of their bodies and the separateness of

95

their minds. "It's an interesting idea," he said suddenly, staring off into space.

"What is?" she murmured, running her fingers up and down his smooth chest.

"A Victorian prostitute, I mean, at the turn of the century in a steamy tropical setting. If you had a garter belt and black fishnet stockings we'd be all set. You could make me a wealthy man!" He turned around and gave her a long, searching kiss.

"Carson, no one else would be interested in seeing pictures of ME like that, except you. You'd never sell them."

He shrugged. "So? I'd be poor and happy. And very turned on. Like right now." He reached over her head and flicked the switch of her battery-powered reading lamp. "Let's go to bed."

He knew this euphoria couldn't last forever. But he was certainly going to make the most of it while he could.

CHAPTER EIGHT

The days and nights passed in a timeless blur. Carson had no idea how long he had been in Mt. Airy or what was happening back at Mango Grove, and he didn't care. He was finally doing the kind of work he had dreamed of doing when he planned this trip to Jamaica – an intimate exploration of the colorful soul of the island. Day after day he recreated scenes of the daily life around him.

To the people who performed these activities they seemed mundane and ridiculous subjects for paintings. The little girls brushing their gleaming white teeth by the outdoor water spigot laughed at him as he tried to quickly draw their images before they were gone. The old woman next door chopping firewood with a machete nearly took his head off with it when she discovered he had painted her in a torn work dress and crushed straw hat. The wrinkled farmer riding astride his mule told Carson he must pay if he wanted to sketch him as he rode by each evening.

One of the most exciting events was the night of the "house moving." Someone was actually moving a house from one piece of land to another; it perched precariously on a flatbed wagon being pulled by mules. People from miles around turned out to watch and the road was lit by excited teenage boys carrying flaming torches. No one paid the slightest attention to Carson who filled page after page with drawings of the crowd and the activity, which he would later turn into large colorful paintings.

Only once did he and Gwen head down to the beach for the afternoon with a crew of Aunt Belle's grandchildren and their friends. It had been an exhausting all-day excursion. A few days later he realized that he had not remembered to check his mail at the Negril post office and had also forgotten to replenish his art supplies from his room at Mango Grove. Gwen needed to do some food shopping at the supermarket, so they left for Negril right after breakfast.

A subdued atmosphere hung over the town; there was a conspicuous absence of well-heeled tourists with vacation dollars to spend. The die-hards were still there, of course – the very tanned, very beautiful, long-haired men and women who would spend their entire winter on the beach living on virtually nothing. But they were not the ones who spent all their money in one week, indiscriminately buying souvenirs and hiring sailboats for sunset cruises. The people scared away by the two murders were the backbone of the local economy and many of the vendors had a hungry look in their eyes as they hawked their goods.

He was not really sure what day of the week it was, but he thought it must be Monday or Tuesday. Molly had been gone for over a week, but there was no postcard from her waiting for him at the post office. There was a letter from his mother, but the details of life at her golf course condominium outside of Tampa did not hold his interest. A letter from a close friend in Jacksonville was filled with news of old college buddies, but it seemed trite and unsatisfying.

There were two letters addressed to Molly; he tucked these in his pack as he headed towards Mango Grove where he planned to meet Gwen and spend a few hours swimming and sunning. He knew Miss Faye would rail at him for not coming around for so long and making her worry so, but he tried to prepare himself to meet her onslaught with a sense of humor.

As usual, George and Emma were sitting in their lawn chairs on the beach in front of Mango Grove.

They were too well-known and entrenched in their Negril lifestyle to allow their comfortable existence be shaken by the pervading atmosphere of fear. A few murders weren't going to stop them from staying in Negril, not after all these years.

"Hey, it's the prodigal son!" George greeted him as he threw himself down on the sand beside them. "When do we get to meet the lucky woman who's held you captive for the last week?"

Carson grinned. "She soon come, mon," he replied. Relaxing, he drank in the immensity of the aquamarine waters stretching endlessly towards the horizon. "But it isn't only she who has kept me hostage for the last week. I've been doing a series of pictures on Mt. Airy. It's a love affair with the island as well, George."

George and Emma exchanged knowing looks and smiles. "It's certainly been quiet down here the last few days," Emma said. "All the bad publicity has scared the tourists right off. It's almost like the old days again."

"What's today? Tuesday?" Carson asked. When they both laughed at him, he went on. "All right, so I've lost track of time. Molly hasn't come back yet, has she?"

"I haven't seen her, have you, Emma? You must be preparing for a showdown of some sort, Carson."

Carson winced at the thought of it. "No, I just wondered. I can't remember when she was supposed to fly back. I think it's sometime in the next few days and I do want to talk to her before she leaves."

"Nope, as far as I know nobody's come back yet. The funeral was almost a week ago; we watched it on the JBC news the night it happened. We were down at the Tamboo Tavern having a drink and it came on the TV there. But Alex hasn't come back yet, nor Jazmo and Dallas for that matter." George wiped some beads of sweat off his brow and then removed his sunglasses. He stood up, preparing for a swim.

"What about those kids that Molly was supposed to meet? Anybody seen them?"

"Kids!" Emma squealed with amusement. "They're hardly that much younger than you, Carson. I haven't seem them, have you, George?"

"You'd have to check down at Paradise Park," he called over his shoulder as he headed for the water.

"It was all right, Carson reassured himself as he walked through the shady mango trees to his room. He wasn't ready to confront Molly anyway.

The stillness of the yard at midday was unnerving. Of course, in the noon heat everyone was always on the beach, but the quiet seemed more intense than usual. It seemed as though it had suddenly become off-season in the middle of the winter.

His room was just as he had left it, although a thin film of sandy dust was now covering all available surfaces. On top of the dresser there was a pile of crumbs where a mouse had chewed through a box of crackers and consumed the entire contents. Molly had obviously not come back yet to claim her possessions; they were still gathered in the basket in the corner.

He rummaged through a drawer until he found where he had hidden her airline ticket and passport. He had been right; her flight home was scheduled for Thursday, two days away. She would be showing up sometime in the next twenty-four hours. He sighed and shoved the ticket back under a pile of underwear before slamming the drawer shut.

They really had nothing to say to each other, he thought as he lay back on the familiar bed. Unless, of course, she was expecting him to be waiting and welcoming, which she very well might be. As long as she returned in the same state of mind which she had departed in, there would be no problem. He would just tell her that he would move his stuff out of the apartment when he got back home to Jacksonville in the spring.

His mind drifted through the possibilities of what might occur. Perhaps she was having an affair with that guy, Robinson Dubois, and feeling equally as passionate about him as he himself felt about Gwen. It was hard for him to imagine Molly feeling that strongly about anything, but nothing was impossible. Maybe she would come back and say she was moving to New Hampshire to live with Robinson. Or maybe she had been swept off her feet by a Rastafarian taxi driver who, instead of taking her to Port Antonio, had taken her up in the hills to his homestead and plied her with sex and weed until she was his blissful, willing love slave and had no intention of ever returning to the real world.

He laughed aloud at the preposterousness of that image, but sobered up instantly as he realized the similarity of his own situation to that ridiculous fantasy. What kind of future was there for him with Gwen? They had never talked about any long range plans. He supposed there really were none. If their relationship was still going strong in a few months they would deal with it then, when it was time for Gwen to go back to her theater camp in upstate New York and for Carson to go back to – to what? Jacksonville?

He wondered if he would follow her north, the same way he had followed her down the beach and then up to Mt. Airy. Would the same arrangement satisfy them in the states, with him playing the role of her live-in lover and artist boyfriend?

A noise in the doorway made him open his eyes and look up. Eva was standing there, tanner than ever. She appeared to have come directly from the beach for her brown skin gleamed with grease and the aroma of coconut oil filled the room. She was wearing her bikini bottom and a skimpy T-shirt over her large unrestrained breasts.

"Pardon," she said in the way of an apology. "I thought maybe Alex..." She groped for the English words.

"No, it's just me." Carson relaxed back onto the pillow but kept his eyes on her. She looked uncomfortable in her error.

"We go in the morning," she explained, backing out of the doorway. "I look for Alex to say auf wiedersen."

Carson could easily imagine what her "auf wiedersen" would consist of. He watched her walk back to her cottage dejectedly, an unusual attitude for Eva. The air in his room felt suddenly still and hot. He changed into his swimsuit, locked the door and headed back to the beach.

He found Emma and Gwen engaged in a lively conversation, as animated as old friends. "You never told me it was Gwen you were staying with, Carson!" Emma scolded playfully as he approached.

"You two know each other?" He sounded like a dumb pick-up in a bar.

"Of course! She's been coming to Jamaica as long as we have. We met on a flight down here years ago," Emma explained. "But we don't see her as much as we used to – she doesn't go in for the wild Negril scene anymore." Emma grinned affectionately at Gwen.

"I usually stay with George and Emma when I'm in the city," Gwen added. "Although it's been four or five years now, anyway. When did you guys start staying here?" She nodded back towards Mango Grove.

"Oh, we helped Miss Faye put the place on its feet about four years ago in exchange for a place to stay each winter."

Carson could see there was no space in this conversation for him, so he dropped his towel on the beach and headed for the water. As he watched the two older women from the sea, he felt like a jealous

102

child. He was disappointed that he wouldn't have the pleasure of introducing Gwen to George and Emma and having them tell him later how wonderful and beautiful she was.

Coming back to Mango Grove seemed to have set his emotions into turmoil. Turning his back on the beach, he began swimming swiftly out to sea, letting the warm water caress his hot, tired body and ease his troubled mind.

Later that afternoon, when they had showered and dressed and were getting ready to go back to Aunt Belle's, Carson heard the familiar scraping noise of the door being opened on the other side of the wall and the thud of objects being dropped on the floor.

He looked up from the table where he was writing a hasty note to Molly just in case she should show up that evening. "Alex must be back," he explained to Gwen. "Just in time, too," he added with a sour laugh.

"Just in time for what?" Gwen was perched on the edge of the bed, looking through an old Time magazine she had found in the corner.

"Just in time for Eva to say her last 'auf wiedersens' and to make Molly's last nights in Negril miserable. She can't stand the guy; he wakes her up banging away at women." He was speaking in whispered tones but Gwen's eyebrows raised in alarm and she nodded towards the open latticework above the wall.

He looked back at his short message. All he had said was that he would be back the next afternoon so they could talk before she left. It was enough. He propped the note up on the dresser and weighted it down with a bottle of suntan oil. Miss Faye would let her in if she showed up.

"Let's go." He kissed Gwen lightly on the top of her head. "Before I know it, I'll be on my way back down here tomorrow." He looked around. "Seems silly for me to keep this room, but I'm rather fond of it."

"Carson-"

"What?" He looked down at her affectionately. Her shiny hair shone a dark auburn in its state of wetness, her nose was freckled and sunburned.

"Nothing. Never mind. You do whatever you want." She shut the magazine and stood up. "Ready?" she asked, slipping her straw mesh bag over her shoulder and picking up her market basket.

Puzzled for a moment, he gazed at her, wondering what exactly she had been thinking. But she was already out in the yard, waiting for him, peering curiously into Alex's open door from a safe distance away.

Alex didn't miss an opportunity to meet a beautiful woman and by the time Carson had locked up, he was already out of his room and making small talk with Gwen. His clothes were wrinkled with the dried sweat of a day's hot travel, yet despite the obvious bags under his eyes, he was mustering up all of his oily charm to use on Gwen. She was gracious but not amused and her relief was visible when Carson slipped his arm through hers and walked her away, calling over his shoulder, "Later, Alex."

They nearly collided with Irena on their way towards the road. She was dashing headlong for the clothesline near the edge of the grove where Eva was taking down clothes that dried. Apparently Eva had not noticed Alex's arrival and Irena couldn't wait to let her know.

"Now there's an evening's entertainment I don't mind missing," Carson commented as he saw Eva's dark gaze flash at Gwen and then back at the building from which they had just come.

Despite a deeply penetrating, full body massage and an earthquake of an orgasm, Carson did not sleep that night. He tossed and turned on the cheap mattress, feeling every sagging broken spring. He knew he was nervous about dealing with Molly and how she was going to swallow the news that as soon as she had walked out on him, he had fallen madly in love with another woman.

He listened as one dog nearby began to bark and as another one joined in, and then farther away another, and another, until pretty soon all the dogs in Mt. Airy were howling and barking. This went on for about five minutes, until the noise level finally began to die down and all was quiet again. Two or three times every night the dogs put on this same performance, but it had never bothered Carson before. Tonight it was just another irksome reason he could not sleep. Slapping a mosquito that was buzzing in his ear, he kicked off the sweaty sheet and sat up.

Gwen found him in that same position when she awoke at dawn. He was asleep with his long thing legs stretched out on top of the sheet, his chin resting on his chest, his sun-bleached hair reflecting the first light of day. Mostly she noticed his fists, which, even in sleep, were still tightly clenched. When she tried to cover him up, he awoke with a start. "What time is it?" he asked instantly.

"Morning," she answered softly, trying to ease him into a more restful position.

"Thank God." Resisting her efforts, he stood up. "I want this day to be over and part of my past as soon as possible."

"Then you can make me breakfast this morning." She snuggled back down into the soft pillows and pulled the covers up to her chin.

The day dragged by slowly at Mango Grove. Molly had not arrived the previous night, so it would probably be late afternoon before she showed up. Carson wandered down to Paradise Park, just in case Rob and Henley had returned and by some slim chance Molly had decided to camp there with them and had not checked in with Miss Faye. But none of the three had been seen. He walked slowly back to Mango Grove, sloshing through the shallow water a few feet from the beach.

He passed the afternoon working on a picture of Hanalei. She was quite intrigued with the idea of being an artist's model and was delighted that Carson thought she was worth painting. But her slim, adolescent figure kept bringing Molly to mind, and he ended up concentrating just on Hana's face, focusing on her large dark eyes and mop of curly brown hair.

After that he went to the kitchen and did several sketches of Miss Faye as she prepared dinner. But his anxiety got the better of him. He finally put his pad away and walked up to the Golden Sunset for a beer. He stayed there until the sun began to dip beneath the horizon, figuring if he was gone for several hours, Molly would definitely have arrived by the time he returned. After a week of not drinking at all, he was really feeling his alcohol as he made his way back home. Everywhere, people had gathered on the beach to watch the fiery sun disappear into the darkening waters, but he could not bring himself to stop and indulge in this daily ritual.

"Hey, cool out, mon!" one dreadlocked Jamaican called after him as he hurried by.

Carson had hoped to be back in Mt. Airy by dark, but he knew that Gwen would understand if he did not return until morning. He had not intended to spend a night with Molly, but now there seemed to be no avoiding it.

However, there were no lights on in his room. A few quick questions and he knew she had not returned. Depressed, he joined George and Emma and the kids in the dining area for dinner.

"It's kind of odd, don't you think?" he commented to George before filling his mouth with curried chicken. "I just can't believe she's going to cruise in here tomorrow, pick up her stuff and cruise out again. Even Molly should know by now that things don't work that smoothly in Jamaica."

"That's just the point," George replied. "If she left Port Antonio this morning, it could easily take her until ten o'clock tonight to get back here. Don't start worrying yet, Carson."

"We better do something tonight to take your mind off it," Emma suggested.

"Carson was going to show me his Mt. Airy series," George reminded him. "I may have a few business deals in mind."

Carson looked at him curiously, wondering what he meant.

"You gonna paint my sister again?" Mickey asked. "If you do, next time paint her from behind so we don't have to look at her face."

"Mickey!" his mother admonished him. "We love that portrait, Carson. You could make a living doing conventional pictures like that."

Carson shrugged. "Thanks, Emma, but I guess I'd rather not." He moved his food around the plate with his fork and then finally pushed it aside. "I guess I don't have much appetite. I'll see you folks in a little while."

As he approached his room, he saw Alex sitting in the doorway next to his own. He was sharing a spliff with the short, fat Jamaican who ran his glass-bottomed boat business for him. "Hey, Carson," he called out, offering him the joint. "Haven't seen much of you since I've been back."

"I'm not around much these days," was his short reply. He really didn't feel like talking to Alex, but, not wanting to appear rude, he accepted the joint and made some light conversation. "How was your trip?"

"Sweet, real sweet. I mean, except for the funeral. That was heavy. But it's good to be back in Negril." He reached for the ganja and shared a laugh with his employee.

"Your girlfriend find you yesterday?"

"Which one?" Again the lecherous laughter. "Eva, yeah, she found me. I'm not sorry to see that one fly home. She was dynamite in bed but, woah, what a temper!" More laughter.

Carson tilted his head and looked sideways at Alex. It was certainly odd talk for a man who had just returned from his dead lover's funeral.

Suddenly he felt that he was wasting his time talking to such a ruthless individual. The ganja made him feel very sleepy and he decided to rest for a few minutes before going back over to George's.

When he opened his eyes he knew instantly that he had slept for more than a few minutes. Reaching for the alarm clock, he held it up to the faint moonlight that came through the windows. Nearly two a.m. The middle of the night and Molly had not arrived.

"Shit." He spoke aloud into the darkness. "What am I supposed to do now?"

There was no point in undressing and getting under the covers. It would be morning in four hours and he was going to have to know what to do.

First he would call the airline. He could find out if she had changed her flight to another day and then he would know when to expect her. That was it, of course. She had extended her vacation and just hadn't bothered to notify him.

But what if she hadn't changed her travel plans - what then? Call the police? They would laugh – find a young blonde woman somewhere on an island that was two hundred miles long and fifty miles wide with a lot of mountains and dirt roads in between? Call the American Embassy? No, they weren't exactly the FBI.

He was being neurotic – there was no reason to worry. But because he knew Molly so well, he had a gut feeling that something was wrong. She was always on time – in fact she was punctual to a degree that drove him mad on occasion. They had to be at the airport an hour early, they were always the first to arrive at a party, she was never late for work. Of course, Molly had not been acting like herself lately, so perhaps she had abandoned her punctuality when she abandoned Negril.

Thoughts like these spun through his brain for the rest of the night. He imagined the worst, he imagined the best. By morning his head was throbbing painfully. He felt a little better after a cup of coffee and two Cafenol, the Jamaican equivalent of aspirin with a name that didn't try to hide the fact that it was mostly caffeine. He didn't want to talk to anybody yet; he didn't know how his anxiety would manifest itself if another person showed interest or sympathy in his situation.

By eight o'clock he was in the phone booth near the supermarket, Molly's airline ticket propped up in front of him, dialing the number for Air Jamaica. He was upset by how much his hands were shaking and tried to attribute it to the Cafenol.

"Air Jamaica. Can I help you?"

"Yes, I'm calling to check on a reservation for today, for Molly McRae. On the 3:45 to Miami from Montego Bay." He gave her the flight information and then waited.

"I have an M. McRae who did not confirm in advance, but there are still some seats available."

Carson was silent for a moment, trying to decide what to do. "Sir, are you still there?"

"Yes, I'd like to change that reservation if I may." After some discussion, he arranged for Molly to be on a flight for the following Monday. If she wanted to pay the extra for a weekend ticket, she could change it herself when she got back.

So what did he know now? He wandered over to the bakery and bought a bun and some coffee. He knew something was really wrong, that's what he knew. He was sure that on-time, do-right Molly knew she was supposed to confirm her return flight seventy-two hours in advance with Air Jamaica. Was she having such a good time that she had just never thought of it? Or was his fantasy of her being held captive by a wild Rastafarian not so far out?

He decided to go back to Mango Grove and discuss the situation with George and Emma. They knew the ways of the island; they would know what to do.

He met them and their kids on the road back into town, loaded down with snorkels, fins and masks. They were headed towards the West End to do some snorkeling on the beautiful coral reef off the cliffs. One look at Carson's strained face was enough to make them stop in the baking heat of the asphalt road and pull him aside.

"What's up? She didn't show?" George looked around for some shade. They all moved into the small dark circle provided by a short mangrove tree, which offered less and less protection from the sun as noon rapidly approached.

"No. And she never confirmed her plane reservation either. It's just not like her, George." Carson shook his head, puzzled. "She's not impulsive and she doesn't space things out."

"Maybe she's having the time of her life in Port Antonio and has decided not to go back for a few months," Emma suggested gently. "That's not unheard of."

"But how do we know she even got to Port Antonio?" There was a silence and then Carson went on. "I mean, no one's heard from those other guys,

110

we don't know if she ever even met up with them. I know I'm being unreasonably neurotic about this-"

"No, you're not," Emma reassured him. "But there's not reason to get nervous yet. She still may show up today."

"And what if she doesn't?"

"Let's just wait and see what happens by evening," George said finally, wiping the sweat off his neck with the tail of his shirt.

"She might be in jail." Mickey's off-hand remark elicited dark looks from everyone, so he elaborated. "I heard about this girl who crossed a customs line by accident on a dock in Ocho Rios and so they made her go through customs again and they found a joint in her backpack and busted her. So then they put her in jail and sentenced her to six months hard labor. Finally she got deported."

"Where'd you hear that?" Emma demanded curiously.

"It's true, I heard it too," Hana piped in. "It was just an accident, it could happen to anybody, that's what everyone kept saying."

Carson shuddered involuntarily. Emma put her hand on his arm before saying in a voice that was just a little too bright, "Well, I'm sure nothing like that happened to Molly. Carson, do you want to come snorkeling with us? Get your mind off all this for a few hours?"

"No, I'm going back up to Mt. Airy." He hadn't really thought about what to do next, he just knew he needed to see Gwen. "I may not be back down until tomorrow morning. So if Molly does show up-"

"We'll take good care of her," George assured him. "And Carson, if you need – I mean, if she doesn't come back – what I'm saying is, we'll help you if there really is a problem."

"Which I doubt," added Emma.

He watched them continue blithely on their way under the blinding brilliance of the hot sun and it was hard to believe that anything might be wrong. After all, this was paradise, wasn't it?

"Well, there's only one thing you can do," Gwen said calmly when Carson had finished telling her what had happened.

They were sitting on a bench under a sprawling naceberry tree that shaded most of Aunt Belle's yard. Carson looked at her in surprise. In the midst of his uncertainty, she sounded so sure of herself. "What's that?" he asked.

"You'll have to go to Port Antonio, of course. And see if you can find her."

"But what if she's not even there? What if she never even got there? Or what if I get clear across the island and she turns up back here after I leave – how will I even know?"

"Now, relax, Carson. You're caught up in this emotionally and you're not thinking clearly. We'll figure it out, we'll answer all your questions, and when you leave, you'll know exactly what you're doing."

"I'm not emotionally involved in this. Damn it! I'm not in love with her anymore!" Gwen's steady rationality made him feel even more agitated.

"For Chrissake, Carson, she's still someone you care about, even if she's not your lover anymore! Who else is going to do this job if you don't?"

Carson did not reply, but his flaming cheeks and his grim, tightened lips spoke to the confusion and anger he was feeling.

Gwen was right. It would be months before anyone back home would suspect anything was wrong. They would assume Molly had just extended her stay in Jamaica to be with Carson. This was his responsibility whether he liked it or not, whether he cared about her or not.

The problem, he was beginning to realize, was that he cared more than he wanted to admit. A cold knife of fear was beginning to dig into his heart. He was afraid that something really bad might have happened to her and it was becoming more than just a nagging worry.

"All right." He sighed heavily. "I'll go. If you'll come with me."

"Oh, Carson." Gwen pulled his head over to rest on her shoulder and put her arms around him. Leaning back against the wide gray trunk of the tree, she held him against her for a few minutes before speaking. "It wouldn't be right," she said at last. "You have to do this on your own. You don't know what you're going to find, or how much she might need you when you get there. I'll be here to help in any way I can on this end and when you get back, I'll be waiting for you. And I'll understand if it doesn't work out between us. You do what you need to do."

He pulled away from her so that he could see her face. "This has nothing to do with you and me." His voice was harsh with raw emotion. "It doesn't change how I feel about you. It only makes it more intense because I'm going to be spending so much time apart from you."

"I know that." She took both of his hands in her own. "Now let's talk about what you need to do first."

CHAPTER NINE

As Carson approached George and Emma's cottage, he could hear their voices raised in loud, urgent discussion. About to rap on the door, he stopped his hand in midair as he became aware of what they were saying.

"Emma, your imagination has been working overtime again. I don't see how you could possible think Molly's disappearance could be connected in any way."

"It's not that crazy! Two women are murdered in Negril within a mile of each other. A third one who, on the very day of the second murder, supposedly left the same place and then didn't return when she was expected. And you can't make a connection? I mean, how do we know Molly didn't get off the bus a mile down the road the same day she left? She might never have left Negril at all."

"You're nuts! Last night you were certain she had fallen in love with that boy with 'the puppy dog eyes'," George did a mocking imitation of Emma's voice, "and that was why she had forgotten all worldly and important things. Today you try to tell me she was murdered by the 'Negril Strangler' before she even left town!"

"Lower your voice! Carson is supposed to show up any minute and I don't want him to worry any more than is necessary."

But Carson had already turned away in a cold daze, having forgotten his reason for being there. In all his worrying, he had never once contrived the horror story that Emma had just spun. Even now he couldn't let himself think that it might be true. He and Gwen had put together a solid, workable plan for finding Molly and in the last twenty-four hours it had given him something to lean on. And now he had to go ahead with their plan so that the seeds of doubt that Emma had just planted in his brain would never take root and sprout.

He stumbled out onto the beach and sat down for a minute to collect himself. He went over the steps of what he was going to do today and tomorrow. As soon as all the loose ends were tied up, he was headed for Montego Bay, where he would spend the night at Aunt Belle's sister's house. In the morning he would go to the Parade – that was where Gwen said all the minibuses dropped people off – and he would ask if anyone had seen Molly get on or off a bus. Then he himself would head for Port Antonio. When he got there, he would go to a particular section of town which George had pointed out to him on the map, where many inexpensive Victorian guesthouses were located. Molly was sure to have stayed in one of them.

At noon each day he would call the phone booth at the Negril supermarket to find out if Molly had finally returned to Mango Grove. Gwen would check Carson's mail to see if there were any letters or postcards from or for Molly that might indicate where she was. If they hadn't found her by Monday...well, then they would go to the police and the American embassy.

Nervously he drew aimless designs in the sand with his fingers as he tried to figure out what else he needed to get together in the next few hours before he left. He needed to dig out any drawings he had of Molly so he could use them for identification and he needed to think about his financial situation.

He had not paid much attention to how much money he had been spending. As the winter progressed, he began to realize that his funds were not enough to see him through comfortably until spring. He had thought about moving up to Mt. Airy to live with Gwen, where he could probably subsist much more cheaply than at Mango Grove. But now that he was going to be traveling...

Shaking his head, he stood up. He had no idea what the future would bring at this point; he couldn't think past tomorrow and Port Antonio. He would borrow an extra hundred bucks from George in case of emergency and deal with his financial problems when he got back.

This time when he arrived at George and Emma's they were sitting on the doorsill, laughing and eating watermelon. There was no trace of the fiery argument they had been having a few minutes earlier.

"Well, there he is at last!" George stood up and wiped his hands on his shorts. "Let's go to your room. I've got some business to discuss with you before you take off."

"You want me to buy you something in Port Antonio?" Carson easily fell into step with George's hurried pace.

"No, nothing like that. I want you to sell me some of your paintings."

"Right now?" Carson stopped short and stared at him.

"I thought you might need some extra cash for your journey. Besides, Emma and I have been very impressed with your work and we think a lot of our friends in New York would be too. I'm sure I could sell any of your art in our imports gallery back home."

Carson was speechless. Finally he blurted, "Are you just doing this because you think I need the money?"

"No, no, no. I've been trying to corner you for days to discuss this, but with everything that's been going on, it's never been the right time. Come on, let's get going. It may take a while."

Carson's face broke into a grin as he clapped George on the back. "George, you're a hero."

By the time he was ready to leave, dusk was approaching and the white egrets were flying home for the night to their mangrove trees by the river. Every evening hundreds of egrets flew in from miles away to roost en masse by the bridge near the roundabout. It was an awesome sight and one of the few things about Negril that Molly had found inspiring. When everyone else headed for the beach to watch the sun go down, Molly had always gone to watch the egrets instead.

Carson could not get this thought out of his mind even though George stood and chatted with him as he waited for a bus. As they watched the road, Alex's battered Toyota turned into the driveway, with a squeal of bald tires and the rumble of a deteriorating muffler, and then disappeared behind a stand of elephant-eared dasheen leaves in the yard.

"A strange guy, huh?" George commented when the dust had settled. "I don't run into very many macho maniacs like him these days."

Before Carson could reply, a slow moving VW bus pulled up and the driver shouted, "Mo Bay! Mo Bay!" Carson climbed into the already crowded vehicle, cursing his mother's tall Swedish ancestors as he tried to fit his long legs between the front and back seat without bumping them into his own chin.

George poked his head through the open window. "If you get to Port Antonio in time, try to call tomorrow, Carson. One of us will be waiting."

"You getting in?" The driver asked George impatiently.

George stepped back and the bus moved out onto the roadway again. He watched its slow progress as the driver yelled, "Mo Bay!" a few more times in a desperate attempt to cram as many bodies as possible into the already overcrowded van.

"Was that Carson leaving for somewhere?" Alex's voice at his shoulder startled him.

"Yeah, he's going to see if he can find Molly." Now that Carson was gone, George did not try to keep the gloom out of his voice.

"In Port Antonio, you mean?"

"Wherever. We don't know if she ever made it there."

"Well, of course, she made it there. I dropped her off myself."

"You what?!" George's jaw dropped.

"Yeah, I found her wandering the streets of Montego Bay and since I had some time to kill before Fawn's funeral, I took her to Port Antonio." Alex's tone was very careless.

George's eyes narrowed with suspicion and he studied Alex for a few seconds before speaking. "How is it that you never mentioned this to Carson?"

Alex snorted. "Carson is a snob. He wouldn't give me the time of day unless I asked him for it and he hasn't been around much since I've been back. Besides, I didn't think he cared, him havin' that new girlfriend and all."

"Damn it, Alex. Haven't you been aware that for the last few days we've all been busting our brains trying to figure out where Molly is? She was supposed to fly home yesterday and she never came back for her ticket." George swore again and stomped around angrily in the dust at the side of the road. "So when did you last see her?"

The two men held a locked gaze for several seconds. Alex seemed offended by the defensive position George was forcing him into and his eyes flashed angrily. "Not since before the funeral," he spat out finally. "Anything else you want to know?"

"Where did you leave her?" Bastard, George added silently. And was she still alive?

"On a fucking street corner. She was going to look for a guesthouse. You tryin' to pin something on me, Goldberg?" Alex moved his face closer and George could smell the odor of stale ganja and rum on his breath. "You're one of those scumbags who thinks I did in Fawn too, I bet. Well, you tell me you think I had anything to do with scrawny blonde bitch disappearing and I'll tell you to take a flying fuck at the moon."

George swallowed hard, trying to keep from becoming irrational and angry before he squeezing all the information he could from Alex. "Did she say where she might be staying or what she would be doing?" he asked in a very controlled voice.

"She said she was meeting that young shithead and his friend, but I really wasn't very interested. She was an ungrateful broad and I was glad to see her go." He stepped aside to leave but George blocked his way.

"Ungrateful for what, Alex?" He could barely contain his simmering anger.

"Ungrateful for the ride I gave her, and the room I got us for the night, and the meals I bought her. The rest of it is none of your damn business!" He shoved past George and stormed off into the twilight.

George picked up a stick and with a cry of rage broke it over his knee before hurling it as far as he could. He should be feeling full of hope – this was the first positive report they'd had that Molly had made it all the way to Port Antonio. At least it blew apart Emma's theory that she might have been murdered before she left Negril. But he didn't trust Alex and he knew he was not telling everything. What could he possibly be hiding? What could Molly have done that would have made him so angry? And why would Molly take a ride with him at all; her hatred of him had always been so evident.

It made even less sense than before, when they had known nothing. Shaking his head, George walked slowly up the drive in search of Emma.

Carson spent a restless night in a narrow bed that squeaked loudly every time he made even the slightest movement. The sheets smelled rather musty, as if they'd been hidden in the bottom of an old dresser drawer for a long time. Aunt Belle's sister, Miss Nadine, insisted that Carson shut the window before retiring so that "duppies and t'ieves not get in." The air in the tiny room soon became so stifling that he opened the top half of the louvers, not caring if Jamaican ghosts and burglars came in or not. He wondered whose bed he was sleeping in, what relative was being forced to double up with someone else in the large extended family. But mostly he wondered about Molly, and what he would find out in the morning.

First light found him packed and ready to go. Despite the early hour many people were up and "abroad," on their way to the vegetable or fish markets, or off to catch a bus to some other Saturday morning destination. Their bright clothing appeared to him as large blocks of color, forming a patchwork quilt in constant motion.

He had little trouble finding the Parade. Although the bus drivers took an interest in his story and passed around his sketches of Molly, not one of them could say he remembered her. One of the drivers, who ran the north coastal route regularly, thought he might have given a blonde American girl a ride. But as Carson eagerly questioned him, it became apparent that the large, buxom, older woman whom he had carried as far as Ocho Rios had not been Molly at all.

One thing he did learn was that there was no bus that went all the way to Port Antonio from Montego Bay. He would have to change in Ocho Rios. When he finally settled into a seat and was on his way, he realized that he'd had no breakfast, not even a cup of coffee. There was nothing he could do about it now, so he rested his head against the window next to him and closed his eyes, trying to sleep.

When the rumbling in his stomach finally awoke him, the minibus was whizzing down a very straight stretch of road that ran beside the sea. To the left, the turquoise waves crashed against the jagged coral reefs; on the right was an enormous hedge of brilliantly blooming bougainvillea that seemed to stretch on for miles.

He leaned forward so that he could speak into the driver's ear. "How much longer to Ocho?" Carson asked him.

"Not too long, mon. Maybe one half hour. Hey-" the driver lowered his voice and spoke secretively- " you looking for some smoke?"

"No, thanks, mon. What I'm really looking for is some food." Carson was beginning to feel lightheaded and remembered now that he hadn't even eaten any supper the previous evening.

"No problem, mon! One lickle shop not far up the road from here where you can buy up bun and soda. It soon come."

Bun and soda was not what he had in mind, but he was too hungry to complain. About five minutes later the driver pulled off in front of a small, one-room building. Through the open doorway Carson could see the traditional glass display case for breads and crackers on one side of a counter covered in green linoleum. Several shelves of canned goods lined the back wall.

Dubiously he climbed out of the bus, trying not to hear the low grumblings of the other impatient passengers in regard to the preferential treatment the driver was showing him. "Right in there, mon. The lady is a friend of mine."

A wizened old lady was sitting on a stepstool behind the counter; she was so tiny, that when she stood up, she could barely see over it. "Good day," she said in a clear voice. "Can I help you?"

Carson could see an open tin of New Zealand cheddar inside the glass case. He hated the bright orange canned cheese with the consistency of Velveeta, but at the moment even the cut piece with its hardened, cracked edges looked appetizing. He ordered a large piece of the cheese and a loaf of spice bread in a sticky wrapper. As she cut the cheese, his eyes ran swiftly across the shelved goods. A dozen cans of carrot juice, several more of tomato soup, a row of pimento condiments and a few jars of mango chutney. He spied a jar of guava jelly that he wanted on the top shelf and then watched painfully as the old woman climbed her stool to reach it for him. She wiped the dust off the lid with her skirt before placing it with the rest of his food. A package of cream crackers and a bottle of D & G orange soda from a picnic cooler completed his purchases.

His arms full, he climbed back into the minibus which took off before he'd even sat down again. Luckily the bus had an aisle down the middle with a row of single seats on one side and double on the other, so he could hunch over in his little one-person seat and stuff his face without feeling overly self-conscious about the hungry eyes that watched him.

It was an odd combination of food and topped off with the sickly sweet orange soda, it did not sit well in his ravenous stomach, or in a bus that needed new shock absorbers. He was glad when the bus finally slowed to a stop in traffic on the outskirts of Ocho Rios.

It was well into the afternoon by the time Carson realized he had never made his call to Negril at noon. When he climbed out of the first bus, he was quickly hustled away by another minibus driver looking for a fare to Annotto Bay, where Carson could make his final transfer for a bus to Port Antonio. When they left Ocho Rios and began heading east, he was quite taken by the lush beauty of the winding coastal road and for a few moments he forgot about Molly and actually began to enjoy himself.

By the time he switched buses in Annotto Bay, he felt as though he had left Negril behind in another country. It had not occurred to him that the rest of Jamaica might be more beautiful than the small western area he was beginning to know so intimately. There were a dozen kinds of wildflowers he had never seen before and off to the south he could see mountains so tall that their peaks were hidden in the clouds.

The young girl sitting next to him was wearing a red plastic digital watch. He caught a glimpse of the time and slapped his forehead guiltily. One thirty. Twelve o'clock had come and gone and he hadn't remembered the simplest part of the plan. He reassured himself with the thought that it hardly mattered. He hadn't found anything out yet anyway.

But what if Molly came back last night, he worried, and he was going all this way for nothing? It was okay, it was a beautiful ride and it wouldn't hurt him to spend a night in Port Antonio.

He argued back and forth with himself, trying to justify the fact that he had forgotten to make his telephone call. He only succeeded in becoming increasingly nervous the closer he came to his destination.

As they entered the city, a large billboard inviting him to stay at the Lorraine Guest House made him realize that the time to get to work was now at hand. The Lorraine Guest House was as good a place to start as any.

The bustling center of Port Antonio had a very colonial atmosphere to it, although it also seemed to have its share of modern banks and supermarkets. It did not take long to drive through the downtown section, and then suddenly the bus was driving up a hill into a quiet residential area where the houses were large Victorian structures, two or three stories high. There was a spacious feeling about them that one rarely found elsewhere on the island. But what impressed Carson most was the element of bygone elegance. Each building had something that gave it away – a sagging porch, peeling paint, an overgrown yard or a broken window. It reminded him of places back home in the South, towns whose glorious antebellum days had ended with the Civil War.

It was also easy to imagine Molly being totally enchanted by the gable ends, the French windows and the long sweeping porches decorated with gingerbread. He tried to see it through her eyes, to imagine which place she would have picked out first in search of a room. Several of the larger houses displayed signs proclaiming them as guesthouses.

The Lorraine Guesthouse was located on the corner of a peaceful side street. He let himself in the gate and walked up onto the porch. There were several white people sitting there, but as he approached them he realized they were speaking German, not English. One of them, a pale fellow with a shaved head and wire rimmed glasses, turned towards him.

"You are looking for a room?" he asked Carson politely.

"Uh, well, yes, sort of." He was not fully prepared for this. "Yes, I am looking for a room. But I'm also looking for someone who may be staying here," he went on more boldly. "Do you work here?"

The German laughed merrily. "No, no. I am on holiday like my friends here. Cecile! Cecile!" He shouted over his shoulder into the screen door which led inside. "Cecile is the concierge," he explained. "But I think she will tell you that the rooms are full."

An attractive, very dark-skinned woman peered through the screen door. "We have no vacancy tonight," she said without bothering to come out or invite Carson in. "We are full up."

Carson set his bag on the floor, and used his thumbs to lift the weight of his daypack up off his shoulders. "I'm looking for a friend of mine. I wondered if you could tell me if she stayed here at all in the last two weeks."

There was a silence during which the woman sized him up, trying to sense whether she could trust him or not. Up until this point Carson had not really thought about what kind of impression he might make upon the people whose help he would need. He rarely worried about what others thought of him. Now he was aware of his white cotton pants covered with paint splatters, the not very clean T-shirt he had been wearing for two days and a night, and his uncombed, shoulder-length hair. He should have let Gwen give him a haircut before he left, but personal grooming had been the last thing on his mind. At least his beard was light; a few days growth was not especially noticeable.

One thing he did know was that women were always fascinated by his eyes. He caught the woman's dark gaze and gave her his most innocent, pleading look. Finally she turned the handle and pushed open the screen door. "Okay. You can come in."

She let him into a dark empty room with plastic couches facing a black- and-white TV that was playing loudly to no one. "What is the person's name?" she asked, crossing to a desk on the opposite side of the lounge. She leaned over to pick up a large red leather ledger which had slipped to the floor, and Carson was suddenly very much aware of the straining seams of the orange double-knit polyester dress tightly encasing her voluptuous body, particularly her oversized behind.

"Molly. Molly McRae. From Jacksonville, Florida."

The woman frowned and shook her head. "What did she look like?"

125

"Short, about this high-" he indicated her height with his hand – "she has long blonde hair, about the color of mine. She wears it in braids."

The woman shook her head again. "Me not remember such a one, but you can look through here and see if she come." She opened the guestbook flat on the desk and gestured towards him.

She stood quite close to him as he leafed quickly through the last few pages. He realized it was no accident that she was pressing those large hips against him – she probably thought he had been coming on to her in the doorway.

He closed the book and handed it back to her. "Well, thanks for your help," he said awkwardly. "Any ideas where else I might find a room?"

She hesitated and then murmured, "I will have a room open tomorrow night. You will come back."

Shit, he thought. What am I doing wrong? "Sure, maybe," he replied cheerfully, backing up to the screen door and picking up his bag. "But where would you suggest I spend tonight?"

"Down the street is the Sea Star Inn. You tell them Cecile has sent you for just one night and then you will come back to me." She gave him a coy smile and he hoped his retreat did not look as hasty as he was trying to make it.

The Sea Star Inn was three stories of gingerbread shutters and latticework porches topped by a dangerously decrepit cupola. A rusty wrought iron fence surrounded the front yard. The old man who ran the place had never heard of Molly and shook his head when Carson showed him his sketches. Despite the quaint appearance of the outside, inside the Sea Star was dark and depressing. Carson moved on.

After a few more vain attempts, he was too tired to continue and decided that he would spend the night at the next place he tried. Lantana House was a large, square-framed building with big, old-fashioned double hung windows. Cracked stone steps led to a porch that ran the length of the building and which was topped by another veranda on the second story.

A very thin, ageless woman sat in a metal porch chair, cooling herself with a folded newspaper fan. "Good afternoon, sir." She greeted Carson in a high quavering voice that suited her wispy figure and hair.

"Hi. Good afternoon." The politeness of older Jamaicans always caught him off guard. "Do you have a room for the night?"

"Of course!" The woman slipped her feet into a pair of old sneakers with broken-down backs as she stood up. "It is just you alone?"

"Yes, just me alone." He followed her into a cool, open hallway. The wooden floor was polished with the red wax that was used in most Jamaican homes. At Aunt Belle's Gwen had shown him how to rub it in with an old rag and then how to polish the floor with half of a water coconut husk.

The woman indicated a few open doors and Carson peered into them uncertainly. The furnishings were shabby but clean and did not fill up the spacious interiors; the rooms were neat but rather bare.

"Wait, I have a room upstairs that I think you will like." She had a quiet voice and an accent that spoke of schooling somewhere in her past.

She led the way up a wide wooden staircase. Opening a door in an identical hall to the one below, she showed him a room very similar to the others. "But see here-" she crossed the room and opened up another door which led onto the upstairs porch overlooking the street and out into the harbor. "You can just step from your room onto the veranda any time you choose!"

Her tone of delight brought a grin to Carson's face. "How much?" he asked circumspectly.

127

His jaw dropped in amazement at the low price she told him. It was roughly equivalent to seven American dollars. There was nothing available for that amount in Negril. "Sold!" he laughed, swinging his bag onto the double bed, and she laughed with him.

"You must come down and register then," she said formally, and taking him firmly by the arm, she marched him downstairs.

As he scrawled his signature into her guest book, his eyes quickly ran over the other names on the page. His pen stopped in midair as the familiar handwriting leaped out at him. "Molly was here?" His voice was no more than a quiet croak.

"Molly? Oh, yes, mon! What a fine girl, Molly." The woman clucked her tongue in satisfaction. "She is a friend?"

"Is she still here?" Carson's eyes were swimming, the names on the page a black blur.

"No, mon, she gone some days now. A funny way she leave me too."

Carson steadied himself and turned around to face her, letting his eyes come back into focus on her kindly face. Crossing his arms across his chest so that she could not see how much he was shaking, he asked, "What do you mean, 'funny'?"

"One morning I get up and make her coffee how she like it, you know, and the sun climb higher and higher and still she not awake. After some hours, I knock on her door and there is no answer. When I open it up, I see she is gone. Just gone." The woman shook her head. "It not like her. All the time that she stay here, she say goodbye to me, even just to go to the market. And she always keep her room tidy-" she stretched out the last word to three syllables and paused for effect – "but this time the room just one giant mess."

She moved closer to him and said in a quiet tone of voice, "You are a close friend of hers?"

Carson nodded speechlessly, trying to absorb all she was telling him. "Yes, she is – was my girl – my good friend, yes." The relief that had at first buckled his knees was giving way to that nameless fear again. "What day was this that she – left?"

"Oh, I don't know, you know, I would have to sit and think. She plan to leave on the same day – she need to get all the way back to Negril she say, to pick up her airline ticket. But like I am telling you, she gone early-early and not one word of goodbye!" She sniffed a little in an insulted manner and then asked, "You will be seeing her in the states?"

Carson swallowed. "I...I assume so. Why?"

For an answer, the woman went quickly out the back door and returned with what looked like a pile of neatly folded laundry. "She leave so fast she forget these things she have hanging on the clothesline in the back yard. Maybe you give her them?"

Stunned and confused, Carson took the pile of clothing she was holding out to him and looked down at it. Like a blast of cold air from a freezer, the familiar tropical print of Molly's favorite skirt seemed to shock him back to his senses. Beneath the skirt was a white dress Carson had given her for her birthday the year before on which he had hand-painted birds-of-paradise and freesias. It was one of Molly's most precious possessions; she would never have forgotten it. Three pairs of tiny cotton bikini underpants and the skimpy red cotton shirt she always wore with the skirt were on the bottom of the pile.

Something is wrong here, Carson thought anxiously, clutching the clothes to his chest. He closed his eyes and breathed in the perfumed scent of laundry detergent. Something is very, very wrong.

"You are feeling poorly?"

Carson shook his head and opened his eyes. "No, I'm okay. I'm sorry, I didn't catch your name?"

129

"Leola Johnston. And you are-" she looked at her guest register and sounded out his name almost phonetically – "Car-son Cor-rig-an. Pleased to meet you." She bobbed her head in an outdated, British sort of way.

"Miss Leola, is there some place we can sit down? You and I need to have a long talk."

CHAPTER TEN

Molly fell in love with Port Antonio. It was everything Negril wasn't – it was safe and inexpensive, with a minimum of tourism. From the moment she walked up Titchfield Hill and saw the quiet streets and the sprawling Victorian houses with their shady, inviting verandahs, she knew she had made the right decision, even though she had been questioning her intuition in the last twenty-four hours.

Lantana House had been the first guesthouse she had come upon. She was so delighted when Miss Leola showed her the high-ceilinged room off the upstairs verandah that she didn't even bother to look further. After a cool shower, she stretched out on the firm double bed and fell instantly asleep, despite the fact that it was high noon. The night with Alex had been a harrowing experience and she needed some real rest to recover.

She spent the next three days exploring the city and the nearby beaches, and the despair she had felt that awful night soon receded to just a small paragraph in the chapter of her life that included all the bad memories of Jamaica before Port Antonio. More than once she awoke, dripping with sweat, from a nightmare taking place back in that seedy motel room outside of Ocho Rios and she would realize then that she was still only suppressing the revulsion she had experienced that night.

Each morning she would drink coffee on the porch and watch the school children walk by on their way to Titchfield High School, built on the site of the old Fort George. The girls wore neatly pressed white blouses and dark blue skirts with white anklets and black shoes. Their individuality was only expressed in their carefully combed hair styles, the most popular being a variation of corn row braids unbraided about halfway down to hang in long, uniformly kinky curls. The boys all wore khaki pants and shirts, like miniature military men.

After breakfast she would explore the town, always visiting the market to buy bananas and tangerines and tomatoes from the beautifully arranged displays. Occasionally she would come back with a prize like a huge avocado called "pear" or a perfectly ripe, sweet little red pineapple called "pine."

Two afternoons she took a bus out to Boston Beach. The small cove with its gloriously blue, crashing surf was nothing like the calm glassy waters of Negril, and she reveled in that difference more than anything else as she swam amidst the waves. One day she took the boat out to Navy Island, the small island that sat in the center of one of Port Antonio's twin harbors, but the only thing about it that was really enchanting was that it had once belonged to the swashbuckling Errol Flynn. Now it was just expensive tourist villas and condominiums and Molly found she preferred the international feeling of the city itself better. There were other white faces in town but very few were Americans; most were Germans, a few were British or Swedish or French.

One evening she treated herself to dinner at the De Montevin Lodge, just for the experience of it. The De Montevin was a fascinating, three-story brick hotel decorated with intricate wrought iron gingerbread painted a gleaming white. It had an ornately tiled terrace, which one crossed to reach the dark lobby, designed and furnished with Victorian flair. On the walls were pictures of Queen Elizabeth at every stage of her life – as a young girl with her pony, at her marriage to Prince Philip her coronation and during her visit to Jamaica. The De Montevin seemed to be a statement that spoke to the glories of the old way of life, when Jamaica was still under British rule. What Molly liked best about the place, however, was the way that the tackiness of the modern world had been incorporated into its vintage panache.

While Molly waited for dinner to be served, she sat on an uncomfortable fainting couch watching a new color TV, which was sandwiched between carved wooden bookcases holding a collection of ceramic dogs. The large white globes hanging from the enormous chandelier were not glowing; instead the room was lit by a dim lavender fluorescent light. After a little bell rang announcing dinner, Molly was seated at a table covered with a snowy linen cloth on top of which were plastic placemats, cracked and yellowing with age, featuring pictures of large hibiscus flowers. Placing her linen napkin on her lap, she laughed to herself as she looked at the menu on the wall. Plastic with removable black letters, it could have come from any diner or sandwich shop in the world – it was another totally incongruous touch.

The only disturbing note to the perfectly served, three-course meal was the JBC-TV evening news. From where she sat, Molly could still see the television in the lobby. Although she was trying not to pay attention to it, she could not tear her eyes away when a large photo of Fawn filled the screen followed by footage of her life and TV appearances.

She couldn't hear the text of the story, but it seemed to be coverage of the funeral which had taken place that day. There were quick shots of Mango Grove, some shots of Fawn's mother and relatives sobbing, and then a short interview with Alex.

Molly's appetite disappeared suddenly and her napkin slipped to the floor as she stood quickly, heading for the bathroom. Passing through a multicolored curtain of round and heart-shaped

133

plastic beads, she had a flashback to Aunt Mandy's Roadside Restaurant where a large backside in red satin jeans had disappeared through a similar curtain. Overcome with loathing for Alex, she stood in the pink bathroom, leaning against the door, until her stomach unknotted and the flush left her face.

When she returned to the dining room, the remains of her pork chop dinner had been removed and a tiny cut glass dish of what looked like coconut custard sat primly in its place. Although she dutifully ate every spoonful, she barely tasted it. In her effort to keep her mind a blank, the sounds of the other diners suddenly became overpowering. Every clink of a fork or clatter of a knife seemed to shatter her shaky self-control. Finally she could not stand it and she headed back to Lantana House to be alone with her thoughts.

She sat on the upstairs verandah, the darkness broken only by the street lamp on the corner. Taking a few deep gulps of an icy Heineken she had retrieved from the fridge downstairs, she finally let the recollections come.

When Molly had returned to the motel room that night, her apprehension of Alex had overcome her exhaustion and she was no longer feeling very sleepy. Alex was still reading the newspaper on the bed. Both pillows were doubled up under his head and various sections of the paper covered the blanket. Molly pulled a book out of her backpack and sat down in the not very comfortable plastic chair, pretending to read. She thought that if she waited until Alex fell asleep that maybe she could then lie down on the bed next to him without him being aware of her presence. He had drunk so much that he would probably pass out soon and sleep very soundly.

Minutes dragged by. Over the top of her paperback, Molly could see Alex's eyes beginning to droop and his head fell forward onto his chest a few times. Finally he yawned loudly, and, folding up the paper, he dropped it on the floor next to the bed and turned to Molly.

"Ready for bed?" he asked, as casually as if they were husband and wife married twenty years.

"No, that little nap revived me," she replied with a false cheeriness. "I think I'll stay up and read for awhile if the light doesn't bother you." She buried her face in the book and tried not to meet his eyes.

"Really? Well, we don't have to go right to sleep, you know." She could not believe the off-hand tone he was using. She had a sinking feeling now that he had been expecting her to have sex from the moment she asked him for a ride. That maybe he thought she actually wanted him and was just shy about showing it.

Out of the corner of her eye, she watched him unbutton his shirt and toss it down on top of the newspapers. She was so tense that her senses were acutely aware of every sound and motion around her. The slightly mildewed smell of the room was sharp in her nostrils; a moth flitting around the light fixture seemed as loud as a helicopter. She could hear at least two different radios playing somewhere nearby, she could mentally tune in one song and then the other, but mostly there was just the clash of reverberating bass lines. The sound of Alex's belt buckle hitting the floor as he dropped his pants was like a fire alarm clanging in her ears.

"Thanks, anyway," she heard herself croak in a little voice. "I think I'll just read for a while."

Alex shrugged and got under the covers, putting one of the pillows down for her next to his own. The little lime green patch on it mocked her as she sat there, stiff and uncertain, waiting for Alex to fall asleep.

For awhile he laid there with his hands behind his head, watching her read, a cocky smile playing

135

on his lips. He was the spider and she was the fly. He was just waiting for her to get caught in his web. Miserably she realized how trapped she already was.

Then, quite suddenly she saw that his eyes had closed and his breathing had become more even. She let the book fall into her lap and just watched him. She remembered Carson telling her about an Andy Warhol movie that was eight hours long and the entire film was of someone sleeping. She wished she could smile now like she had then at the ridiculous notion of it. Now she was in her own, real life, avant-garde film.

Cautiously she stood up and tiptoed across the room to the light switch. The loud click of it made her jump. Taking two or three deep breaths, she slowly sat down on the edge of the bed, and the old springs sighed loudly beneath her. Alex stirred, rolled away from her and then was still again. She carefully stretched out on top of the blanket, not removing any clothes.

With the lights out, all the sounds of the night were magnified and Molly resigned herself to a sleepless night. She tossed and turned, telling herself that at least she was getting some rest, if not sleep.

She did not realize that she had drifted off until she was awakened by a feeling of suffocation. A heavy weight seemed to be bearing down upon her chest. Opening her eyes, she saw the outline of Alex's face a mere inch from her own. She gasped and he took the opportunity to thrust his tongue into her open mouth and give her a hard, probing kiss.

Pinned down beneath his bulk, she could barely get her hands free to push him away. Pummeling him on the shoulders with her fists only seemed to spur him on further and he began grinding his body against hers. She finally grabbed the back of his head, and pulling his hair with both hands, jerked his face away from her own.

"Ow!" He howled with pain. "You little bitch! What do you think you're doing?"

"What do you think YOU'RE doing?" she shouted back at him. "Get the hell off of me or I'll scream rape."

He laughed unpleasantly. "Feisty little thing, aren't you? Did you know fighting turns me on even more?" With one arm across her chest to hold her down, he raised himself onto his knees, using his free hand to fumble with the zipper of her pants.

"Alex, no! Stop it! Get away from me!" She knocked his hand away from her crotch.

"Don't tell me you haven't been asking for this, baby," he whispered, grabbing her wrist, trying to guide her hand to his groin. She resisted with all her might, clenching her fists fiercely. "Come on, why'd you come with me if you didn't want to make love?"

"Make love!" she exploded. "Is that what you call this?" She tried to wrench her arm free but he was much stronger than she was and he forced her hand up until it grazed the burning hardness between his legs.

The last bit of anger and fear burst inside her brain. She never knew if her reaction was voluntary or involuntary, but her knee shot up, catching his balls from behind. Bellowing, he crumpled up and fell over beside her. Even in his pain, he did not relinquish his hold on her.

"All right, all right!" He gasped. "You win. I believe you. You're a fucking crazy broad, you know that?"

She tried to wriggle out of his grasp but his fingers tightened around her arm. "You can stay there. I won't try anything again, I promise."

Hot tears began to trickle out of the corners of Molly's eyes. She wished she knew where she was so she could just walk away. But the dark night in this strange place was too much for her to tackle. Never

137

before in her life had she felt so small, so vulnerable. She sniffed loudly and Alex looked up.

"Oh, for Christ's sake, what the hell are you crying for? I didn't hurt you, you little hellcat. I'm the one who should be crying!" He released her at last and turned away disgustedly.

Wiping her eyes with the back of her hand, she slowly got up off the bed and crossed the room to the door. As she groped for the key in the lock, Alex was quickly there, grabbing her around the waist from behind. "Hey, where do you think you're going?"

For one second her whole body trembled uncontrollably and then she was incredibly still. When she spoke, her voice was calm and icy. "I want you to unlock the car for me. That's where I'm going to spend the rest of the night."

"Oh, come on, Molly. All right, already. What do you need, an apology? I'm sorry. Okay?"

"Alex, unlock the car."

"You're a nut case, lady. I'm not gonna stand here arguing with you all night. If you wanna sleep in the car, feel free." He crossed the room to where his pants lay in a heap on the floor. He didn't bother to put them on, he just pulled the keys from the pocket and strode out of the now open door. After unlocking the front car door on the passenger side, he pushed past her, back into the room and, without another word, got back under the blanket on the bed.

Molly grabbed a pillow and her purse before slamming the door behind her. She did not care how funky the inside of Alex's car was. She could lock herself in for the remainder of the night and be safe from everyone. Except him.

Now, as she sat thinking about it on the verandah of Lantana House, it seemed amazing to her that she had come out of the episode unhurt and not raped. The endless and stuffy hours spent trying to sleep in the car, the sullen silence between the two of them the next morning as he drove at breakneck speed on the winding road between Ocho Rios and Port Antonio, her fear that he would take revenge on her in some way... it was all an anticlimactic epilogue to the scene at the motel.

Most puzzling of all was the way he had acted when he finally dropped her off in front of the old courthouse in the center of town. "So, I'll drop in on my way back from Kingston, see if you need a ride back to Negril," he said, reaching over the back of the seat and passing her bag to her.

She stared at him in disbelief. What could he possibly be thinking - that she would ever go anywhere with him again?

"I'll find you," he said confidently. "This is a small town when it comes down to it."

"I'm meeting friends," she replied stiffly. "Thanks for the ride." She turned abruptly and walked briskly away.

It made her shiver a little now to think that he might reappear some time in the near future. Well, if she didn't meet up with Rob and Henley in the next few days, she would have to leave on her own. She had noticed a small airport on the coastal road into Port Antonio. Maybe she would fly back to Negril.

Walking down the hill to town the next morning, she finally spotted them coming out of a small local restaurant generally frequented by German students visiting Port Antonio. Totally engrossed in their own lively conversation, they didn't even see her until she stopped right in front of them, blocking their path.

"Molly! Hey! How are you?" Robinson and Henley each hugged her in turn. "We were just gonna start looking for you. We got in late last night. Where are you staying?"

Molly felt a warm flood of relief coupled with a sense of security she hadn't experienced for days. Before she knew it, she was swept away with the two of them, off to pick up their snorkeling gear at the Lorraine Guest House, back to get her bathing suit and camera from her room, and then onto the coastal bus which would take them to the Blue Lagoon.

They chatted non-stop the entire time, Molly telling them about what she had done in Port Antonio (glossing quickly over her trip with Alex), and Henley and Robinson taking turns describing the wake and funeral in Kingston. At times Henley seemed to carry on both sides of the conversation single-handedly, unaware that Rob and Molly were silently contemplating each other. Every now and then their eyes would meet and hold for a few seconds until Molly would look away, feeling searched and explored in a way she had never experienced before.

The Blue Lagoon was the color of midnight and a calm, one hundred and eighty feet deep. It was a sharp contrast to the crashing surf along the rest of the North Coast and, although there was a restaurant of the same name built right on the edge of the water and all kinds of hustlers in the parking lot, it still had a special, peaceful quality about it.

Rob and Henley took turns sharing their snorkeling equipment with Molly, but since Henley was much shorter than Robinson and of a slighter build, his fins fit Molly much better. Consequently, while Henley lay in the sun on the dock, the other two snorkeled across the lagoon, enjoying the myriad of brightly colored fish and unusual formations of coral, until they finally climbed out on a tiny stretch of white sand on the opposite shore from the restaurant and bar.

Pulling off their masks and snorkels, they relaxed in silence for a few moments before speaking. Molly wasn't really sure what to say; there seemed to be so many layers to Rob's personality that she was uncertain as to where to begin getting to know him better.

He began talking about the funeral again and how hard it had been for him, particularly since Alex was the one getting all the attention for being Fawn's closest male friend.

"Tell me how you and Fawn met," she suggested gently, steering him away from the subject of Alex.

"We were in the same English Comp class. She was in it for the second time." His face softened a little as he remembered. "She didn't have a very good background in grammar and she couldn't type." He laughed. "She was so beautiful and I was so infatuated that I would do anything to meet her. So, in a reversal of usual stereotypes, I offered to type her papers. One weekend I invited her home to my aunt's house on Lake Winnepesaukee, but as it turned out, my Aunt was gone for the weekend and..." He tossed a seashell into the water and watched it sink to the bottom. "...the rest is beautiful history."

"You live with your aunt?" Molly asked confused.

"Well, right now I live in an apartment off-campus with Henley, but I grew up in my aunt's house."

"What about your parents?" She knew it was a prying question, but she wanted to understand him and knowing his past would help.

He gave a wry laugh. "What about them? My mother was pregnant and married by sixteen, divorced four years later and then decided she couldn't get back on her feet and find a new husband with a wild five-year-old tying her down. So she took me to live with my aunt for a few months that turned into a few years. When she finally got married again it was to an abusive truck driver who didn't like children. A few years turned into my whole childhood." There was no denying the bitterness in his voice. "I can't say she didn't do the right thing.

141

I'm sure I had a much more stable and normal childhood with my aunt and uncle and their three daughters than I would have had with her and Fred. But even so..." He broke off and Molly, who had been watching him carefully, could see his face flooded with dark emotions.

She had a feeling that perhaps she had opened a door to a room she wasn't ready to see yet. She could not imagine what it must feel like to be rejected by one's own mother as a child, but she was sure the reverberations echoed throughout the rest of life.

"So how much longer do you have at college?" Once again she changed the subject abruptly.

He blinked at her for a few seconds as his brain switched channels. "This is my last semester." His face relaxed again.

"And then what? What are you studying?" She hated asking these questions that she herself had such difficulty answering even now that she had graduated, but at least it was neutral ground for discussion.

"I'm a psych major, but so what? There's not much you can really do with a degree in psychology except keep going to school until you can become a high paid therapist of some sort. There's a halfway house where I might do an internship for a while, but that's more for the experience than the money."

Molly thought to herself that it was curious how the most confused people seemed to take the greatest interest in psycho-therapy as a career. "What about Henley?" she asked, looking across the water at the reclining figure wearing a pair of brightly patterned, loose cotton shorts.

"Henley? He doesn't know what he's doing from one week to the next. He's changed his major five times. First he was into Education, then Literature, then he did Theater for a long time. After than he became practical and studied Computer Science and now he's taking Business courses. He'll probably be in college for years!"

They chuckled together at the thought of Henley, the permanent student. "No, seriously, Henley is great – I don't know what I'd do without him. He keeps me laughing when things get too heavy and I keep him in line when he gets too crazy." Robinson yawned. "Boy, I'm exhausted. I haven't been sleeping well lately. What do you say we swim back so I can take a snooze on the dock?"

Standing up, he extended his hand to help her to her feet. Their eyes met and held again, this time for a long minute. Molly thought how easy it would be to lose herself in the feeling and passion she saw there; she found the idea equally scary and exciting.

"I really like you," he said in a matter-of-fact voice that did not quite match the intensity of his gaze. "I don't really know you, but I feel like we have some sort of connection. As though it was more than just a coincidence that you and I happened to be in the same place at the same time."

Molly was thoughtful as she swam back across the beautiful lagoon.

For the next two days each of them courted her in his own fashion, vying for her attention in the ways they knew best. Henley entertained her, telling her funny stories, impersonating celebrities, and doing ridiculous things like a soft shoe on the beach with a bamboo cane and a coconut shell for a top hat. Robinson wooed her with deep philosophical discussions and intensely passionate looks, touching her occasionally in a way that sent electricity to the deep private centers of her body.

Afraid of hurting one by encouraging the other, she responded enthusiastically to both of them, enjoying all the attention lavished on her. At times Rob seemed to be very much on edge; he would become grumpy and irritable, and Molly noticed that sometimes his hands would shake violently.

"Is he all right?" she asked Henley privately.

"What do you mean?" Henley gave her an odd look.

"I don't know, sometimes he seems as though the stress of the last week has been too much for him. Like he's about to have a nervous breakdown or something."

They were exploring a ruined mansion called "The Folly" near the little Port Antonio lighthouse. Built at the turn of the century by an American millionaire, it was Greek revival style with large columns, symmetrical stone staircases and beautifully tiled floors. Unfortunately, salty sea water had been used to mix the cement from which it had been constructed. The building had begun rusting structurally before it was even complete and no one was ever able to live in it.

"He's been pretty strung out since – since Negril." Henley kept looking over his shoulder to see if Rob might be within earshot. "He's always had trouble sleeping, at home sometimes he only sleeps three or four hours a night, but he seems to be really mentally tortured since we got here."

"Can't he take some sleeping pills or something?" From where she was standing on top of the ruin, she could see Rob inspecting the broken tiles in a room down below.

"Yeah, he usually travels with some downers, but he used them up already. One of the German guys where we're staying said he could get us some more, but he hasn't come through yet." He turned suddenly to snap a picture as a herd of goats ambled by, each one more enormously pregnant than the next. "Hey, pose for me down by that pillar, will you?"

She giggled. "What do you want me to do?"

"I don't know. Look Greek. Wrap a towel around yourself like a toga and put some flowers on your head."

When Robinson rejoined them they were engrossed in a hilarious photo session with Molly stripped down to her bikini and draped in Henley's large white beach towel with a wild wreath of oversized hibiscus in her hair.

"How about lying on the top of these steps and be Cleopatra now. Rob, go find something to fan her with. Here – put this belt around your waist. Take the towel off first, for crying out loud! Cleopatra has to look sexy and alluring, here hang some of this stuff around your neck-"

They didn't leave until they were exhausted from laughing and Henley had used up all the film in his camera. As they walked back to town, Molly could not remember the last time she had felt so relaxed and contented. She was sorry she would be leaving this end of the island in a few days to collect her airline ticket and go home.

As they ate supper that night in a little coffee shop that served full Jamaican-style dinners for under $3 US, Henley suddenly dug deep into his pocket. He quietly laid a couple of pills on the table next to Robinson's beer. "I forgot I copped these for you this afternoon," he explained.

"Rob's eyes shot up questioningly. "Tu-ies?" he asked.

Henley nodded, filling his mouth with deep-fried red snapper.

"What's a tu-ie?" Molly asked curiously.

"Tuinol. Something to help Rob get to sleep tonight."

"Are there more where these came from?" Rob asked as he washed them down with a mouthful of Red Stripe.

"Mmmm, Hans knows where to get them and he seemed to have a large personal stash."

145

Molly watched Rob closely. By the time they had finished eating, he was already beginning to slump in his seat a little and he had a foolish grin on his face. "Maybe we ought to walk back to your guest house," she suggested.

Rob did not seem totally in control of his limbs on the short walk back to the Lorraine Guest House and Molly put her arm around his waist to steady him. The warmth of his body against her own made her realize how much she had missed having close physical contact with another person for the last week.

At the door to the room, he couldn't quite make the key match up with the keyhole and finally Henley laughed and unlocked the door for him. "I'll go see if I can find Hans in case you need some more to get you through the night," he said, and then disappeared down the hallway, leaving Molly and Rob very much alone.

Molly led him to the edge of one of the beds and then released her tight grip around his waist. His body seemed to melt like liquid onto the mattress, miraculously ending up with his head on the pillow. "Wow, I can feel sleep coming down to meet me," he said softly, stretching his arms above his head. "In a few minutes I'm going to be in a sleep sandwich with sleep all around and me in the middle..." His voice drifted off and she thought he had already fallen asleep. But as she turned to go, he spoke again. "Molly, don't leave me yet."

"I'm still here, Rob." She took the hand he was stretching out towards her and sat down on the edge of the bed next to him.

"Will you stay with me until I fall asleep?" He sounded like a small boy.

She smiled. "Of course, if you want me to."

"Will you give me a goodnight kiss?"

This time she laughed aloud. "Sure." She leaned over to give him a quick peck on the lips, but suddenly both of his arms were around her and his lips were enveloping her own, his childlike innocence erupting into the passion of a man. His kiss had the same style with which he seemed to approach everything. It was deep and searching, asking for more.

When she pulled away and sat up, she felt dazed. Robinson's eyes were still closed but he had a satisfied grin on his face. "Thanks," he whispered. "Now I'll have pleasant dreams."

Henley burst back into the room at that moment, oblivious to the mood he was shattering. "Hans, what a dude he is, man!" He spilled a handful of pills onto the night table next to Rob's bed. "You owe me, Rob. This cost me - " He stopped talking abruptly as he became aware of how close Molly was sitting to Rob on the mattress. "Am I interrupting something? What a touching tableau! Just tucking our boy in for the night, mother?"

"Henley-" Rob's voice was barely audible, a mere mumble that scarcely moved his lips- "Eat shit, will you?"

"Well, my dear," Henley said a few minutes later as they closed the door on Robinson who was now sleeping soundly, "It looks like you and I will have to paint the town alone this evening. What do you say we find some place to do some drinking and dancing?"

"Sounds good to me." Anything that would keep her from thinking sounded good right now. She felt very confused.

The club they went to was dark and smoky, and did not serve banana daiquiris. Instead they drank rum and cokes while they waited for the music to begin and played a few archaic video games that lined one wall of the place. The band was terrible when it finally began playing, but by then they didn't care. Molly had already exceeded her usual quota of drinks and she would have been happy dancing to a jukebox full of scratchy forty-fives. Rob and his passionate nature seemed a part of her distant past. All that existed for her was right now, and the lighthearted, good time she and Henley were having together.

"Henley. Is that your first name or last?" She spoke into his ear as they danced close together during a slow number.

He grinned. "Middle. Arthur Henley Harrison. The third, no less. Pretty ritzy name, eh?" He spun her around in a flamboyant manner, and then resumed the slow two-step they had been doing.

"Sounds like a ritzy family too. Old money? If I may be so bold as to ask."

"Very old. Too old for me, sometimes it's more of a headache than it's worth. Boston Brahmins and all that goes with it."

Molly wasn't quite sure what a Boston Brahmin was, but before she could ask he whirled her around again, and then she was too dizzy to do anything but cling to him and giggle. Probably just what he had in mind, she thought.

"Should have gone to Harvard," he went on. "But, hell, that would have been too much work. UNH suits me fine and puts me over the state line from Mom and Dad." As the song ended, he purposely stopped dancing abruptly so that she nearly fell over and was forced to throw her arms around his neck to keep from losing her balance. "Didn't know you cared," he joked giving her a big hug. "I like dancing with you, Molly. You're just the right size for a short guy like me."

Over his shoulder, Molly caught a glimpse of a familiar face across the room. She felt her chest begin to tighten with fear and she quickly averted her eyes. The person leaning against the bar was focusing his attention completely on them. It didn't make any sense – what was Alex doing here in Port Antonio now?

He had said he would come back and find her to see if she wanted a ride back to Negril. She had been hoping never to see him again, and especially not right now. She was having such a great time, she did not want it spoiled by him.

She looked up again and their eyes met for just a fraction of a second. It was long enough for Alex to know that Molly had seen him, that she knew he was there and watching her. She shuddered at the thought of confronting him. Henley turned his head to look at her questioningly.

She had been clinging to Henley like a life preserver, but he didn't seem to mind. "Let's keep dancing." Her voice sounded loud and nervous to her own ears. "I like dancing with you too, Henley."

In an effort to forget about Alex, she gave herself up completely to the insistent beat of the music, and kept her gaze on Henley's beaming, youthful face, responding to his carefree mood as much as possible. When they finally sat down several songs later, Alex had disappeared. As she gulped down a fresh rum and coke, Molly tried to convince herself that it had just been her imagination and she turned her attention fully on Henley again.

She had no idea what early hour of the morning it was by the time they stumbled out the nightclub, and by then she didn't care. With their arms around each other's waists, as much for support as for anything, they made their way back to her guest house, letting the cool night air dry the sweat left on their brows from the vigorous dancing. Molly's hair was damp with perspiration and beneath her arm she could feel Henley's T-shirt soaked through to the skin.

When they arrived at Lantana House, they sat on the wide stone steps, their arms still around each other, reluctant to end the good time they were sharing. Leaning her head against his shoulder, she closed her eyes. Almost immediately her rum-fogged brain began spinning.

"Wow, I'm really dizzy." She sat up straight and looked him in the eyes. "Thanks for a great evening, Henley." She started to stand up but he pulled her back down again.

"It doesn't have to be over yet." The salty taste of his lips did not surprise or disturb her. It just felt like a natural extension of the closeness they were feeling. "I bet your double bed is more comfortable than these cold stone steps," he said softly and then kissed her again, laying her down on the step to prove his point.

"You're right about that." Molly barely recognized herself in the hungry girl who was responding to him.

"Want me to take you up there?"

"Sure." But she was not ready when he literally swept her off her feet and carried her into the building and up the stairs. "You're crazy!" she whispered furiously, trying not to laugh too loudly. "You'll hurt yourself! Stop it!"

"Come on, you're a lightweight. I lift more pounds than you at the gym." He stopped in front of the door to her room and put her down. "I'd be a real hero and kick the door open, but I'm sure it's locked."

Once inside, they peeled off their clothes without a break in the frenzy of hot, wet kissing. As they eased down onto the bed, Molly dimly realized that this was the first man she'd been with besides Carson in years. It seemed important; she wanted to stop and think about how special this was, what a turning point in her life. But Henley began doing things to her that drove all conscious thoughts from her mind, and she was forced to go along with the pleasure of the moment.

150

Yesterday didn't matter and neither did tomorrow, she told herself. All that counted was that right now two people were making each other feel as good as they could possibly feel.

Afterwards, as she drifted off to sleep curled up in the curve of his body wrapped safely around her own, she felt a twinge of something like guilt, but she wasn't sure who or what she should feel guilty about. Peaceful exhaustion enveloped her at last and together they fell into a deep, companionable sleep.

CHAPTER ELEVEN

They sat on the upstairs verandah while they talked. Carson was drinking a cold Heineken from Miss Leola's fridge, she was drinking a Pepsi. He had so many questions to ask her, he could not figure out a place to start.

"How did Molly get here?" He might as well start at the beginning. Did a taxi drop her off?"

Miss Leola shrugged. "She just come walking, me nevah tink to ask her how she carry to Port Antonio. Most of dem come by bus from Kingston. We not get many from Negril side."

"Who did she hang out with while she was here? I mean, did she make any friends, go places with anybody you remember?"

"Oh, yes, mon." Miss Leola chuckled. "After she been here two, maybe three days, two nice white boys come for her every day. She seem quiet and sad before they get here, but afterwards she seem brighter, you know, laughing more."

Carson didn't trust his own reactions to that statement, so he pushed on. "These two guys, was one tall and skinny with dark, curly hair and the other shortish with spiky hair standing straight up?"

"Yes, that is them. They stay by the Lorraine Guest House."

Frowning, he tried to recall if he had seen their names in the guest book there. Robinson Dubois and Henley...well, he didn't know Henley's last name. Perhaps he had signed the book for both of them or maybe Carson had only had eyes for what he was looking for. He realized Miss Leola was still talking and refocused his attention back onto her.

"They were good to her – I think they both want to be her boyfriend. She such a nice girl, it seem that many men like her. The night before she left-" she lowered her voice in a confidential manner and Carson leaned towards her to catch her words- "one of them spend the night here with her!"

Her loud whisper seemed to reverberate through the caverns of his exhausted brain. "Which one?" he asked in a flat, emotional voice, giving away everything and nothing.

Miss Leola settled back into her chair, like a little bird readjusting her wings in the nest. "I don't know, you know. I don't pry into the life of my guests. But she come back late-late and I could hear them laughing...man's laugh and woman's laugh, you know. I keep busy in de kitchen until him gone in de morning, so as nobody embarrass."

He felt sick to his stomach, not able to identify what emotion he was feeling. Anger? Jealousy? He had no right or reason to feel either. Perhaps just a sense of loss, the losing of something personal and precious.

"Have you seen these guys since Molly left?"

"No, they nevah come back since then but she tell me they were leaving same day as she so I nevah expect to see them again. One other man did come."

Carson choked on a mouthful of beer. "Another man? Looking for Molly?"

She nodded vigorously and then said nothing, enjoying the way she was holding Carson's attention, preening like a sparrow in a birdbath.

"Who was he?"

"Me nevah ask him name – me not like him much. Him come twice but him nevah find her. He come de afternoon before she leave, but she gone out to beach and then he come back next morning, but by then she already gone."

"What did he look like?" Who else could Molly possibly know in this town? Maybe she had met somebody in her first days alone here, it was probably just some casual acquaintance.

153

"Not very lovely – him older than she, darkish white man, dark white man hair, kind of fat right here in front." She mimed a beer belly over her own.

Carson shrugged and slumped back in his seat gloomily. The description could fit anyone and it probably didn't matter anyway. He didn't know what he had expected to find here. What he knew now was that Molly had left on the day she had planned, but at some early hour without saying goodbye or taking her laundry down. That she had fallen in love with Robinson Dubois, just as he had expected she would. Probably she had bought a ticket back to New Hampshire and had gone home with him and that's why she had never come back for her ticket to Miami. He guessed there were ways to re-enter the country without having a passport, perhaps saying it had been lost or stolen during your travels.

He felt a little foolish as this idea solidified itself in his mind. But it still didn't explain her sudden departure. Another thought occurred to him. He had never called home to see if maybe she had just bought another ticket to Miami and left the country without returning to Negril. Maybe she figured she would cash in the other half of her round trip when he returned with it.

He knew he was grasping at straws, but he'd never thought of calling home to Jacksonville to see if she was there. "Do you have a telephone?" he asked, standing up so suddenly that Miss Leola started visibly in her seat.

"No, you must go down to de square. There are public phones by de court building."

He took a quick shower and changed into some clean clothes before hurrying back down the hill. Two of the phones didn't work, and then it took him ten minutes to get through to an operator on the third one.

In his mind he could picture the green wall phone in the kitchen of their apartment as its familiar ring went unanswered. It was almost suppertime; she was probably at work already. "There is no one home, will you try again later, please?"

"Wait – operator – damn!" Carson slammed the receiver of the phone against the wall. Now it would take another ten minutes to reach an operator again.

This time he tried calling Molly's best friend, Melissa Truman. He questioned the wisdom of this, knowing Melissa's loyalties would lie with Molly if there was any reason that Molly didn't want Carson to know she had gone home. But he had no choices left, only chances.

"Melissa, hi, it's Carson. Listen-"

"Carson, are you back? When did you get in? Did you guys come back together?"

Melissa's excited voice had already told him everything he needed to know. "Molly isn't back yet?" he asked, trying to sound nonchalant.

"No, we've been expecting her. The restaurant was pretty mad; they had to reschedule everybody to cover her hours again. When did she leave?"

"I don't know. That's what I'm trying to find out." He didn't have the energy to explain the situation to Melissa on a long distance credit card call.

"Where are you calling from? Jamaica? Were y'all near that place where that girl was murdered in Negril?"

"Listen, Melissa, I can't talk now. If Molly should show up just tell her I called looking for her, okay?"

"Sure thing. You know, Carson, I thought maybe she'd stopped to visit her parents for a few days on the way home. You might try calling there."

Molly's parents were the last people he wanted to talk to about the possibility that their daughter was missing. He leaned his head against the side of the phone booth, wondering what to do next.

He supposed he should go back to the Lorraine Guest House but he dreaded another confrontation

155

with that woman, Cecile. But perhaps she could shed some light on how and when Rob and Henley had departed, and if they had a girl with them.

His stomach rumbled; he hadn't had a decent meal in days. He crossed the square to a shop that appeared to be a Jamaican version of a fast food restaurant. There were pieces of deep fried chicken and fish inside a glass case, pans full of sweet potato pudding, cut pieces of cheese, all kinds of breads and cakes, and a freezer full of ice cream. Munching on a chicken leg, he headed back towards Lantana House hauling a heavy bag of food.

A full stomach had the opposite effect from what he had expected. Instead of rejuvenating him, he felt immediately heavy and sleepy. Twilight lit the room with a hazy grayness as he stretched out on the bed for a short nap. He would get up in a few hours and continue his detective work. He knew that napping usually didn't work for him the way it was supposed to, but he was so tired there was nothing else he could do.

Several hours later he awoke to a loud insistent knocking. Disoriented, he sat up, trying desperately to remember where he was. It was dark, but light from the hallway filtered through the latticework transom over the door and illuminated the room, jarring him back to the present.

"Who is it?" He had no idea what time it was, and the quietness of the street outside led him to believe the night was fairly well advanced.

"Carson! You have a visitor! Wake yourself up!" Miss Leola's high voice was as commanding as it could be.

"A visitor? Who the hell would visit me here?" he muttered, fumbling with the key in the darkness.

"Carson, it's me." A familiar feminine voice made his heart beat faster and his fingers trembled as he worked the lock and opened the door at last.

Her golden-red hair seemed to reflect all the light from the naked bulb overhead, blinding him with its shimmering brilliance. Despite the hint of dark circles that were beginning to appear beneath her eyes, her full mouth twitched with laughter at the anticipation of surprising him.

"Gwen! What are you doing here? How did you get here? What time is it?" His head hurt from trying to figure out what was going on.

Miss Leola and Gwen both burst into peals of laughter. Wiping the tears of merriment from her eyes, Miss Leola said goodnight and tiptoed back downstairs to her own room.

Still speechless, he took a few steps backward. Framed by the doorway and so brightly lit from above, she reminded him of nothing less than a shining angel from heaven. "May I?" she asked again, picking up her bag and moving hesitantly towards him.

For an answer, he folded his long arms around her and buried his face in her neck, losing himself in her softness and warmth. He no longer cared why she was there, just as long as she was. Covering her mouth with his own, he kissed her deeply, feeling himself immediately aroused by his passionate desire for this woman.

He kissed her chin and her throat and then the sunburned vee between her breasts that swelled just slightly above the low neckline of her sundress. Swiftly unbuttoning the top few buttons, he slipped both of his hands inside to caress her. As he began to gently lift her breasts out of the dress, Gwen protested laughing.

"Carson, you're so crazy sometimes! I've just traveled clear across the island and burst in on you unexpectedly in the middle of the night, and here you are, undressing me with the door wide open, standing up no less! Aren't you just a little curious why I'm here?" She grabbed him by the wrists to stop his roving hands, which were now slipping the straps off her shoulders, and tried to make him look her in the eye.

He said nothing. Instead he shifted positions with her, his hands still on her bare shoulders, her hands still gripping his wrists. When they had rotated a half circle and exchanged places, he kicked the door shut with his foot, never taking his eyes off her.

Once again the room was in semi-darkness, lit only by the hall light coming through the latticework above the door. "You're demented!" she laughed as he began covering her with kisses again.

"No, just possessed. This is what happens to me when I'm in your presence." Slipping free of her grasp, he went down on his knees to continue the work of unbuttoning her dress.

"I came here to tell you something really important." She was obviously not quite as carried away with the passion of the moment as he was.

"Can't it wait until I'm finished?" Her dress fell open and as he buried his face in the softness of her belly, his fingers found her underpants and slid them off her hips; they dropped softly in a heap around her ankles.

"Why does sex with you seem so... pornographic at times?" she asked as he moved her slowly backwards towards the bed. She let out a little shriek as the underpants tangled around her ankles. She tripped and fell sprawling onto the mattress.

"Pornographic?" The word slowed him down, and he stopped with his own pants half off to look at her. "What do you mean?"

"You always seem to be setting me up for some sexy pose in a picture or something similar." She relaxed back against a pillow and closed her eyes.

"Must be the artist in me." He chose to ignore her disturbing choice of words. Admiring her soft, voluptuous body as she stretched out on the bed, he let his animal instinct take over. Laying down beside her, he continued his erotic worship of the goddess he loved.

Much later, as they lay spent and sweaty, Gwen's head against Carson's shoulder, he whispered softly, "Now tell me; what news could be more important than that?"

"It can wait until morning." Gwen was ready for sleep, but Carson was wide awake now, having slept since suppertime.

"But I can't. Tell me now and then you can sleep." With his mind clearer now, he wondered why she hadn't just waited until he called Negril at noon the next day.

"I can't just tell you, I have to show you as well. It's a postcard you got from Molly." Gwen's voice gave the impression she was about to drop off at any second.

"A what? When? Where is it?" His relaxed body was suddenly stiff with excitement.

"In my purse. It came this morning. I was going to tell you about it when you called at noon but you never did. So George and I talked about it for a while and we decided it was important enough not to waste any more time and that we'd better come right away and help you find Molly."

"WE? Did George come here with you?" Carson was more amazed by the moment.

Gwen smiled without opening her eyes. "Yes, and lucky him, he's probably already asleep in his room downstairs. George decided we would rent a car-"

"You rented a car?!" He was sitting up straight now, staring down at her restful expression.

"Just for a day. From one of the big beach hotels. They need it back by Monday morning because it's been promised to one of their guests. It was George's idea and his credit card."

Carson was now out of bed, once more searching vainly for the light switch by the door. He connected with it at last, flooding the room with forty watts from a dim yellow bulb. Gwen's purse was right by the door where she had dropped everything. He rummaged through it until he finally found a rather dog-eared postcard. One side was a typically staged scene of a colorful Jamaican man riding down a country road on a donkey that was wearing a beribboned straw hat. Turning it over, he saw the back was covered with Molly's familiar neat handwriting.

"Dear Carson, It really changed my perspective of Jamaica to get away from Negril. Port Antonio is truly paradise, I love it. This is about as far from the Negril scene as you could possibly get on the island. Remember my conversation with George at the dance about my excursion that day? Well, it's just like that here. It's O-K-4-me, I'm doing fine on my own. Your father was right when he said I would love the tropics. See you soon? Love, Molly."

"My father?" Carson spoke slowly. His mouth felt like rubber. "She never met my father! He's been dead since I was eighteen!"

"Don't you get it, Carson? She's trying to tell you something, but for some reason she can't say it outright. We wondered what that part about your father meant, but that just confirms it. She probably just threw that in to make sure you would read the card a few times and not throw it away." Gwen realized she was not going to get any sleep until she went through everything with Carson, so she continued. "We thought it all made sense at first and that she really was here in Port Antonio until George noticed the postmark."

Carson held it up to the light. "It looks like Montego Bay! What's the date? Wednesday. But-" He shook his head and sat down on the bed again. "It's possible, but it doesn't make sense. She WAS here, you know. Right here in this very room, right here in this very bed, until early Tuesday morning."

160

Gwen leaned forward and looked into his face as though she was wondering if Carson was truly crazy. He quickly explained to her all he had discovered so far from Miss Leola. "So it is possible that she herself mailed this from Montego Bay and that this trip all the way across the island was for nothing. She is probably building snowmen in New Hampshire with Robinson Dubois right now."

"Do you really think so? Then what do you think she meant by this line?" Grabbing the postcard out of his hand, she read, "'Remember my conversation with George at the dance about my excursion that day? It's just like that here.'"

"Probably just what she says. But how should I remember her conversation with George; I wasn't even there!"

"Precisely. She knew you would have to go talk to George about it and maybe you would figure it out. George said he thought they had talked about her trip to the Negril lighthouse."

Of course, Carson remembered now. That was the day she had refused to go to Savanna-La-Mar with him and had walked out to the lighthouse in the West End. "But then what does she mean 'it's just like that here'?"

Gwen sighed. "If we knew the answer to that one, we'd know where she is. George and Emma and I dissected this for a few hours before we decided to rent the car and come right here. Emma is sure that Molly wrote the card this way because someone else was going to mail it and she didn't want that person to understand her message. But you know how dramatic Emma can be."

"What do you mean?"

"Emma has this idea she's being held captive somewhere, kidnapped or something like that, and that the postcard was not only to keep you from worrying about her, but to let you know in some cryptic way where she is."

"Good God, I'm not smart enough for this kind of cloak and dagger detective work! I'm just a dumb picture painter." He threw himself backward on the bed and stared glumly at the ceiling.

Gwen kissed him tenderly on the forehead. "And that's why George and I came out here to help you, dear."

In the morning, over a breakfast of ackee and "sal'fish", the three of them once more discussed the tattered postcard in the middle of the table. Carson's breakfast went untouched, although he usually loved the Jamaican substitute for bacon and eggs. When the red outer pods of the ackee, the national fruit tree of Jamaica, explode open, the yellow meat is cleaned away from the shiny black inner pods and then is cooked up into what resembles a greasy version of scrambled eggs. Although Carson knew it had none of the protein value of eggs and could be poisonous if eaten raw, he enjoyed its delicious natural flavor.

"I think the lighthouse angle is the one to follow," George was saying. "She mentions it twice in that one line and then says, 'it's just like that here.' Wouldn't that lead you to believe..."

"So where's the nearest lighthouse?" Carson slumped down in his chair, still feeling rather cynical about the whole idea. He was almost sure Molly was enjoying her Sunday morning coffee in New Hampshire between the flannel sheets of Robinson Dubois's bed.

"Right over there, mon," an older man at the next table answered him. Startled, they all looked in the direction the man's brown finger was pointing. Sure enough, across the harbor was a small red and white lighthouse at the end of the opposite point.

The coffee shop where they were eating had one wall open to the view of the harbor with a two foot high cement barrier to prevent customers from falling down the steep cliff below. They all crowded to this short wall right now to study the little lighthouse.

"Does anyone live there? It doesn't look full size." Gwen's comment echoed Carson's thoughts exactly.

The man chuckled. "No, mon. No one live IN de lighthouse. Dey live beside it."

"Can you drive out there?"

The man nodded in the same vigorous way as Miss Leola. "Yes, a good road go out dere. Past de Folly. But lighthouse is government property, you know. It fence off – you must ax permission to go in."

George shook his hand. "Thank you, mon. You have no idea how much you've helped us." He turned to Gwen and Carson, both of who were still staring out across the harbor. "Ready to go?"

Carson shrugged. "It's worth a try, I guess."

The road to the Port Antonio lighthouse started out impressively, cutting between the two old pillars built for The Folly, which was on the same road. It quickly lost its glory in huge, water-filled potholes through which the rented Toyota Starlet bounced on worn-out springs, bottoming out several times. They could see the crumbling ruin of the Folly up on the hill, but Carson's normal attraction to such a curiosity was not there today. He sat numbly, alone in the back seat of the car, as Gwen and George speculated wildly about what the building might have been. There were ruined outbuildings right up to the sturdy, five foot high mesh fence that ran around the entire lighthouse property.

Silently they got out of the car and peered through the fence at the peaceful scene beyond. It was definitely the home of a family, with laundry on the line, a well-tended vegetable garden, and goats tethered in the bush. Two small, fierce-looking dogs announced their arrival.

"Doesn't look very promising," Carson muttered gloomily.

"Don't be so negative. Anybody home?" George shouted.

Five minutes later they were on their way, having been reassured that the lighthouse was government property and no one could stay there but those officially sanctioned. The lighthouse keeper also informed them that there were no other homes on that peninsula, but that people did come regularly to explore The Folly and swim at the little beach below.

"Well, so much for that lead. What's next?" Carson asked as they bumped along the road back to town.

"Maybe she's some place with a view of the lighthouse or with the word 'lighthouse' in its name," Gwen suggested.

"I think we should check back at the Lorraine Guest House and see if any of the guests there know if she left with Rob and Henley." In his tired and twisted mind, Carson was now imagining Molly gaily mailing that postcard at the airport as she headed towards the departure gate on Robinson's arm. "If she left with them, we might as well forget it."

"Don't be ridiculous! What's wrong with you this morning?" Gwen scolded him.

"You know what the first thing I'm going to ask Molly when we find her?" George said in an overly cheerful voice. "I'm going to ask her what the hell she was doing accepting a ride with Alex all the way from Montego Bay to here. I've been wondering that for two days now. I mean, we all know how much she hated the man. What could–"

"Alex? What are you talking about?" Carson came to life suddenly. "Alex from Mango Grove?"

George looked at Gwen who swallowed guiltily and said, "I forgot. There was so much else to tell him and it didn't seem that relevant..."

"Forgot what? What's going?" Carson was hanging over the back of the front seat now, looking accusingly from one face to the other.

164

"Remember the night you left for Montego Bay and Alex drove in just as you got on the bus? Well, when I told him where you were going, he told me he had personally dropped Molly off on a street corner in Port Antonio. When I tried to question him further about it, he got rude and surly. To tell you the truth, Carson, I was ready to believe Alex was our man. If you know what I mean." George was silent for a moment. "We got this postcard from Montego Bay and all we had was Alex's word that he had brought her this far, not to mention that Port Antonio is not exactly on the way to Kingston."

"But it doesn't make any sense! He was one of the reasons she left Negril!" Carson shook his head in bewilderment. "Well, Miss Leola said Molly arrived alone and she didn't see anybody except Rob and – no, wait a minute. She did mention some older man coming by to look for Molly the day before she disappeared, but Molly wasn't around and then he came by again the next day, but she was already gone. I wonder if that could have been Alex?"

"He told me he never saw her again after he dropped her off," George answered. "But that doesn't mean he was telling the truth. He seemed really mad about something. He said he thought she was ungrateful for all the stuff he'd done for her."

"What would HE have done for her? Turn here." Carson pointed out the road which led to the Lorraine Guest House.

"He said he bought her meals and got her a room for the night-"

"She spent a night with him? He must be lying. He probably made the whole thing up!" Carson's voice had become shrill with disbelief. He was frightened by the thought of someone like Alex being involved in Molly's disappearance. His idea about Molly going home with Robinson may have been a bitter and sordid little fantasy, but at least it was safe. "He came by the Lantana looking for her after she left. Why would he do that if he had anything to do with her disappearing?"

"He probably didn't." Gwen's flat statement did not dispel Carson's desperate feeling. "This looks like the place. Pull off here, George."

Cecile was standing in the doorway with a disapproving look on her face as she watched the three of them walk up the path to the porch. "I only have room for one," she called crossly to Carson in lieu of a greeting.

"We're not looking for a room, thanks anyway," he replied politely. "We wondered if you remembered two Americans who stayed here this week named Robinson and Henley?"

"Yes, mon! Dey stay by me but dem long gone. Hans!" She called down the length of the porch to a young man in his early twenties who was seated in a chair at the other end, reading a book. "When de Americans dem gone?"

Hans looked up and removed his wire-rimmed reading glasses. His emaciated appearance deep wracking cough indicated he was either about to die from a serious illness or about to recover from one.

"Tuesday, mid day," he said at last in a thick German accent. "They pack up a little red rental auto and they go."

"They rented a car? That's interesting. Doesn't sound like the same boys who camped on the beach," murmured George.

"Did they have a girl with them when they left?" Carson asked.

"The small blonde one? I did not see her the day they left, no." Hans shook his head. "They are friends of yours?"

"Yes." Carson did not know how much to say. "We're looking for the girl, actually. You say you did see her with them?"

"Ya, many times. She came back vith them when they rent the auto the night before leaving. I am not –

166

not- " he searched for the right English word – "listening over, you understand, but I heard them talk about all going together the next day. They must have picked her up after they leave here. She didn't stay here vith them, you see."

"But they didn't pick her up," Carson said in a low voice to Gwen and George. "Not if they didn't leave until mid day."

"Are you sure they didn't leave first thing in the morning?" George asked Hans loudly.

"Yes, I am quite sure." Hans' voice was emphatic. "I vas sitting right here vatching as they put their things in the auto."

"He true, you know," Cecile interjected gruffly. "I couldn't clean dem room until pas' noon. De should pay me for another day if dey stay so long."

Just to make sure, Carson described Rob and Henley to Hans. "That is them," Hans assured him. "I know them, one night I give the short one sleeping pills for the tall one and then the short one takes your blonde girl to a night club."

"Henley? Took Molly?" Even though it was a minor detail, it didn't fit into Carson's scheme of how things had been.

"Maybe we ought to go back to Lantana House and rethink this," George put in hastily, before Carson could get entangled in his new train of thought. They thanked Hans, who assure them he would be happy to answer any more questions that might come up.

"We don't seem to be getting very far, do we?" Gwen commented as they turned the car around and headed back down the road. "What do we do next?"

"Maybe we should go to the police," Carson suggested.

"I supposed it's not a bad idea," George admitted. "Although I think in this case, it's probably the American Embassy who should be called."

Neither the police nor the embassy proved to be much help. The information was dutifully recorded at the police station in a ledger filled with illegible cursive writing. They really had no ideas, however, except one idle officer, leaning against a desk, who suggested mockingly, "Perhaps she has a Jamaican boyfriend she is staying with in the hills?"

The police helped them get a call through to the American Embassy in Kingston, who in turn recorded the pertinent facts and said they could check to see if Molly had been on any flights leaving the country for Miami (or Boston, at Carson's insistence) in the last five days. Carson was to call the Embassy back later that afternoon to see what they had to report.

"And what now?" Carson asked as they left police headquarters. The sun was high overhead by this time and beating down mercilessly on the paved roads of downtown Port Antonio.

"Let's find someplace to swim, I'm roasting." George pulled out a map of the island as they opened the doors and windows of the car to let it cool off before getting back inside. "Sheesh, no wonder there aren't any tourists here; there isn't a beach for miles!"

"Oh, of course there is. It's probably just not on the map." Gwen walked back into the police station and in a few minutes they were on their way to San San Beach about four miles from town.

After they had cooled off in the clear, refreshing water, George spread the map out on the sand and began studying it again.

"I'm still stuck on this lighthouse lead, you know," he explained. "She made too big a deal of it in the postcard. It's got to mean something."

"So where else are there lighthouses on the island of Jamaica?" Carson squatted next to him, drops of water from his wet bathing suit trickling down between his legs.

168

"Well, let's see... there's one on this end, there's one on that end, there's one down here, Portland Lighthouse. But look, the one here in town is only on the small inset map of Port Antonio. And I know for a fact that there is one right here by the airport in Kingston, the Plumb Point Lighthouse, but it's not even marked. You can see it when you land there, I know it's there. So a lot of good this does us." He tossed the map aside disgustedly and Carson caught it as it was about to blow away.

"Let's write down what we know and see what we come up with," Gwen suggested, fishing a pad of paper out of her large straw handbag. "We know that Molly was gone by 6:30 on Tuesday morning. We know that Rob and Henley didn't leave until noon the same day. We know that Alex came looking for her after she was already gone."

"We don't know that for a fact," Carson interrupted. "It might not have been him."

"Well, we'll look into that one. Okay, what else do we know? That she mailed you a postcard on Wednesday from Montego Bay."

"We know that the postcard was mailed from there," George reminded her. "It doesn't necessarily mean Molly mailed it."

"Why don't we just wait and see what the Embassy finds out about airline flights? I mean, if we find out she's already left the country, we can call off the search." Although Carson's statement made sense, none of them believed it.

"What do you think, Carson? Do you feel like she is still here in Port Antonio or not?" Gwen's question was met by a long minute of silence.

"I don't know," he answered finally. "But I'm not ready to give up just yet."

"Then you won't be driving back to Negril with us this evening?" Although George tried to keep the emotion out of his voice, it was obvious to Carson that George thought he was a fool to stay on.

He turned to Gwen who sat crosslegged on a towel and studied her for a minute. She had braided her thick hair and pinned it up high on her head for swimming; she said it took forever to dry once it became wet. Her crown of braids gave her an Old World appearance, like an Irish milkmaid who had been dropped into the 1980s and outfitted in a shiny spandex swimsuit. Her frank gaze, however, was nothing but modern and very perceptive.

Carson sighed. It was hard to deal with his fears and feelings about Molly when this other woman whom he cared for so deeply was here. It was confusing; two very different kinds of love, although he was not quite sure just what the difference was yet. Until he had journeyed to Port Antonio, he had been so sure of what he had wanted to say to Molly. But the more he worried about her safety and her life, the less certain he was about what he really felt.

"No, I'm not going back with you, George. I think there may still be some answers here."

"Do you want me stay on with you, Carson?" Nothing in Gwen's eyes gave away what she might be feeling. "It's up to you, you know. If you need my support, I'll stay."

He reached out for her hand and then looked away and out to sea. "I know. But I think this something I need to do on my own. I'll be back in a few days. I know where to find you."

"Carson, if – if- " Gwen faltered a little and Carson glanced at her quickly, alarmed at the uncertainty in her usual self-assured manner. "If, when you find Molly, or if you come back to Negril and find her there, if you don't want to come back up with me...well, it's okay. I'll understand. That's all."

He squeezed her hand tightly. "Nothing's changed that way. I still feel the same way about you, about us. I have a responsibility towards Molly. But it's as though she were my sister, not my ex-girlfriend."

He reminded himself that she still had been his girlfriend when she left on her trip and that she probably still thought she was. And he knew that it was probably guilt more than anything else that was forcing him to continue this crazy pursuit.

CHAPTER TWELVE

The first thing Molly saw when she opened her eyes was Henley's sunburned arm flung protectively across her chest. His body was curled around hers, his front to her back, and everywhere she could feel the warm contact of his skin pressing against her own. She tried to luxuriate in the sensuality of the moment, but something didn't feel quite right. She was not exactly sure why.

Perhaps it had to do with the pounding in her head and the queasy feeling in her stomach. Too much rum and coke the night before; she had known that even as she was drinking it. She lay perfectly still, trying not to disturb her tenuous equilibrium, and listened to the even, rhythmic sound of Henley breathing.

Eventually she carefully peeled her body away from his, cautiously slipping out from under his arm so as not to awaken him. Wrapping a shirt around her shoulders, she sat back down at the foot of the bed and studied him while he slept.

Instantly a smile broke out on her lips as she remembered all the funny things he had said to her the night before. He looked so peaceful and boyish in his sleep; his exuberant, high energy personality did not show itself in his relaxed features. Only his spiky hair hinted at his love of the bizarre. She tried to imagine what he would look like with his hair slicked down, wearing a suit and tie. She could picture him wearing red sneakers with it, just to make a statement, and the image made her laugh aloud.

She hadn't meant for this to happen. She was not sure what their commitment to each other was expected to be now. After all, in a few days they were both leaving the island for different destinations. She

172

didn't think she wanted to put any more energy into something that would just be over in a matter of hours. There was no point in forming attachments to people you would never see again. It hurt too much.

But now her mind was made up. She did not regret a minute of what she had done the night before, she had enjoyed herself thoroughly, but that was that. When he woke up, she would tell him.

Henley stirred in his sleep and felt around for where he thought Molly should be. His eyes fluttered open as he realized she was not there. He shot up to a sitting position, his pale blue eyes not really focusing yet. Seeing her sitting cross-legged at the foot of the bed, he sighed with relief and fell back on the pillows.

"My God, woman, you scared me," he said, looking at her through half-closed eyes. "I thought you'd run out on me. Stolen my wallet and flown the coop."

"What a good idea! Would it be worth my while? Do you have some major credit cards?" As she teased him, he grabbed her by the arms and pulled her back down next to him.

"But of course, ma cheri," he replied, affecting a French accent. "Take what you want. All that I have is yours." She knew he meant it, in a joking sort of way. For a crazy second she wondered what the future might be like as the girlfriend of Arthur Henley Harrison, the third. Lots of good times with money as no object, no more slaving away at waitress jobs, dozens of cozy mornings like this one. Resolutely, she pushed the thought from her mind.

"Henley, we need to talk," she said as his fingers ran lightly down her back and came to rest on her bottom.

"Uh-oh, sounds heavy. What's wrong? You can't be pregnant already." But he lay still and waited for her go on.

"Well, it's just this." She began to speak very quickly, not because she thought he would interrupt her, but because she wanted to say it all before she changed her mind. "I really enjoyed being with you last night, but I don't think we should get any more deeply involved. In fact, I don't even think we should sleep together again. I mean, in a couple of days we'll each get on our own planes and go our own ways. I don't want to be emotionally involved with someone who lives a thousand miles away; there's no point to it."

Stopping to catch her breath, she glanced warily at him to see how he was reacting and saw that he was regarding her with amused interest. Damn! she thought. She'd bared her soul and it had probably just been a one night stand for him. He had been planning to leave the affair behind him as soon as he left the room.

"Fine," he replied after a moment. "If that's how you want it."

"I'm just afraid of getting serious-"

"You how I hate being serious." He moved his hand up to her shoulder and squeezed it. "But we're still friends, right?"

"Of course! I really like you a lot. I'm just not ready for the next step yet." She only half-believed her own words, but she did feel a great relief having spoken them.

"Okay, that's cool." He shrugged. "So what are we going to do on our last day in Port Antonio?"

Later that same day, as she fell in and out of a sun-baked sleep on the beach at San San, she found herself wondering how differently things might have turned out if Rob had gone dancing with them the night before.

Rob sat sullenly on the blanket next to her, a deep scowl on his face as he watched Henley's attempts at windsurfing on a rented board. He had

174

been in a black mood since morning, when she had walked over to the Lorraine to meet the two of them. Henley confided that he thought Robinson was mad because they had had such a good time without him, but Molly knew there was more to it than that.

She knew how Rob felt about her. Although an eternity had transpired in her own lifetime since she had tucked him into bed and kissed him goodnight, he had done nothing but sleep and awaken with the memory of a sweet bedtime kiss lingering on his lips. He had not expected to find out that his best friend had slept with the girl he was falling in love with.

Groaning, she rolled over and buried her face in her arms. The painful look in his soulful eyes made her feel like a cheap tramp. Damn him, she didn't belong to him or anybody. But at the same time, she felt a little bit as though she had betrayed her own feelings. After all, it had been Robinson whom she had thought she felt a deep, passionate connection with all these days.

Oh, what did it matter anyhow... In another day she would never have to see either of them again if she didn't want to.

She sat up, her head still throbbing from the effects of rum and coke and made an attempt at cheerful conversation. "So, Rob, you must feel better after a good night's sleep."

Robinson turned his head slowly and looked at her as though she was mad. Without replying, he returned his gaze to Henley's antics in the water.

"I can't believe Henley feels well enough to do that," she went on bravely, ignoring his response. "After all he drank, he should be sick as a dog today." She was saying all the wrong things, but she didn't care.

Robinson snorted. "He's never hung over. He has a high tolerance for unnatural and illegal substances." He did not look at her as he spoke.

"Well, he sure knows how to party hearty." Impulsively, she reached out for his hand. "Robinson, don't be mad at me. We were just having a good time, you know how it goes. I didn't mean to hurt you."

His expression was one that she'd seen before, back in Negril. The lines of his face were hardened with anger, a red spot appeared on each cheek as if he'd been stung by something, his eyes were smoldering. Now she remembered when it was; it had been when Alex had him down on the floor at the dance. They had been fighting about Fawn, the night before she had been murdered.

She shuddered unconsciously at the memory. Robinson had been through so much in the last few weeks. She felt badly that she had unthinkingly hurt him again.

Overcome by compassion, she leaned over and kissed him on the cheek. His features softened somewhat and his eyes focused in on hers. Once again she felt drawn into the depths of his complexity and it was only through extreme concentration and willpower that she was able to resist him as his lips moved towards her own.

"No." Her voice was a ragged whisper as she abruptly turned her face away from his. "Not here. Not now."

Hey guys!" Henley's shouting made them both look up at him. He was splashing through the shallow water, dragging the windsurfing board after him. "I've got a great idea! Listen to this!"

Dripping wet, he stopped in front of Molly and Robinson, thrown off for a moment by their physical proximity to each other. Molly moved aside uncomfortably and put her hands up to cover her flushed cheeks.

Henley threw himself down on a towel between the two of them. "I know what we'll do to get back," he went on excitedly when no one had responded to his exclamation. "We'll rent a car!"

"Don't you need a credit card for that?" Molly asked dubiously.

"He has one." Robinson's flat statement said more about what he thought of Henley's wealth than he would have liked to admit.

"It ought to be worth it for the three of us. I mean, it would cost about fifty bucks for the day and it'll get us all the way to Negril and back to Montego Bay faster than any bus possibly could."

"Why do we have to go back to Negril?" Robinson would not let on yet how he felt about Henley's idea.

"To get Molly's stuff she left there. I think we should rent the car right now so that we can leave first thing in the morning. Then we can spend the rest of the day seeing places here that we haven't been able to before." He got up and immediately began packing up his gear.

"Henley, I don't need to be in Montego Bay until Thursday. But you can just drop me off and I'll find my own way from there to Negril." She felt more relief than excitement at the prospect of getting back across the island safely and quickly.

"What's wrong with you two deadbeats? Get off your asses and let's go!" Henley was actually running down the beach, carrying the sailboard towards the rental shop. Despite her mood, Molly smiled as she began stuffing things back into her bag.

Within an hour, they were driving away from National Rental in a shiny red Honda Jazz, a square little model not available in the States. Henley was like a small child with a new toy and his enthusiasm was catching. Even Robinson perked up as they headed towards Titchfield Hill.

"Your hotel, madam? Or will you be accompanying Mr. Dubois and myself to our quarters?"

"No, no. Home, James." Molly sat in the back seat, trying to peer through the front windshield between their heads. She could see a battered wine-colored Toyota parked in front of Lantana House. "Oh, my God," she murmured. "Slow down, Henley. And do me a favor; don't stop. Just drive by very slowly."

She slumped down in the back seat so that only her eyes and the top of her head were visible through the back window.

"Anything you say, madam. Rather kinky, isn't this?"

"Hey, isn't that-" Robinson's jaw dropped and then he looked sharply back at Molly hiding in the narrow back seat.

"Shhh! Yes, it is him. He must be looking for me." There was no mistaking Alex as he stood on the verandah of Lantana House talking to Miss Leola. "I don't want to see him."

"Why is he looking for you?" Robinson asked.

"I don't know why. He told me he was going to come back here and find me after he went to Kingston but I told him not to bother. I saw him last night at the dance, but I pretended not to see him. He must have followed us home. Shit."

"Want me to go back there and tell him to fuck off?" suggested Henley.

"I don't think that would help matters any. You remember what happened in Negril." None of them spoke for a moment and Henley pulled off the road a short way down the block past Lantana House. They all watched as Alex got back into his car and started it up.

"I think he was the one who murdered Fawn," Molly said quietly. "But I bet he never gets convicted." All three of them ducked down instinctively as he drove by.

"I still don't understand why you can't just tell him to get lost," Robinson went on, sitting up again.

"I supposed I could," she signed. "I just didn't ever want to see his face again."

"But I thought he gave you a ride here because you knew him from Mango Grove. Aren't you friends?"

"Friends?" Molly choked on the word. "No, I'm not usually friends with someone who tries to rape me."

"He what?" Two pairs of eyes turned to stare at her incredulously.

"He tried to force me to have sex with him."

"So what did you do?" Henley's voice was anxious.

"I kicked him in the balls and slept in the car." She said it very matter-of-factly, as though it was an everyday occurrence in the life of a very strong woman instead of the terrifying experience it had been for a frightened and very petite one.

"The bastard," Robinson growled. "Maybe you better come stay with us tonight, Molly."

For a second the idea made sense, but then the thought of what she would have to deal with emotionally if she spent a night the two of them overcame her. "No, that's okay. I'll be all right. I'll tell Miss Leola not to let him know I'm there if he comes back. If I do see him, well-" she hesitated and then added defiantly, "I'll just tell him to fuck off."

Henley and Robinson exchanged glances and she knew they were thinking about persuading her to change her mind. "Would you take me back there right now?" she asked quickly, before they had a chance to speak. "I have some laundry to do and if I hang it out now, it will be dry by the time we leave in the morning."

Without a word, Henley put the little car in reverse and backed it up the street. "We'll come back and get you in a couple of hours," he said as she got out. "We'll go some place special for sunset and dinner."

179

She left them early that night, wanting to be alone for an hour or two before bedtime. Sitting on the verandah, enjoying the light breeze coming in off the harbor, she thought about going back to Negril and Carson.

Carson had been in the back of her mind for days. She had not wanted to think about him or about life with him back home. Or about life without him for that matter. It had been an easy, mindless existence for her. She had been in love with his easy-going beauty and his intriguing talent. Her identity had been as his girlfriend. If she got back together with him, it would have to be on different terms.

By tomorrow night she would be back at Mango Grove and have to resolve it all. Sighing, she got up and went inside, locking the door between her room and the verandah. The air inside was hot and still, and despite Miss Leola's warnings, she always slept with the large, old-fashioned double-hung window open. Because it opened onto the porch, there was never any chance of rain coming in.

Wearing only a T-shirt, she crawled between the sheets. She lay on her stomach in a comforting position from childhood, and with her hands beneath the pillow, she fell into a dreamless sleep.

She did not know how many hours she had been asleep when she awoke to a strange sensation. It felt as though someone was tickling her feet as they stuck out from the bottom of the sheet. She tried to pull them up and back under the sheet, but something seemed to be holding them down. Thinking that she must be tangled up in the bedding, she gave a hard jerk. Her ankles banged together as something tight cut into them.

A cold stab of fear struck her heart. She tried swiftly to sit up, but before she could, a heavy weight descended onto her back, preventing her from moving at all. She gasped as the realization of what was happening to her sunk in. Someone had tied her feet together, had lashed them to the iron bed-frame and was now sitting on her back.

"Who's there?" she croaked, trying to crane her head around to see who was behind her in the dark.

A hand stroked her hair in a gentle way that made her scalp and the nape of her neck tingle with fear. "Who are you?" She could not project her voice beyond a whisper because her chest was being crushed by the weight of the body on her back. "What do you want?"

The hands were lifting the hair off of her neck now and strong fingers were massaging the muscles of her shoulders. As they moved in towards her throat and then began closing around it, she gasped again, realizing at last what was really about to happen.

"Who are you?" She began to squirm, trying to escape the firm grasp. "Why me?"

"Because you rejected me, Molly." The whispering voice sounded familiar, but was not distinct enough for her to recognize. Her brain went wild trying to think of who she might have inadvertently rejected. Three or four people came to mind almost instantly. "I wasn't good enough for you. People like you shouldn't be allowed to exist." The hands began to tighten.

She thought she knew who it was now. "No, you don't want to do this! Not again!" She struggled to free her hands from beneath the legs that were pinning them down.

The fingers hesitated momentarily at her words. The blood was pounding so loudly in her head that she could barely hear the whispered reply. "...not again?"

"Yes, you killed Fawn, didn't you? Just like this. Why would you want to do it again? Do you want another murder on your conscience as well?" She was stalling for time, holding desperately onto the

slightest hope that she could talk him out of it..
Maybe someone in another room would hear them.

The fingers came together around her throat again. "If you know that much, I have no choice. I can't let you live to tell everybody."

She was having trouble breathing and could barely speak. "If I rejected you, I didn't mean to. Please – don't-" She gagged as she struggled for air.

From what seemed like a great distance away she heard a crash. "What the hell do you think you're doing?" a voice shouted. And then she lost consciousness and the rest was darkness.

CHAPTER THIRTEEN

Before George and Gwen took off, they all had a drink together at the Bonnie View hotel which was high up on a hillside overlooking Port Antonio's twin harbors. The splendid view took their minds off their troubles for a few minutes and allowed them to make the same mindless remarks as the other tourists around them about how breathtakingly beautiful this emerald island was.

Carson had just gotten off the telephone with the American embassy, who reported that no one using the name Molly McRae had departed via Montego Bay or Kingston during the last five days. As it was Sunday, there was not much they could do officially except put feelers out to various police stations around the island to see if there were any suspicious stories that matched up with Molly's disappearance. Carson suspected the police were not ready to launch a large scale, island-wide investigation. He didn't really blame them, despite his overwhelming sense that, if something really terrible was happening to Molly right now, then precious minutes were ticking by.

At some point during the course of the afternoon George had unwittingly made a remark about "white slavery" and Carson had not been able to get this new idea out of his head. Molly was so small and vulnerable and could be so easily overpowered...

"Carson, we need to be going. Drink up." Gwen's voice cut through his thoughts and he focused his attention on the table in front of him. George had once again spread out the map and was identifying landmarks on the small inset of Port Antonio within the view spread out below them.

"That must be the hospital, that roof down there." He pointed down and off to the left.

"I suppose I should check there. Maybe she got hurt and has been there all this time," Carson remarked halfheartedly, not cheered by the thought of another dead end street. "I believe I'll stay here and have another drink and then walk back to town. It should be easy; it's all downhill. Why don't you leave me that map, George and I'll find my way to the hospital."

They said their goodbyes, George reminding Carson to call them the next day at noon, the same way they had originally planned. "Don't forget this time," he warned. "We don't want to be chasing all the way across island again to find you."

"Here – take this." Gwen quickly undid the leather strap of her wristwatch and pressed it into Carson's hand. "That should make it a little easier," she whispered in his ear as she threw her arms around his neck and held him in a strong but swift embrace.

"You know me so well already." He laughed lightly and kissed her soft lips before letting her go. "I'll see you soon."

He slipped the watch into his pocket as they drove away down the steep, narrow road, and then returned to the table, map and postcard in hand. Taking another sip of his beer, he looked at the picture side of the card. Such a perfect picture of paradise. The happy man on his friendly donkey riding through the beautiful countryside. It showed nothing of what life was really like on the island. Too bad it wasn't a picture of where the man was coming from, or where he was going. Turning it over, he reread the message for the hundredth time.

"This is about as far from the Negril scene as you could possibly get on the island...."It's O-K-4 – me..." That part bugged him; it just didn't sound like Molly.

She didn't go in for cutesy phrases with initials in them.

He opened up the map again and studied it. He'd never actually even seen a map of Jamaica until he'd arrived in the country. He'd had only a vague idea of where Negril was on the island and he was really quite surprised to see just how far it was from Port Antonio. It was nearly at the opposite end of Jamaica, as far from Negril as one could get on the island. But the farthest point was actually the fat little peninsula way out to the east.

He turned the map over to read the "Sightseeing Guide" with its points of interest. "Cockpit Country (D-2); Hilly wild densely thick area...", "Port Antonio (J-3)...", "Blue Hole (or Blue Lagoon) (J-3); a seemingly fathomless lagoon...the water is crystal clear but incredibly blue..." He read on until the end of the description and then decided to see how close it was to Port Antonio. The two places had the same coordinate points and it might be worth a trip in the morning.

He ran his fingers across the grid lines of the map. In one direction it went from A to K, the other way from 1 to 4. A-1 to K-4. He was looking for J-3...He found the square he was looking for, but stared at it sightlessly. Something in the back of his brain was clicking away at the sound of these letters and numbers, something very important.

Suddenly his eyes shot back over to Molly's postcard. "O-K-4 – me." He held it up to the light. If you studied it, the dash between the O and the K really looked more like a comma which gave that silly phrase another meaning entirely. "O, K-4 – me."

Dropping the postcard, he went quickly back to the map. His trembling fingers traced K-4, right to the easternmost point of the island. Right to the Morant Point Lighthouse.

"Holy shit!" he shouted, jumping up and overturning the metal chair he had been sitting in.

185

"That's it! That's as far from Negril as you can possibly get!"

Several people turned to regard him with disapproval as he destroyed the serenity of their sunset cocktails. But he was jumping up and down by this time, unable to contain his excitement. He had figured it out, he knew where Molly was, now all he had to was go get her.

When he had calmed down, he looked more closely at the K-4 section of the map. There was nothing on that peninsula but a long, unimproved road leading through what looked like a swamp and ending at the lighthouse. He frowned as new, puzzling questions began to attack his brain. What the hell would Molly be doing all the way out there? And how would she have gotten there? And why? And was she still there?

There was only one way to find out. First thing in the morning he would head for the lighthouse.

Back at Lantana House, Carson tried to work out a plan in his head as he showered off the day's grime. He was still impressed with the power of the water pressure in Port Antonio compared to the trickle that came out of the showerhead at Mango Grove. As the cold water beat on his scalp, he realized that what he should do was what everyone else did. He would rent a car and just drive to the lighthouse in the morning.

Lightheaded from the ease with which he'd solved his traveling problems, he spent a few hours doing a watercolor of Miss Leola on the verandah of Lantana. He went to bed feeling rather smug and self-assured. In the morning he would drive off to rescue Molly.

At nine a.m. he was waiting outside the door of United Auto Rental, but of course they did not open on time. It was close to an hour later that a woman arrived, murmuring apologies that had something to

186

do with a roadblock on the A-4 outside of Drapers. He followed her into the office.

A few minutes later he was back outside, his self-confidence fully blown away. It had been a matter of seconds before she had asked him what credit card he would be using.

"I don't have a credit card," he had replied.

"Then we will need a cash deposit in Jamaican dollars equivalent to two thousand US dollars," the well-modulated and very bored voice informed him.

"Two thousand dollars! Well, I don't have that. Thanks, anyway."

Depressed, he headed back up the hill to the guesthouse, not sure what to do next. He would have to take a bus as far as he could and then walk the rest of the way. He consoled himself that it would still be fairly simple, it would just take a little longer.

As he looked around the room trying to figure out what he needed to bring with him, he was overwhelmed by the big question looming ahead. He had no idea what he was getting into, he didn't even know exactly where he was going, and he didn't know if Molly would even be where he didn't know he was going.

Realizing it might take a few days, he packed a change of clothes for himself, his sketchbook, his drawings of Molly, the map and the postcard. After some thought, he included one of Molly's dresses. Just in case...what, he didn't know.

He told Miss Leola he was headed for the Morant Point Lighthouse and that if he was not back in three days to send the police after him. "You will find my girl and bring her back to me, won't you now?" she clucked, taking his hand and pressing it between her own gnarled brown ones.

"Yes, ma'am," he assured her with more confidence than he felt.

As he went out the front door, he remembered Gwen's watch and bounded back up the stairs to retrieve it from the windowsill next to the bed. As he strapped it on, it reminded him of the phone call he was expected to make in just a little over an hour.

"Shit," he said aloud. It meant that he would not be able to get on a bus out of the city until after noon. His plans of driving off in a rental car into the sunrise and returning by sunset were in tatters now. It would probably be dusk by the time he got there.

To pass the time he went to a supermarket to load up on a few supplies but nothing seemed appropriate. Finally he bought a loaf of bread, a box of juice and a bag of bright orange cheese puffs. He stopped in at the open air market for a grapefruit, some bananas and a large avocado. By then his daypack was full and it was nearly noon.

He had to wait to use the phone booth at the old courthouse and when he finally got through to Negril, the line there was busy. It was close to 12:30 by the time he heard it ring at the other end and by then he was dripping with sweat, partly from the midday heat, but also from the frustration of using the Jamaican telephone system.

"Carson, is that you?" George seemed to be shouting into the phone. Carson could hear motorcycles revving up in the background.

"Yes, George, listen! I've figured it out!"

"Figured it out? Be quick about it, I'm being roasted alive out here in this parking lot. I feel like a hot dog inside a glass rotisserie cooker."

Carson explained it all to him as briefly as possible. "I've wasted half the day," he finished up. "And now I've got to get going."

"Damn, Carson! That's amazing! I can't believe we didn't see that before!" George continued sputtering his astonishment until Carson cut him off.

"Look, George, I'm outta here. I'll call you tomorrow if I can." The uncertainty of the future made Carson's stomach tighten up. He had no idea what he would discover in the next twenty-four hours. "But don't wait up, if you know what I mean."

After hanging up the phone, he shouldered his backpack and headed for the large dusty parking lot at the edge of the harbor which served as the town bus depot. An unsuspecting tourist might have thought it was a graveyard for junked buses, but Carson knew that despite their dented and disintegrating appearance, these sacred vehicles traveled every passable road on the island. They were the lifelines that linked poor, backcountry people with the market and the rest of the world.

Even though it was the hottest part of the day, there were passengers waiting inside the driverless buses, assuring themselves of a seat on the impending ride. Carson had to look at his map to see which town was closest to the lighthouse and then still had to ask someone which bus to take.

"Golden Grove? Any Morant Bay bus carry you ah Golden Grove." A battered red and blue one was pointed out to him. Although a few people sat inside, it did not appear to be about to leave.

"How soon will it be going?" Carson asked in frustration.

"Soon, mon! Not to worry. It soon go!"

Carson had been in Jamaica long enough to know that "soon" could mean any time in the next twenty-four hours. Reluctantly, he swung himself through the open door, flopped down in a seat on the shady side and tried to be patient. He could see the ground through a large crack where the side of the bus met the floor.

It was over an hour later when the engine choked to life and the bus finally roared off along the coastal road, headed east. He had forgotten how the big bus had to stop for any passenger along the road, no matter how full it was; this seemed to be an unwritten law. Within a few minutes there were school children filling up every available space and the number of stops and starts the driver made were too numerous to count.

Another hour passed this way, until they jolted to a stop in a fairly sizable town and Carson ventured to ask the woman on his left where they were.

"Long Bay," was the reply.

Carson looked it up on his map and was distressed to find they'd only traveled about fifteen miles in all that time. He slid down in his seat and closed his eyes. This was going to take forever.

It was close to 4:30 by the time he stepped stiffly off the bus in Golden Grove. To the east, green cane fields stretched flatly towards the horizon. Westward there were hills that would eventually, farther inland, become the Blue Mountains. Smoke from cook fires dotted the countryside as people fixed their suppers so that outdoor kitchens could be cleaned up before dark.

A blond white man was clearly an unusual sight on this remote end of the island. Carson took the opportunity to ask one of the young boys staring at him which road led to the lighthouse.

"Lighthouse?" His tone indicated that he thought Carson's question quite odd. "That way, mon." He gestured vaguely towards the cane fields.

"Well, where's the road?" He had no intention of bushwhacking his way to the coast.

"Not far. A little way on down." He pointed towards the paved stretch of road into town.

Carson thanked him and took long strides in that direction until he came to a crossroads that headed east into the cane fields. He stopped another boy who was riding by on a rusty bicycle with a wooden seat. "Is this the way to the lighthouse?" he asked him.

Another blank look before comprehension. "Yes, yes, the lighthouse is that way," came the sudden affirmative reply. "You just keep on going, you will get to it."

Carson began walking down the road that cut through the vast fields of sugar cane. In a short while he came to another crossroad, but he just stayed on the same eastward-bound road. The sun was setting so rapidly behind him that it was easy to tell which direction he wanted.

The road took an odd turn north but since there was no other way to go, he stuck with it. Just as he was beginning to think he was lost, it turned abruptly eastward again.

At first a few cars had passed him, headed back into town and a few ragged, barefoot men shouldering machetes had eyed him suspiciously before giving the usual greeting of "Good night." The mention of the word "night" made him more nervous than the sharp blades of their curved knives. It was getting dark and the farther he walked through the endless cane fields, the more isolated and alone he began to feel. He didn't know how far he had to go or even what he would find when he got there.

The road had turned to dirt some distance back and his footsteps were quiet thuds against its hard-packed surface. He was surprised when he came suddenly to an intersection with an identical dirt road running perpendicular to the one he had been traveling. A crude wooden signpost, hand-lettered with "Amity Hall", pointed north. One beneath it pointing the other direction read "Port Morant."

In the fading daylight, he quickly pulled out his map and found where he was. He found it odd that the sign should indicate Port Morant, which was so many miles and so many different roads south, but he convinced himself that it was okay because it was the biggest town in that direction. There was nothing to indicate that the road he was on led to the lighthouse except for the long thin line on the map leading away from this intersection.

It had looked like such a short distance to cover when he had gleefully studied it back in Port Antonio. Now seeing the small distance he had come compared to how far he had to go, his heart sank. He would never make it tonight.

He sat on the road and ate a couple of bananas while he tried to decide what to do. He measured the distance with the scale of miles on the map. It was only between five and ten miles not counting a few odd bends and turns. He should be able to walk that in a couple of hours if he put his mind to it.

Determinedly he set off again. He could see a few stars appearing now in the purple twilight of the sky. As it became darker, the shadow of the rippling sugar cane against the sky helped him to find his way. Where it parted in the middle of the horizon was where the road cut through it.

He cursed himself for not bringing a flashlight, but he had not expected to be making this part of the journey at night. Now that he could not see the ground in front of him, he had to walk much slower. His anger at himself grew when he thought about all the hours he had wasted in the morning waiting to rent a car. He should have left at dawn!

The darkness around him was like nothing he had ever experienced before. So complete, without the hope of a street lamp in the distance or the glimmer of light behind the curtains of a house. Occasionally a rustling in the cane or a scurrying across the road made him stand still with a pounding heart. Then he would convince himself that it was just a mongoose or a goat or a rat and he would continue his snail's pace through the night.

Probably he should turn around and go back to Golden Grove, but it seemed too late for that now. At the rate he was going, he wouldn't get back to town until midnight and then he would just have to retrace his steps in the morning.

He berated himself for not hiring a taxi or paying someone with a car to bring him out this way. But the thought had never even occurred to him. It had seemed as though it would be a short and easy walk.

Thrown off balance as his right foot stepped down into an unseen hole, he found himself suddenly sprawling in the road. Exasperated, he just lay there on his back, trying to decide what to do next. The only sounds were his own uneven breathing and the night crickets and frogs.

He knew the only sensible thing was to stop walking and wait until dawn to continue. He could probably stay right where he was on the road and be perfectly safe until morning. Visions of predawn cane trucks rumbling down the road with dim headlights quickly changed his mind about that idea. But he didn't relish the thought of camping in the ditch that ran between the road and the cane fields, especially when he couldn't see.

Taking off his backpack, he rummaged around in the front zipper compartment until he found a pack of matches. The one he lit burned down before it illuminated much more than his hand and his arm. He ripped a piece of paper out of his sketchbook and set a match to it. Holding it above his head like a torch, he moved quickly towards the ditch at his right. Soon enough the flame was licking at his fingertips and he had to blow it out. But he had seen enough. He knew the place he wanted to be was beyond the ditch, between the first two rows of cane.

It was an odd sensation, settling in between the cane, one he would probably have enjoyed if he'd been sharing it with a friend. When he sat down, the leaves of the rows met above his head, hiding the sky from his view. The uniformly planted stalks on either side of him were like two walls of widely spaced bamboo poles. On one side he could see the shadows and shapes of the moonless night, on the other was the utter darkness of miles of sugar cane.

He put on his jacket and then, using his pack for a pillow, he stretched out on the ground and tried to relax. But he was not tired and his mind was racing as fast as his heart. It was still early in the evening and the hours until daylight stretched out endlessly ahead of him. He let his thoughts roam over the events of the last few weeks in an effort to understand why he had ended up sleeping on the ground between rows of sugar cane on the deserted eastern end of the island of Jamaica.

Various scenarios of what he would find in the morning played over and over in head. After picturing himself coming across a band of Jamaican rebels armed with machine guns and wearing belts of ammunition, he was certain he'd made a mistake coming unarmed and alone. He tried to laugh it off.

He kept wondering why the postcard had been mailed from Montego Bay. If Molly was here, someone else had mailed the card for her. Someone who knew where she was and wanted her to stay there. But why? It still didn't make any sense. He only hoped he wasn't on a wild goose chase. One of the worst scenarios that went through his mind was that he got to the lighthouse only to find that Molly had just left or been moved the day before and that no one knew where she had gone.

When he finally fell asleep, his subconscious fears surfaced to create the nightmare he really feared. A skeletal Molly, with someone else's face and hair, chained to a wall in a dungeon, hanging limply with no breath of life left in her. Carson awoke with a scream and sat up. Dripping with sweat, he shivered in the cool night air.

It was just a dream, he told himself over and over. But alone in a cane field in the middle of the night, it was hard to feel calm and safe. He lit a match and looked at Gwen's watch. 3:05. Only a few more hours until dawn. He would survive.

CHAPTER FOURTEEN

Molly seemed to be rising up out of a deep black well of swirling sleep, propelled higher and higher by the throbbing pain in her head. When she finally broke through the surface into consciousness, she was aware of a great heaviness in her limbs as though gravity was trying to pull her back down into the dark depths again. It was a struggle just to open her leaden eyelids and when her vision focused on a strange ceiling in a room she had never seen before, she did not even have the energy to care where she was. As she slipped back into the shadowy, spinning void, she dimly realized how sore and dry her throat had become. But sleep overcame her before she could search for a glass of water.

When she awoke again, it was night and this time she felt much clearer, although the darkness around her made it impossible for her to see her surroundings. Gingerly she sat up, acutely aware of a pounding headache and a parched, aching throat. She seemed to be in a narrow bed with a stiff straw mattress. She ran her fingers over the rough, loosely woven blanket that was covering her and then, with sudden alarm, she slipped her hands beneath it. Her relief at finding that she was wearing a T-shirt and shorts was quickly obscured by a growing fear inside of her.

Where was she? And how did she get there? She couldn't seem to remember anything, let alone where she should be. If only she could recall where she was supposed to be; then maybe she might know where she was.

Her eyes were becoming accustomed to the darkness now and she could make out a window in the wall at the foot of the bed. The louvers were slightly opened and a light breeze was stirring a single curtain pushed to one side. Cautiously extending her left hand, she almost immediately touched a wall of unfinished wooden boards. There was something tacked to it, a piece of paper or a picture.

Swinging her feet off the bed she felt cool floorboards against her soles. But the sudden movement made her feel sick and dizzy and she sank back down on the bed, her only familiar territory. She needed some water badly; in a minute she would have to find some.

In her mind she pictured herself walking down the upstairs hall of Lantana House, opening the bathroom door, crossing to the sink and turning on the cold water faucet. Suddenly memories came hurling at her like a freight train, images that made her gasp with fear, some clear, some vague and cloudy. Slowly reaching up to her throat, she poked and probed a little and found the very bruised and sore places where fingers had tried to –

Tried to what? Choke her to death? It was too horrible to be true, she wanted to believe she had dreamed it, but the painful areas on her neck meant it must have really happened. Holding her face in her hands, she tried to remember more. Someone had saved her at the last minute, someone had stopped – him –

A raspy sob slipped out of her and she tried to sniff it back. She couldn't remember anything after that – no, there was something else. Someone making her drink something that tasted bitter, a pill being forced down her throat, but for some reason she couldn't see who it was. Had she struggled? Desperately, she tried to remember more.

Yes, she had struggled, but her hands had been tied behind her back, and something stuffed inside her mouth. When she had been picked up bodily, she had struggled harder until whoever was carrying her lost their grip and she had fallen head first to the ground, hitting her head. And that was the last she remembered.

Touching the throbbing area of her forehead, she found a huge lump. Well, no wonder. That explained at least part of her headache. But that was all it explained. She still didn't know where she was or why she had been bound and gagged and blindfolded. And drugged.

She lay perfectly still as another fearful thought occurred to her. What would be done to her when it was discovered that she was awake? Would she be forcefully drugged again?

For several minutes she battled internally over the choice of facing the unknown or dying of thirst. Before she could come to a decision, she heard the sound of a bolt sliding open and the click of a door unlatching. She froze with one arm flung across her face; that way she could see without it being obvious that her eyes were open.

A wide beam from a large square flashlight arced across the room and came to rest on her face. In the blinding glare she could see nothing; she tried to breathe calmly and look asleep. The sound of footsteps crossed the room and then someone stood next to her, training the light on her face. A hand rested on her forehead for a moment. Then the footsteps moved away again, there was the click of a lighter, a clinking of glass against metal and then the room was softly illuminated by a kerosene lamp that sat on a small table.

Molly watched as a tall black man dragged a straight-backed chair across the room, but when he got closer she was no longer able to see from beneath her arm. She heard him sit and then the sound of water dripping from something. When his fingers closed around her wrist, her heart began beating faster, but her merely moved her arm off her face and carefully laid it at her side. Seconds later she felt a cool wet washcloth placed very gently on her forehead.

Having prepared herself for something brutal, the very kindness of the gesture startled Molly so much that her eyes opened automatically in astonishment. Gentle eyes in a dark, handsomely bearded face looked back at her with overwhelming compassion.

"So. You finally awake." His voice was deep and pleasant.

She tried to ask for water, but only a small rasping sound came from her throat. He quickly left the room and was back momentarily with a plastic cup full of water. She drank it in great gulps that made her choke and sputter a little.

"Thank you," she whispered, sinking back down on the mattress again. "Where am I?"

"In a safe place. You not to worry. No one will hurt you now." He took the cup from her and set it on the floor next to a wash basin full of water.

"Well, who are you?"

"Derrick." He wrung out the washcloth and sponged her face again.

His short replies did not answer her question, yet there was something about him that made her believe he was interested in her well-being, that she could trust him. "How did I get here, Derrick?"

"You must not ask so many questions," he warned half-jokingly. "I promise you, you will be all right. But you must be patient for now. How do you feel?"

"My throat hurts and this bump on my head-" she winced as he touched it.

"You want to eat a little something? I will bring you some tea and biscuit." He picked up the flashlight, started for the door and then turned. "There is a chimmy under the bed if you need it."

"A what?"

He reached down and pulled out an enameled metal chamber pot. "Okay?"

"Yes." She was embarrassed. "Thank you."

The scraping of the bolt sliding back into place on the door seemed incongruous after their conversation. Why was she being locked in? How was she safe if the bolt was on the outside of the door?

While he was gone, she looked around the room in which she was apparently imprisoned. It was the typical eight-by-eight foot room that comprised half of a two-room Jamaican house. In the wall opposite the bed, she could see the door that led to the other room, no doubt locked from the other side. She seemed to be in a sparsely furnished bedroom. There was a two drawer dresser with only one drawer, some clothes hanging from nails on the wall and a metal footlocker beneath them. In one corner was what looked like a pile of motorcycle parts; a broken rim, a few inner tubes, a busted seat and a few unidentifiable engine parts.

If it was night again, she must have slept all day. What day of the week was it, anyway? Tuesday? She should be back in Negril now. Her need to know where she was gave her the strength to cautiously get out of bed again. Holding onto the wall, she made her way to the window and peered out.

Nothing, only blackness. She could hear crashing surf nearby and for a second she almost believed maybe she was back in Negril. Crossing to the other window she could see a dim light coming from an outdoor kitchen where Derrick was humming to himself as he fixed her tea. Who was he? Was he the person who had saved her?

The peaceful quietude surrounding the house made her more curious than before as to where she could possibly be. Everywhere she had been in Jamaica had sounds of other life around it at every hour of the day or night. She was either in some very

200

remote place or it was three a.m. in an extremely quiet neighborhood.

She was sitting on the bed, resting her back against the wooden wall, when Derrick returned with a tin mug full of steaming liquid and a package of crackers. "What time is it?" she asked innocently.

"Early evening. Eight or nine o'clock." He sat down in a straight-backed chair again to watch her eat.

"Really? How long was I asleep?" She wondered if her tone was too ingenuous to be believed.

"All day, mon! Me start to worry when night fall and you still sleep on. Drink up your tea, now."

She sipped it cautiously, not enjoying its unfamiliar herbal taste. "What kind of tea is this?"

"Bush tea. It will make you well."

"Bush tea?" She tried not to laugh aloud. "What kind of bush?"

"All kinds. You laugh now, but you will see. If you would like, in the morning I will show you where it come from."

"In the morning...Derrick, what's going on? Where am I anyhow?"

He laughed and leaned forward in his chair. "Ah, me darlin' girl, you are far, far from everything and everyone in Jamaica. You are very safe here, no one will find you or hurt you."

Molly's head swam a little as she tried to understand what he was saying. Why shouldn't she want to be found? Obviously there was someone who had tried to hurt her and maybe she was safer if he didn't know where she was. Finally she spoke up. "I need to get back home. To Florida. I'm supposed to fly back on Thursday."

"Well, I don't think you will be leaving here so soon. You will have to take a different flight home." His voice was calm yet firm.

"But why? Why can't I just get up and leave in the morning?" She sounded like a petulant child, her tone rather high and whiny with fear.

"For two reasons. One is because I have been told you stay here until I am informed otherwise. The other reason – well, in the morning I will take you to the lighthouse and show you why."

"Who told you I must stay here?" she demanded angrily.

"I am not at liberty to say." His musical Jamaican accent made everything sound more mystifying than it might have sounded otherwise. "A man tried to kill you and, until it is safe for you to go back, you are to stay out here with me. We have had too much killing. If I can stop it from happening one time more, I will."

What he said made sense to Molly, but she didn't understand the mystery surrounding the whole situation. "There will be people who will miss me in a few days." Resting her head against the wall, she closed her eyes. "They will probably get the police and start looking for me."

His laugh was short this time. "They will never find you here. Come now, me girl, you mustn't look so sad. This is not such a bad place to be. You will stay here for some days and then return to your own country, alive and well." He reached over and plucked the empty cup from her hand. "You'll see."

"Carson will be worried. I don't know what he will do." What would Carson do? Would he even realize she hadn't come back when she said she would? She had never even sent him a card. "I should at least send him a postcard and tell him I'm okay."

Derrick's forehead wrinkled in a frown. "Maybe so. We will talk about it in the morning time. If you need me in the night you can bang on the wall. I will be sleeping on the other side." He stepped through the door and then stuck his head back in again. "You see your things there? At the bed foot. That's right. Good night."

As the bolt slid back into the lock, Molly stared in amazement at her suitcase and purse which were sitting on the floor at the foot of the bed. Still rather unsteady, she slid off the bed and sat down to quickly rummage through her purse. Her money was still there and her traveler's checks. She looked in her wallet again. There seemed to be more cash than she remembered having. Not feeling quite clear in the head yet, she put it aside and unzipped her suitcase.

Her clothes had been stuffed in unceremoniously, not carefully folded and packed as she would have done. More like dirty laundry pushed into a gym bag. Her toothbrush, shampoo, and damp bathing suit had all been hurriedly shoved in with the clothes. It looked as though someone had just swept up everything around her room at Lantana House and dumped it into her suitcase. To make it appear as though she had packed up and left in a hurry, of her own free will, in the middle of the night.

Unable to fathom why all this should be happening to her, she lay down on the bed again and watched the light of the oil lamp cast flickering shadows on the ceiling. She was surprised at how drowsy she felt again after sleeping all day. Bush tea, hah, she thought, rolling over and closing her eyes.

At some point in the night she awoke and thought she heard low voices talking outside. But she was still too drowsy to care. There was nothing she could do in her locked room anyway.

Noises from the other side of the wall awoke her before the daylight streaming through the window did. Still rather dazed, she moved stiffly across the room to look outside.

The house seemed to be situated in a grove of trees, but through the low-growing foliage she could see an expanse of white beach and the ocean beyond that. The sun was hovering fairly close to the horizon, which meant she was on the eastern end of the island. Derrick came into view wearing a pair of yellow gym shorts, a towel thrown over his shoulder. He immediately saw her eyes peering at him through the louvers of the window and his teeth flashed white as he grinned.

"Good morning, lady. You promise not to run if I let you out to see the day?"

Running away had not even occurred to her yet, but it would certainly be an interesting idea once she felt better. "I promise."

With an odd feeling of excitement, Molly stepped through the opened door into the morning light and looked around. She had been right about the house; it was a two-room structure of unpainted wood with a corrugated tin roof. A battered motorcycle leaned against the side of the building, under the overhanging eave. The small clearing in which the house sat was mostly hard-packed red earth, but there seemed to be a vegetable garden of some sort at one end. A narrow sand road led out to the deserted beach.

"Is there some place I can wash up?" she asked, looking around for a water standpipe.

"Over there." He gestured toward a crude bench on which a plastic basin sat. "Me fetch watah fah you." Like most Jamaicans, he seemed to slip easily back and forth into patois. He returned with a red five gallon container and poured some into the basin. "I have to haul watah on de motah bike," he explained. "No pipe will reach to here." He laughed at the idea of it.

"I-I'll get my towel and soap," Molly said uncertainly. She wondered how she would take a whole bath, but decided not to tackle that at the moment.

After a quick wash-up and a change of clothes, she felt much more human. Peeking into the other room, she saw that Derrick had set out two places at a small wooden table. As she ate the toast and eggs he placed in front of her, she assessed this half of the house. Sparsely furnished, a couch with torn red plastic cushions took up most of one wall and the sleeping bag rolled up in one corner made her realize guiltily that she must be sleeping in Derrick's bed.

"You live here alone?" she asked, although the answer seemed obvious.

"Yes, mon. I like the peace here. After growing up in Kingston, I can never get enough of this fresh countryside."

"How far are we from Kingston?" She stared into her cup of instant coffee, not meeting his eyes.

"You can't trick me into telling, you know." His warning was not mean. "On the island of Jamaica, one is never very far from Kingston. After breakfast I will take you some place that will show you what you are near to."

Molly realized that her questions were not getting her any answers. She could probably learn more by keeping her mouth shut and her eyes open.

Molly sat behind Derrick on the small blue motorbike. As they took off with a jerk down the path towards the beach, her arm flew instinctively around his waist. With a detachment she did not usually possess, she thought how odd it was that she was entrusting her safety to a man she'd only met last night, a man who was holding her captive "for her own good." But some part of her mind was telling her that if she remained calm, it would all work out.

The pristine beauty of the white sand beach took her mind off of her problems. As they drove along the wet sand near the water's edge, she took in how gloriously clean the crescent shaped cove was – no empty bottles or dried orange peels or soap boxes to greet the waves rolling slowly in to the gently sloping shore. The dark green of the palm trees against the blue of the cloudless sky, the aquamarine water curving into the golden sands...it was more perfect than any picture postcard she'd sent home. It was the Jamaica every tourist dreamed of finding but, of course, never would.

At the end of the beach there was a rugged dirt road. They turned left and stopped at what, at one time, must have been a bridge. Apparently washed out by a storm, all that was left now were the stone parapets that had once held it up. Molly held her breath as Derrick lined up the front wheel of the bike with one of the stone foundations and then, without hesitation, roared across. They continued along through a flat, sparsely vegetated area until stopping abruptly at a gate that blocked the road.

"Open it for me, please," Derrick commanded. Molly was surprised to find her legs trembling a little as she climbed off the motorbike. She stopped at the gate, delighted by what lay ahead.

The grassy road was lined on either side by broken cinder blocks painted white. A short distance beyond, the road ended at some outbuildings next to a tall, red and white striped lighthouse. It looked just like the small lighthouse she had seen from the porch at Lantana House, only several times larger. It reminded her of a giant candy cane, misplaced in the greens and browns of the dry, flat countryside where goats and cows grazed and wandered. A sign off to one side told her it was the Morant Point lighthouse.

Molly looked back at Derrick who was waiting expectantly for her to open the gate. She wondered if he had been told of her interest in lighthouses or if this was just a coincidence. It was best to say nothing, she decided as she pushed the gate open and waited for him to drive through.

"My friend Henry works here," Derrick told her as they rode the final few feet. "He will take us up to the light." After parking the bike in the shade of a building, he turned to look at her. "Better for you not to say why you are staying with me."

She bit her tongue to keep from asking why and followed him into the office. An old man sat behind the desk. "Henry here?" Derrick asked.

"At him own place," the man replied, eyeing Molly with interest. "Good day to you. You are from the States?" Molly nodded, not knowing how much to reveal. "So how do you love our country?"

Visions of all the bad times she'd had in Jamaica exploded in Molly's brain, but as she felt Derrick's arm pressing against her own, she answered blankly, "Very much, thank you."

"We must go find Henry. Later." He nodded to the old man and steered Molly out the door again.

"Why?" she asked him as they walked across the yard. "Why don't you want him to know about me?"

"Do you want someone to try to murder you in your sleep again? Best for no one to know or wonder."

She stopped walking and waited until he turned to look at her. "Derrick, you don't know me. Why are you doing this for me?"

"I am doing it for a friend. And I am doing it for someone who is already dead, someone dear to me. Now – no more questions! Come."

He led her into another small concrete building. "Henry, wake up! Morning come!" Derrick called loudly as the screen door banged shut behind them.

"Who goes? Derrick?" Henry's voice came thick with sleep from the next room. "You too early, mon. Why you call on me so early?"

"I want to take Molly up de lighthouse. Door is open, then?"

"Who?" Henry appeared in the doorway, fumbling with the catch on a pair of cut-off trousers with a broken zipper. Seeing Molly he turned away, embarrassed. "You not tell me was lady friend you bring!"

"What kine name Molly fah boy!" Derrick and Henry began a fast exchange in patois that Molly could not follow. Looking around the room, she saw a road map of the island tacked to the wall above the table. While they conversed, she casually ambled over to the map and looked at the eastern end of it.

Morant Point Lighthouse – there it was, way out alone on a peninsula of land. Miles from Port Antonio. And as far from Negril as you could possibly get and still be on the island of Jamaica.

"Ready?" Derrick's voice made her look down and pretend to be studying the girlie magazine that lay open on the table.

"Sure." She shut the magazine and followed him and Henry out the door and across the yard to the lighthouse. They climbed a set of stairs on the outside of the building, and then Henry opened a small door and they went in.

The air inside was several degrees cooler, but the refreshing feeling was offset by the loud noise of the diesel generator that sat in the base of the structure, creating electricity for the lighthouse and its outbuildings. By the time they had climbed the last of several flights of circular stairs, Molly felt quite dizzy again and the bump on her head was throbbing.

The "light" was not one giant bulb as she might have imagined but several sealed beam lamps, looking like so many car headlights, mounted in rows pointing in every direction. Stepping out onto the circular concrete landing at the top, she breathed easier until the spectacular 360 degree view made her realize why Derrick had brought her up there.

In one direction, stretching as far as she could see from north to south, was the sea and the shoreline. She could see the beautiful white sand beach they had traveled on, but she could only guess where Derrick's house was located. In the other direction the narrow dirt road cut a crooked line through flat, dusty green countryside, eventually becoming a thin ribbon that disappeared finally into the distance. Far off were the hazy shadows of the Blue Mountains.

"Not many close neighbors, I guess," she said softly, joking.

"None. We are miles from anywhere. It is a long, long walk to town. You see all that green there way out? Cane fields. A person who didn't know their way could be lost for days." Molly knew he was saying all this for her benefit, so she wouldn't get any ideas about running away.

Gazing out at the wide expanse of uninhabited wilderness, she had no illusions of making her way to town. Probably the dirt track led right to civilization, but she was not about to find out. Not yet, anyway.

"It's very beautiful. Thanks for bringing me here."

"But you understand what I am saying?"

She nodded and walked around the other side to gaze out at the blue waters of the Caribbean as they crashed violently against the coral reef below. Alone for a moment, she took several deep breaths and told herself that she would stay calm, she was still alive, and she would continue to live to tell about it.

"Let's go down." They went back inside where Henry was waiting for them, leaning against a window with his eyes shut. Derrick laughed. "You drink too much Appleton's last night, Henry?"

"Mmm." Henry led the way back down the circular staircase to ground level. As he held the door open for her, Molly glimpsed the time on his wristwatch. She was surprised to see that it was only nine o'clock. She must have been up since dawn.

"We have things to do so we must run. Maybe come back tomorrow and collect whelks off the rocks for some whelk stew." Derrick pronounced the word "well-ick" but Molly knew what he meant.

"Tomorrow then." Henry watched them ride off on the motorbike and then stumbled back into his house.

"What do we have to do?" Molly asked as they bumped along the path. "It's still early."

"You need to write a postcard to your friend in Negril and then I will take it to be mailed."

"You mean tell him where I am?" Just thinking of Carson gave her an overwhelming feeling of homesickness.

"No, just tell him you are okay so that he doesn't worry. Let him think you are still in Port Antonio. If it says anything about you being here, Molly," he slowed the bike down and looked over his shoulder at her, "I won't mail it."

He left her alone in the bedroom with the battered postcard he had produced. She wondered where he'd found it. She'd already composed part of her message to Carson, trying to make him remember her trip to the Negril lighthouse and the conversation she'd had with George that night about all the lighthouses on the island. Even if Carson was too spaced out, she could count on George to remember. Digging through the front zipper compartment of her suitcase, she found her road map of Jamaica and tried to figure out what she could say that would lead him right to Morant Point without giving it away.

Finally settling on the coordinate points as the best clue, she added the corny, "O,K-4 ME" but wasn't sure if Carson would do much more than glance at it. She had to write something that would make him look twice, but that would not look suspicious to Derrick.

"Hurry up!" Derrick called through the window. "I must be some place by ten o'clock."

Not able to imagine what kind of appointment Derrick would have to keep out here in the bush,

Molly racked her brains for a last line that would be totally off the wall. Say something about Florida, something Derrick would know nothing about. Something about her family, no, his family. Make up a relative...

She was just finishing a line about a suggestion given to her by Carson's dead father (whom she'd never met) when Derrick burst through the door.

She hoped he thought she was sweating from the temperature inside the close little room as she handed him the postcard with damp fingers. While he read it slowly a couple of times, she stepped outside and paced around the yard, trying not to let her apprehension show. Finally he flashed his brilliant grin and slipped the card into a shirt pocket.

"Soon come back," he said as he straddled the motorbike again. "You are okay?"

"Yes, fine!" she shouted as he gunned the engine. Relieved that he had not felt the need to lock her inside, she wandered down the path to the beach. As she walked, she realized that all the tire tracks in the sandy soil were not his. The wider double tracks of a car were quite apparent.

Not that it made a difference at this point. Of course she'd been brought here in a car. Now all that mattered was what she was going to do with herself for the next few days while imprisoned in this tropical paradise.

The days ran together in a pleasant blend of relaxation and boredom. Sometimes Molly could not remember how long she'd been there or even why. Once or twice as she lay on the beach in the bright midday glare of the sun, she allowed herself to think back to the dreadfulness of that night and tried to piece together just exactly what had happened. She remembered one point in those few black moments being so sure that she knew who it was assaulting her. In retrospect she couldn't believe she had been right. She wouldn't allow herself to think about it, it only made her feel nervous and insecure. Besides, there was nothing she could do about it right now, anyway.

With little to do, she found herself retiring early every evening and sleeping well into the mornings. Most nights she had distorted dreams of Carson rescuing her. Because she had nothing or no one else to think about, he became her white knight, whisking her away, back to their old normal life in Jacksonville, and making everything all right again. Only once did the memories come and this time, as the air was being squeezed out of her throat, Derrick shook her awake and then held her and soothed her until the pounding of her heart stopped echoing in her head.

She did not understand this strange, kind Jamaica man. He did not act like the bold hustlers on the beach in Negril who seemed to assume that having sex with one of them would make any woman's vacation complete. And he did not act like other Jamaican men she had met in various places, who would whisper or mumble vulgar endearments that were supposed to turn her on and make her long for their "Big Bamboo." Instead he gave her his bedroom, never tried to take advantage of her and cooked meals for her as well.

At times he would take off on the motorbike and leave her alone to amuse herself for hours on end. She did not know where he went or why, but sometimes he came home with bread or coffee or tinned milk and she knew he had been to town. Most of what they ate came from the trees and the yard. There were a few scraggly wild chickens that roosted in the bushes and a goat tethered on a rope that reached just short of the garden.

When he announced on Saturday that he was going to market, she forced him to take some of her money to buy food for both of them.

212

"I insist! You've been so damned nice, but I'm sure I've got more money than you, so take it."

He did not return until after sunset and the half empty bottle of gold Appleton rum spoke to how he had spent most of his day. Derrick built the cookfire that night, but Molly cooked the dinner and while she worked she poured herself a cup of rum and squeezed the juice of a fresh orange into it.

They sat on the plastic couch that night, listening to the radio with its newly acquired batteries, drinking rum and laughing and talking. He tried to teach her some patois. "You know what in mean in Jamaica to 'draw card'? It mean to fool somebody. You know what a duppy is? It a ghost. How about your batty? It your bum-bum, girl!"

Molly knew that if there was ever a chance for her to find out more about him, this was it.

He told her about growing up in Kingston in his grandmother's house with his cousins and aunts and uncles, "everybody all sleeping same room, same bed, sharing same bedbug and same hunger." All through his childhood he felt suffocated, unable to breathe or move except when the Sunday School took the children on Easter picnics to the beach or to harvest celebrations in the country. When he was a young teenager, he ran away to live with his grandmother's sister in Mavis Bank, high in the mountains, finding work in the Blue Mountain Coffee factory there. But even the mountains made him feel closed in and he longed for the sea. He saved his money, and many years later, was able to build his homestead on the beach.

"What about a wife or girlfriend?" The soft warm glow Molly felt from the rum matched the golden light of the kerosene lamp.

"Yes, I had one back in Mavis Bank. We never marry, but she have two babies of mine. I can't have just one woman. I can't be closed in that way. I like to live alone, come and go, not have to answer to wife or girlfriend." He leaned towards her, the whites of his eyes gleaming in the dim light, and grabbed her hand in a way that made her heart leap into her throat. "You know what I mean?"

"Yes, I know. " For some reason she laughed and then he laughed, releasing her hand, and everything was okay again. And it was true, she did understand what he meant. She almost felt the same way. "If you need to be alone so much, why are you keeping me here?"

He threw his head back and laughed merrily again. "You think you can get me drunk and make me betray my confidences? What a girl you can be. Why can't you trust the way I trust? This is for the best and soon enough we will all know the truth."

When she did not reply, he went on. "I don't mind your company, you know. From what I know of you, I think maybe we are a lot alike, you and I."

Just contemplating the vast difference in their physical appearances made Molly burst out in laughter. She tired to envision what life with Derrick would be like and as she thought about, she realized that she already knew. They were living it day to day here, very compatibly, but it would never be enough for her. She wanted to do more with her life than peacefully exist in the Jamaican bush.

Suddenly she was impatient to get on with it all. She was ready to go back and start over, alone, without Carson. "Derrick, how much longer must I be captive here?" she asked.

"You are not enjoying your visit?" he teased softly.

"I would enjoy it more if I had come here on my own and could leave when I was ready."

"What today is – Saturday? Let me see, maybe three, four days more. But it could be two weeks."

"How will you know when it is safe?"

"I'll be told by one who knows. And if I don't hear in, say, one month's time, I will take it on myself to let you go."

A month. She felt a sinking depression at the prospect of spending that much more time here, even though it was probably one of the most beautiful places on earth. Freedom, no matter how dangerous it might be, seemed much more appealing to her.

The pleasantness of the evening was over and she stood up. "Guess I'll go to bed," she sighed.

"Molly – some day when this is far, far, in the past, you will come back to visit to me? As friends?"

"Once I get away from this island, I don't know if I'll ever come back." The fierceness in her voice was a surprise even to herself. "But if by some piece of bad – if by some chance I end up here again, I will certainly look you up."

"You won't hold it against me?"

"Never."

As she lay down on the rough blanket, she felt lonelier than ever before in her life. She wanted someone's strong arms around her, a shoulder to snuggle against, a chest to fall asleep on. If Derrick had walked through the door at that moment, she would have welcomed him into her bed without blinking twice. Instead she rolled over and thought about the men in her recent past. Robinson... Henley...and finally settled on an image of herself and Carson, safely sleeping, arms and legs entwined, in their queen-size bed back home in Jacksonville.

CHAPTER FIFTEEN

Carson rolled over in his sleep and the cold, crumbly feel of dirt against his cheek awoke him instantly. Wiping the back of his hand across his face, he looked quickly at Gwen's watch. Almost 8 a.m. In the tunnel beneath the two overhanging rows of cane, the first rays of dawn had not awakened him as he had expected. Crawling through the stalks, he stepped out into the ditch at the side of the dusty road and into bright sunlight at last.

He felt like shit but there was nothing odd about that considering where he had just spent the night. His back and his neck ached, his eyes felt crusty and his throat was like a desert. As he urinated into the ditch, he noticed that he was also filthy, both his clothes and body. But that was to be expected too.

Sitting at the edge of the road, he breakfasted on grapefruit and cheese puffs, resolving to save his warm box of juice for later in the day in case he needed it more at that time. And then he was on his way, walking briskly in the direction of the rising sun.

In a short amount of time the cane fields ended and the road followed along a narrow strip of beach where a couple of old fisherman sat making nets outside of a ramshackle hut. They waved at him, big curious grins on their faces.

"Lighthouse is this way?" he shouted to them.

"Lighthouse - yes, mon! Just keep on de road!"

Soon the cane fields appeared again and Carson trudged on, trying to keep his mind blank. The strap on one of his sandals broke and, cursing himself for not wearing sneakers, he went on, barefoot. At times he almost forgot why he was doing this and when he remembered, it seemed like some crazy dream from someone else's life.

Finally the cane fields came to an abrupt end and he found himself on the edge of a vast savanna of scrub brush and golden grass. It reminded him of pictures of West Africa. A thin and dusty ribbon of road cut through this landscape. Shading his eyes, he could see something several miles away in the haze of the horizon that quite possibly could be the lighthouse.

It was not as far as it looked. In less than an hour he had covered the distance and was standing at the junction of a beautiful white sand beach and what appeared to be a washed-out stone bridge. The road continued on the other side of the gully that the ruined bridge had once spanned and, although it was hard to believe, there were tire tracks continuing out the other side.

Carefully crossing what was left of the foundation, he had barely started off again on what he felt sure was the last lap of his journey, when the sound of a motorcycle engine behind him made him turn in surprise. A small motorbike shot suddenly off the beach and disappeared up the road he had just come down. Well at least there were some signs of life out here. He shrugged and went on.

Like a mirage to a thirsty camel, the red and white striped lighthouse manifested in front of him, an oasis in the desert. He could not believe he had finally made it. He hesitated at the gate, however, trying to sort out what he was going to say.

He was almost afraid to enter, afraid to find out that it had all been in vain, that Molly wasn't here at all. Then, driven by the crazy positive intuition he'd been riding on, he hurriedly opened the gate and walked swiftly towards a group of buildings in front of him.

217

"Hey! Oy!" A dark man milking a cow in the shade of a tree hailed him with one hand. "Come here!"

Obediently Carson crossed the grass to him.

"How can I help you?"

The greeting was not unfriendly, but it was not very welcoming either. Carson knew that by this time his appearance might put the most open-minded person off and he tried not to expect too much. "I'm looking for someone who might be staying here," he began.

"You might know someone staying here?" The man repeated his words in a mocking way. "And who might that be?"

"Her name is Molly McRae. She's about this tall with blond hair and–"

His laughter interrupted Carson's words. "No, mon, she is not staying here. No woman stays at the lighthouse now."

Carson could feel a lump in throat beginning to form. "Have you had any woman visitors here in the last week or two? Perhaps you might remember if she came by here. Or maybe you weren't here the day she came–"

The man laughed again, cutting off Carson's nervous chatter, not unpleasantly but still in a condescending way. "You not listen to me, mon. I say she not stay here."

Carson stared at him dumbly for a few seconds. "You mean she came through here but didn't stay?" he said at last.

The man nodded. "That is right." He looked down at Carson's dirty, bare feet. "How you get here, mon?"

"I walked."

Hoots of laughter followed his reply. "You? A white man? I can't believe it!"

"So where is she?" Carson asked impatiently.

"Who are you to her?" His tone was full of suspicion now.

218

Carson looked into the man's distrustful eyes and then replied without hesitation. "Her brother."

"Well, all right then. She stay with a friend of Henry's, name of Derrick. Him live down the beach you pass by. You just follow the beach along, you can't miss it." The man went back to milking the cow, his interest in Carson gone now.

"Thanks a lot, man. Catch you later." Not waiting for a reply, Carson headed back in the direction he had come.

He tried not to let the new questions in his mind affect him, knowing that he would have the answers in a matter of minutes. But he could not keep from wondering who Derrick was and why Molly was there. Something in the man's attitude had given him the uneasy feeling that perhaps Molly and Derrick were lovers. He wondered what uncomfortable and sticky situation he was getting into now.

After Derrick left for town, Molly spent the morning washing her clothes in a small plastic tub, trying not to think how many more times she might have to wash them this way before Derrick would tell her that she was safe to go. She was tired of being an inmate in this palm tree prison. A few times she had gotten out her map and tried to calculate the distance to the main road, but she didn't have the nerve to try running for it yet. She also didn't want to bear the brunt of Derrick's temper if caught up with her.

She had only seen him angry once in the week she'd been here. That was when the pig had gotten loose and eaten up the chicken stew that was simmering over the fire in the kitchen along with a loaf of bread, a bunch of scallions and a roasted breadfruit. When his misbehavior had been discovered, Molly had cowered in her room listening to Derrick explode in anger as he beat the pig and put the kitchen back to rights, barely able to recognize the gentle man she thought she knew. For the rest of the day he had been moody and silent. Molly did not think Derrick would ever treat her the way he had treated the pig, but she was not quite ready to find out.

A few days earlier she had asked him to buy her a notebook and pen in town. When she had finished doing her laundry, she took the black and white school composition book and headed out to the beach. It consoled her a little to write her thoughts down, to plan for her future, to write letters to friends back home even if she would never get a chance to mail them. In a long, unfinished letter to Melissa, (and in an effort to understand why someone had tried to murder her), she tried to outline everything that had happened to her since she left Negril.

Having spent long hours going over the events of that night, she was fairly certain now of who it was. And one thing was for sure - he knew that she had figured out he was responsible for Fawn's death and if he knew where she was, he would not let her live to tell the world. She was not sure she would even be safe going back to Jacksonville; surely he would easily track her down there.

As she lay on the beach, wondering how much of her suspicion she dared to even put in writing, something moving down the beach broke into her abstract reverie. Shading her eyes, she saw now that it was a person walking towards her, a rather ragged and filthy-looking man. She stood up, excited and fearful at the same time, not sure whether or not she should run back to the house and lock herself in.

There was something familiar about those long limbs and that loping stride. Suddenly she screamed in disbelief and throwing down her notebook, she ran down the sand, shrieking with joy. She threw her arms around Carson's neck as he lifted her in the air and spun her like a child, his whoops of delight mingling with her own.

"You came! You came! How did you get here? I can't believe it!" Her shouts were no louder than his.

"You're okay! You look fine! You're not dead!"

Putting her down at last, he stepped back to look at her, the smile fading from his face. She looked well-fed and relaxed, in fact she looked better than she had when he'd last seen her. It didn't make sense. "So what the hell's going on here, Molly?"

"I still don't get it." Carson had stripped down to his shorts and was stretched out on the beach, face down with his eyes closed. Despite his weary appearance, he had been listening to Molly's story with intent amazement. "For one thing, why would anyone want to murder you? Secondly, why would someone else go to all this trouble to keep you, quote, 'safe' when they could have just gone to the police? It doesn't add up. Haven't those questions run through your mind?"

For an answer Molly burst into tears. "You pig! Do you think I've thought about anything else for the last week? There aren't exactly a wide variety of distracting activities at this high class resort, you know."

"I'm sorry." But it was hard for Carson to feel sorry for her when she looked so clean and rested and he felt so disgusting and exhausted. "So what conclusions did you come to?"

She sighed. "None. Derrick knows who brought me here, but I'm sure he doesn't know who tried to kill me. He seems to have something personal invested in this, but I can't quite figure out why."

They were both silent for a while and then Carson said, "This 'rejection' thing is what really throws me. This guy who tried to kill you, he said that you had rejected him. That sort of rules out any old maniac off the street, doesn't it."

221

There was a sarcastic edge to his voice that made Molly feel very defensive. "Not necessarily. It could be some guy in a restaurant or something who thought I should be paying attention to him when I never even knew I was ignoring him."

"Well, that's pretty farfetched."

"Well, so is this whole damn situation!"

Both of them lay there, inwardly fuming at each other. Here they were, together again, and after only a few minutes they were already fighting. Finally Carson said, "Let's just forget it. What's done is done. Right now you should go pack up your things and walk out of here with me."

"How many miles do you think it is?"

"I don't know - it probably took me four hours. Maybe fifteen miles. But it's all flat, an easy walk."

"I can't carry my suitcase for fifteen miles. I'd have to leave most of my stuff behind." Molly had an odd, faraway look on her face.

"Your stuff doesn't matter. The main thing is to get you out of here, isn't it?"

Molly stood up and wandered slowly up the beach until she was a good distance from Carson and then sat down again. Somehow this had turned out all wrong. This was not how she had imagined Carson sweeping in and rescuing her. And now that he was here, she was not so sure she even wanted to go with him.

Carson knelt behind her and put his hands on her shoulders. "What's wrong?" he asked gently. After their initial encounter he was fearful of getting too close to her physically, afraid it might break down his resolve to tell her about Gwen.

"You don't really understand, Carson. In a certain way I'm afraid to leave here. It might seem strange to you, but I trust Derrick. I believe him when he says I should wait until he know it's safe for me to go."

"Are you lovers with him?"

"What?" She burst out laughing and jumped up, turning to face him. "No, we are not lovers! Maybe it's hard for you to believe, but he's just a kind man who took care of me when I had a huge bump on my head and bruises around my neck. A man who gave up his bed for me and has slept on the couch for a week." She laughed again. "But I suppose that's hard for a 'passionate man' like you to understand."

Carson was suddenly flooded with memories of how Molly had been acting towards him before she left Negril. He realized it would not be hard to tell her their relationship was over. She had known it before him.

"Is there any place here I can wash up while I think this over?" he asked. Maybe if he was cleaner, he would feel better.

She shook her head. "Not really. The only place to take a bath is in a big enamel washtub, and there's no running water. You can do it, but it's not easy."

"Anything would be better than the way I feel. You can pack up while I wash."

Her lips pressed together in a thin grim line, Molly led him silently up to the house, contemplating how strange it was that she had so anxiously hoped for Carson's arrival, and now that he was here, he was taking charge of her life in just the way she hated. But it might be her only chance to leave here and no matter what her better judgment told her, she would do it. She would go with him. But it would have to be immediately. If Derrick found out that she had contacted Carson, well, who knew how he would react.

While Carson stood in the washtub behind the house trying to figure out how to wash up with a gallon jug of water and a bar of soap, Molly nervously stuffed as much as she could into her day pack and into her purse. She had just ripped a sheet of paper from her composition book to write a message to

Derrick when the sound of his motorcycle pulling into the yard made her freeze.

Carson was just coming around the corner with a towel wrapped around his waist as Derrick drove down the path. Stepping back, he instinctively flattened himself against the wall. He hadn't prepared himself for a confrontation and certainly not with this large, imposing black man.

Derrick immediately noticed Carson's backpack and dirty clothes where he had unceremoniously dumped them on the ground outside the door to the bedroom. He stopped motionless in his tracks, looking around sharply. Then, with one long stride, he was inside calling Molly's name.

"Molly! Who's here? Are you okay?" It seemed unusual to Carson that Molly's captor should sound so concerned about her.

"I'm right here, Derrick. You don't have to shout."

"Sorry. Whose things are those outside?"

There was a second of silence and Carson held his breath, waiting for her reply. "My friend Carson is here," she answered at last. "He's around back washing up."

"Your friend Carson? The one you sent a postcard to in Negril?" Carson could not hear Molly's reply. "How did he find you here?"

He cringed mentally as he waited for Molly's answer. It seemed to be a long time coming. "Molly-" Derrick's voice has a very unpleasant edge to it now- "How did Carson find out that you were here?"

Exhaling, Carson stepped around the corner and asked loudly, "Molly, where do want me to put this soap? Oh, hi," he said lightly as Derrick's eyes flashed at him. "I'm Carson. You must be Derrick." The large frame filling the doorway blocked his view of Molly. "Hey, thanks for taking such good care of her, but it's time for her to get back to the States now. She might lose her job if she stays away any

224

longer." Carson gave a half laugh and tried to step into the room, but Derrick had no intention of letting him pass by.

"Who told you she was here, mon?" His low voice growled with suspicion.

"Some guy at the lighthouse." Wearing nothing but a towel, Carson was overcompensating for how vulnerable he felt. He turned his back and pulled his shorts on as Derrick puzzled over his answer.

"Morant Point lighthouse?"

"Yeah, the one right down there at the end of the beach." Carson carefully folded up his dirty clothes and put them back in his bag, wondering just how far he could go with this double talk.

"That lighthouse not on the way to anywhere, mon. How you happen to end up there from Negril?"

"Well, I'm a painter, see. And I have this thing about lighthouses. So while Molly was off traveling by herself, I thought I would just go from lighthouse to lighthouse around the island. I'm on my way to Kingston next. You can imagine my surprise when I heard that Molly was staying right here, when all this time I thought she was in Port Antonio." Carson felt as though he was listening to another person babbling, it sounded so unlike his usual self.

"Just a coincidence then?" Derrick did not sound convinced.

"Yeah, pretty unbelievable, huh?"

Derrick leaned against the doorframe. Crossing his arms, he studied Carson. "Pretty unbelievable. In fact, I don't really believe it all."

"So, anyway, this is great!" Carson went on, trying to sound enthusiastic and oblivious. "Now Molly can come with me and we can finish up our trip together before we go home."

Derrick threw back his head and laughed loudly. "Not a chance, mon! You might as well have your little visit and be on your way."

"Derrick-" Molly's voice came timidly from inside the dark room. "Wouldn't I be safe if I was with Carson?"

"Don't even think about it. You are not leaving here until I know it is the right time. And if I have to make sure of that, I will."

An ominous silence followed his words. Neither of them doubted his sincerity. Finally Carson said, "Okay. That's cool. But I'm really beat. It wouldn't hurt anything if I stayed the night here and left in the morning, would it? Molly could use some company for a day, don't you think?"

Derrick stepped out of the doorway and came face to face with Carson. As they eyed each other, Carson was surprised to realize they were the same height - Derrick seemed so much bigger. It was clear to both of them that they didn't trust each other. "How much do you know?" Derrick asked him in a tense, quiet voice.

"Just what Molly has told me. How much-" He had been about to throw Derrick's own question back at him, but he bit his tongue. It was wiser not to cross this man. "How much else should I know?"

"You and I will talk later. You can stay, but no funny business. Understand?" Derrick walked away abruptly. He crossed to a corner of the house where he stooped to pull a machete and a strop out from a pile of tools he kept underneath the building. Seating himself on a bench across the yard, he began purposefully sharpening the curved blade, blatantly displaying a don't-fuck-with-me-mon attitude.

Carson went inside where Molly was sitting on the bed, her head in her hands. "I bought us some time," he said softly, putting his arm around her. "Don't worry, we'll figure something out. I'll get you out of her somehow. Even if I have to come back with the Jamaican National Guard."

"He's a really nice guy, Carson." Molly did not lift up her head. "I don't want to see him go to jail."

Through the window he could see Derrick taking his anger out on the machete. It was hard to understand why Molly would want to protect him when he had been holding her prisoner for the past week.

His next thought sent a chill up his spine. Derrick must realize that Carson was not going to walk away from here and keep this incident to himself. So why had he agreed to let him stay? Stranger still, why had he agreed to let him leave? He was probably sitting out there right now trying to figure out how he was going to keep Carson quiet. Perhaps permanently.

He leaned back against the wall, pulling Molly back with him. "Well, Molly, what are we going to do?"

They spent the next few hours stretched out beside each other on the narrow bed, quietly discussing what to do next. Carson was in favor of overpowering Derrick somehow, tying him up and taking the motorbike. "When we get to town we'll send someone back, so it'll only be a few hours that we'll leave him like that."

But he could think of no way to do it, let alone separate the man from his machete. "Does he sleep soundly?"

"How would I know? I've never tried to sneak away before." She thought for a moment. "One night I was having a nightmare and he did wake up and come in here. So he doesn't sleep that soundly."

"Do you have a flashlight here?"

"Derrick does. Why?"

"If we had a light we could probably just walk away from here in the middle of the night and be back to town by morning."

"Oh, Carson." Molly got up and walked to the window.

"'Oh, Carson' what?"

227

"The door to this room locks from the outside. He can lock us in at night if he wants to. And I'm sure he will."

A loud terrified squawking from the yard made Carson leap up and join her at the window. With his gleaming machete, Derrick had chopped off the head of one of the chickens, which was now running headless around the yard.

"Do you think he's trying to tell us something?" Carson asked glumly.

"No, I think he's going to cook a chicken for dinner." Inside the small room with its tin roof the air was suddenly stifling. "Let's go back down to the beach, Carson. I'm suffocating in here."

As they headed towards the beach, Derrick called to them. "Oy! Wait a minute! Molly, you go on. I want to talk to this man alone."

The bloody machete in his hand left no room for argument. Carson walked obediently over to where Derrick stood waiting. "Come around here to the back of the kitchen with me while I pluck this bird." Derrick motioned with his head for Carson to follow him.

While Derrick sat on a bench pulling the feathers out of the chicken, Carson stood opposite him, nervously shifting his weight from one foot to the other.

"It really doesn't matter how you found Molly here," Derrick said at last. "What matters is what are we going to do with you now that you are here."

Carson just looked intently at him and said nothing.

"I guess the question is -" Derrick continued- "whether or not I can trust you not to tell anyone that Molly is here. The safest thing would be to keep you here as well. But I don't know how many more days we are talking about, you know. And I don't think you would be such an easy guest as Molly."

"Trust ME? You're the one holding my girlfriend hostage here and you're asking if you can trust me?" Carson had not meant to lose his cool, but it was too late now. "Who the hell are you, anyway? What difference does it make to YOU if someone tried to strangle Molly? And what kind of mysterious sign are you waiting for before you tell her she can go?"

Carson was shouting now, but he didn't care. "You know what I think, man? Forget this good Samaritan business. I think you know who did it and I think that person is paying you to keep Molly here so he can get far away from this island before anyone starts looking for him."

Derrick's eyes narrowed to angry slits as he listened to Carson's ravings. "You are crazy, mon," he said in a low, very controlled tone. "You don't realize how lucky Molly is that she didn't end up like Fawn Farrell. Fawn - she dead, mon!" His voice cracked a little and he looked away. "You can leave whenever you want, mon. Me na care what you do, just don't fuck wit de plan. Molly, she stay."

The emotion he showed when he spoke of Fawn aroused Carson's curiosity. He knew she was a well-loved symbol of Jamaica, but this seemed more personal somehow. "Did you know Fawn?" he asked.

"Yes, me know her." Derrick went back to plucking his chicken.

"I knew her too."

"You? How you know her?"

"She was staying next door to me at Mango Grove. Before she was killed." He watched Derrick's face closely. There was some clue here if only he could figure out what it was.

"Then you should know what I am saying! You want to see Molly like that?"

Molly had mentioned something about accusing her assailant of killing Fawn as well. He wondered if Derrick was making a connection between the two incidents because of something he knew or because of something Molly had told him.

"You think it was the same person both times?"

"I know so. But that is all I know. Now - the best thing would be for you just to leave and pretend you know nothing of this. I will make sure Molly gets back to you when the time comes."

Carson watched Derrick work for a few moments, wondering what to do. How could he leave Molly here? He would stay the night, bide his time, and think of something. "I'll stay the night if you don't mind. I'm really kind of tired."

"All right then. In the morning I can carry you part way on the bike if you would like." Placing the chicken in a plastic tub, he carried it to the kitchen, indicating that their conversation was over.

Carson walked slowly back to the beach, not really knowing what to do next. If he wanted to find out more about Derrick, he would have to win his confidence somehow.

By the time supper was ready, Carson had finished a detailed ink drawing of the two room house, a close-up of the black pig as he scrounged in his feed pan, and a sketch of Molly with the sweeping curve of the palm-lined beach as background. He presented them to Derrick before the meal.

In exchange for dinner," he explained. "I thought you might like a little art work for your place."

Derrick studied the pictures, a pleased yet surprised expression on his face. "These are very good, mon. This is how you make your living?"

"Well, yes, I guess so." Carson was slightly embarrassed. He told Molly how George had bought several pieces of his work before he had left for Port Antonio.

"You should take care of those drawings," Molly advised Derrick. "Someday they may be worth a lot of money."

230

Derrick was intently studying the picture of the house. "Yes, mon. You have captured it. I would never sell these pictures. Thank you, Carson."

As they ate the delicious meal of curried chicken, yams and breadfruit, Derrick's attitude towards Carson was decidedly warmer. Carson noticed that Derrick was eating his meal with a large spoon out of an old pot that was missing its handle and felt guilty as he realized that he and Molly must be using the only plates and forks.

"Do you play dominoes?" Derrick asked him suddenly as they were carrying the dishes out to the kitchen afterwards.

"Well, yes, I mean, I don't know-" Carson laughed uncertainly- "I know how to play, but I've never played the way you do here." Images came instantly to mind - dimly lit, open air bars where men clustered around a tiny table were boisterously slapping their dominoes down with large masculine gestures and loud cries of outrage or triumph.

"After we clean up here, we will play a game."

"All these nights I've been here and you never asked me if I wanted to play dominoes," Molly complained.

Carson cringed at the response he knew was about to come.

"Women not play dominoes," Derrick replied with a smile.

"And why not?" Molly launched into a tirade against Jamaican sexism and did not let up until Derrick agreed to let her play with them.

Clearing the small table, he pulled a paper bag out from under the couch and emptied a pile of wooden dominoes onto the table. Within a few minutes they were intensely involved in the game. They were laughing so much that they did not hear the car driving up the beach until it turned into the path.

All laughter stopped and eyes widened at the sound of an overheating engine and the scraping of branches against metal as the vehicle forced its way down the narrow path. Then, at the same instant, all three of them stood up and streaked out the door to see who the unannounced visitor might be.

"Ah, at last," Derrick said as he recognized the driver and moved quickly forward. Molly was on his heels but Carson hung back, unsure of what effect his presence was going to have on whatever was going to come next.

"Hey, dude, what's happening?" rang out a familiar voice. "Hi, Molly! You're looking as good as ever."

Carson started forward as he realized who it was. "Hello, Henley," he said evenly, pushing past Molly who was staring dumbfounded into the car.

A look of shock crossed Henley's face as he saw Carson standing there, but he quickly regained his composure. "Fancy meeting you here, Carson!" he remarked gaily. "What's a nice guy like you doing in a place like this?"

"Funny, I was just about to ask you the same question, Henley." Even though he was aware of Derrick closing in on him, Carson opened the door on the driver's side and reached in to turn off the engine. Stepping back, he crossed his arms across his chest. "So why don't you just step out and do some explaining?"

CHAPTER SIXTEEN

Henley lifted a half-empty bottle of Red Stripe off the seat next to him and drained it before speaking. Then wiping his mouth with the back of his hand, he belched loudly and said` "Well, that's a fine welcome for someone who's just driven here straight from the Kingston airport and who's been travelling since 6 AM this morning." As he opened another beer for himself, he asked, "Anybody else like one? Carson? Derrick?"

"I'll have one," answered Molly. "But you're not going to buy us off with beers, Henley. Get out of that car right now and tell us what's going on."

Carson and Derrick looked at Molly in surprise, but Henley responded immediately. After handing them each a Red Stripe, he stretched and walked around a bit, obviously stiff from a day of travel. "It's nice here, isn't it?" he said in a pleasant voice. "The perfect picture of paradise, huh?"

They all followed his gaze through the trees to where the sea had taken on the rosy afterglow of sunset. "Don't try to distract us, Henley`" Carson said evenly. "So what's wrong with this picture?"

"You, for starters." Henley turned to face him. "I don't understand what you're doing here at all."

"I think your story comes first," Carson replied. "Or are you going to wait until we go to sleep so that you can finish the job you started?"

"You make me sound like a two-bit gangster, Carson. I'm not on trial here. I came here to take Molly back to Negril and see that she gets home safely. You're welcome to come along for the ride."

They all stood there in silence for a moment as twilight began dropping its skirts around them. "Let's go inside," Molly suggested, slapping at a mosquito.

"Because I'm not going anywhere with you, Henley, until you answer a lot of questions."

Even in the warm light of the kerosene lamp, Henley looked pale and frightened as he perched on the arm of the plastic couch and looked around at the three waiting faces. "I tried to do the right thing," he said at last, addressing himself to Molly. "And I think I did okay. But you have to understand, he's my best friend, I've known him a lot longer than you-"

"Robinson? Is that who we're talking about?"

Henley nodded, taking another swig of beer to fortify his courage. "He's always been an extremist. When he does something, he throws himself into it passionately, totally, and when he's through with something he gives it up completely. He's especially that way with his love life. If he has his heart set on someone and they aren't with him one hundred percent, it makes him wildly morose, almost manic depressive. He's been like that since he was a kid and his mother abandoned him." He took a deep breath before continuing. "I didn't realize how unbalanced he had become until-"

"Until what?" Molly asked him gently.

"Until I walked in on him trying to strangle you." When he exhaled, they all breathed with him. "Oh, I admit I suspected it when that prostitute turned up dead after the Yellowman concert, but I pushed her out of my mind because I didn't want to believe it."

"What prostitute? What are you talking about?"

"You had already left Negril for Port Antonio, but Carson knows what I'm talking about. Out of all the hookers on the beach that night, Robinson picks out this real young one who says she won't do it with him because she doesn't like his face. He's still feeling so sensitive over Fawn's rejection of him that he can't deal with this one at all. I left them on the beach arguing and, well, you know the rest. Even though I suspected him of killing that girl, it never

234

even crossed my mind that it might have been Robinson who...who-" he glanced warily at Derrick- "who had murdered Fawn-"

All three of his listeners sat forward in their seats. "Did he?" demanded Carson.

"Yes, I'm sorry to say, he did. I guess I didn't know him as well as I thought I did. If I only had guessed what was churning in his restless brain that night, I might have talked him out of it."

"You can't blame yourself for something like that," Molly interjected.

So where is the psychopath now?" Carson demanded.

"Carson! Let him finish what he was saying!"

"Actually, when told me he couldn't sleep that night until he'd talked to Fawn again, I never thought it would end like that. So you're right. I guess you can't stop something that you don't expect is going to happen."

Nobody said anything for a few minutes but it was a charged silence. Finally Molly asked, "When did you figure it out?"

"Not until he tried to kill you. I just didn't want to believe that he was that crazy. I mean, he loved Fawn so much, it just didn't seem possible that he would- would- want to harm her, even if she had told him to lay off because she was hanging out with Alex. And then, once he cracked, every woman who rejected him brought back how much Fawn had hurt him, including you."

"Why did you follow him to my room that night?" Molly asked.

"Well, you remember how weird he'd been acting all day. When he said he was going for a walk, I just didn't trust him. I thought he might hurt himself, you know, get into trouble somehow because he was so mad that you and I-" He cut himself off and shot an uncomfortable look at Carson, whose eyes widened suddenly with a greater understanding of

Henley's role in this situation. At a shrug from Carson, he went on.

"Anyway, when I saw him enter Lantana House, I thought that maybe I should go home and mind my own business. But I watched him climb in your open window from the verandah, and there was something in the way he did it and how the lights didn't go on afterwards that made me a little nervous."

"Another minute and you would have been too late," Molly said in a low voice.

"As soon as he saw me he seemed to snap out of it. It was as though he was stepping back into himself and looking at what he had been doing with the same horror that I felt. We stood there looking at each other, not knowing what to do. Somehow it came to me at that moment that what I needed to do was get him home and into a nice private mental health clinic where he could get some professional psychiatric care. I did not want to see him end up stark, raving mad in some Jamaican slammer. The only problem was that I didn't think you'd go along with trying to salvage the life of someone who'd just tried to murder you."

"So you tied her up and drugged her?" There was no mistaking what Carson thought of Henley's plan.

"It was all I could think of on such short notice. I hated doing it! You've got to believe me." He searched each of their faces, but all three were fixed into stony, unreadable masks. "My first thought was to bring her with us, but that would have been more than I could have handled. Robinson had already turned into a shaking, weeping wreck of a human being. We wracked our brains to think of who we knew on the island that could be trusted with such a heavy responsibility and in the end it was Robinson who thought of Derrick."

All eyes turned to Derrick now. "We met at Fawn's funeral in Kingston," he explained. "I tell them how to get here in case they want to visit some time. Henley, him say there not enough action out this way for him, but thanks just the same." He turned to Henley suddenly, his eyes blazing with hurt and anger. "Why did you never tell me it was Robinson all the time? Him just sit in de car and say nothing while you tell me this whole story about Fawn's murder and keeping Molly safe. If I had known, I would have crushed him with these very hands." He let out a bellowing cry of pain. "My cousin's killer right in me own yard and me never know!"

"Your cousin?" Molly said slowly, light dawning on her. "Fawn was your cousin?"

Henley's face was twisted with conflicting emotions. "Derrick-" he reached over and caught the black man's arm. "I never lied to you. I told you that I would come back and get Molly when it was safe. That I would see to it that Fawn's killer got what he deserved. And that's what I did. Robinson is getting what he needs and no one has to fear his passionate nature again."

There was no sound for a while but the sputtering of the kerosene lamp. Each person was lost in their own thoughts, working it out for themselves, now that they knew the facts.

"You're an accessory to the crime," Carson said at last. "What do you think about that?"

"No, I don't think I am." Henley spoke from a deep and private place. "I think I'm an accessory to a new beginning. Personally I think justice is being done." He stood up. "I didn't think I would ever have to explain any of this to anyone but Molly and I thought she would probably see it the way I do. So now it's up to you guys, Carson, Derrick. You can turn me in and get Robinson locked up or we can keep this between the four of us here."

Derrick was the one who broke the ensuing silence. "If I should go to the police, I would also end

237

up in jail because I kept Molly here against her will. In a courtroom it would be kidnapping."

They all nodded in agreement with this line of reasoning and then, one by one, the attention shifted to Carson. "I don't know what I think," he said angrily and then stood up suddenly and stormed across the room and out the door.

"I don't get it." Henley shook his head and relaxed back in his seat now that Carson was gone. "How did he find you here, Molly? I read that postcard before I mailed it from the Montego Bay airport and he couldn't have figured out where you were from that."

Molly grinned for the first time in what felt like hours. "But he did! I gave him some very specific clues." She explained to Henley what she had written and how Carson had figured it out.

Henley gaped in amazement and Derrick laughed aloud. "She one smart girl, dis Molly," he said admiringly.

"Henley- I don't understand why I had to be kept here for a whole week. Why couldn't you have told Derrick to let me go in just a few days?"

"I thought I would be able to get back sooner, but after three or four nights without sleep as well as the whole strain of getting Robinson committed..." he faltered uncomfortably on the last word,"... I just collapsed, I guess. Slept for two full days. I didn't realize how much time had gone by, and besides that, I guess I just wanted to come and explain the whole thing to you in person. When I saw him in there that night...on your back with his hands around your neck..." He cleared his throat a few times. "Well, I guess I just wanted to see you alive and well, I wanted to make sure for myself that you were okay."

Silence settled again, separating them and leaving each one alone with personal thoughts and feelings.

Molly spoke up at last. "I think I knew it was Robinson all along. But I didn't want to admit it, even to myself. I really liked him. Truthfully, I was rather infatuated with him. Even in the short time we knew each other we had a deep connection and I knew he felt I'd betrayed that. I just didn't know how - how sensitive he was."

"He did something to me on the plane ride home that sort of explained to me what he's been going through. I was listening to a reggae tape on my Walkman and all of the sudden he reaches over and turns the volume all the way up so that the music is just blasting in my ears. So I pull the headphones off and still the bass line is just reverberating in my head. And I said, 'What the hell'dja do that for?' and he just reaches over and turns it down again and says, not looking at me, 'That's what it's like for me a lot of the time. Sometimes the music inside my brain just gets so loud that I can't think straight. Sometimes it becomes so deafening that I can't hear the words for the tune.'"

"Poor Robinson." She sighed. "I guess you did the compassionate thing, Henley. I'll never tell anyone about it."

He reached over and gently touched the black and blue mark on her forehead. "I'm sorry about that," he said. "I didn't mean to drop you, but even tied up you were more than I could handle. I didn't mean to knock you out like that."

"Yeah, sure."

"It true, mon. Him nevah leave here until him sure you wake up and not have concussion."

Molly remembered the voices she had heard talking outside that first night and realized that Derrick was right. She knew Henley must have stayed around until the next morning as well because he had mailed her postcard to Negril. Suddenly she was confused and tired of talking. "I

239

think I'd better find Carson," she said and stepped out into the night.

Once her eyes became accustomed to the dark, it was not hard to see his silhouette sitting on a bench across the yard. "Carson?"

"Yeah, I'm over here."

"Are you okay?"

"Yeah, I'm all right."

"What are you thinking about?" She felt for the solid plank of wood and sat down next to him.

"Actually I wasn't thinking about any of this craziness we heard about tonight." There was a funny edge to his voice she could not identify.

"No? Then what?"

"I was thinking about a woman I met after you left Negril. And I was wondering how to tell you about her."

After fighting over who would sleep where, they settled down to a restless night. Molly insisted that Carson have the bed because he had spent the previous night sleeping on the ground. Henley, having anticipated spending the night, had brought an inflatable air mattress with him from the states. He would not hear of Molly making a bed out of a thin blanket on the hard floor and he insisted on her using the air mattress. Derrick overheard the argument from the other room and solved the problem by giving Henley the couch to sleep on and saying he would head up to the lighthouse and sleep in Henry's spare room.

Typical Jamaican hospitality," Henley commented as Derrick packed up to go. "Give up your own bed for a guest. You won't find too many Americans willing to do that."

Despite the comfortable air mattress, Molly did not sleep well. Like a roulette wheel, her mind would spin and then stop on something she had learned that evening and before she had thought it through, the wheel was off and spinning again, only to stop on another new discovery. More than one chapter of her life had ended in the last few hours and she felt a little sad, but a little excited at the same time.

Carson, on the other hand, slept more soundly than he had in many days. After telling Molly about Gwen, he felt light and relaxed. He had found Molly and everything had turned out all right. He fell asleep instantly.

Derrick awoke them at dawn with johnny cakes and coffee." You must be on your way if you want to make Negril by dark," he advised.

It did not take them long to prepare for departure. As anxious as Molly was to put the lighthouse beach behind her, she felt badly about leaving Derrick. He was startled as she threw her arms around his neck and leaped up to kiss him on the mouth.

"Crazy as it seems, I'll miss you," she confided.

"You know I say I want no woman in my life, but you make me think I wrong. You must come back as a friend, Molly."

She let go then and shook her head. Turning to gaze down the path, she could just glimpse the blue waters of the sea sparkling in the early morning sun. No," she said solemnly. "I don't think I'll be back." And then she laughed. "I mean, don't hold your breath. Who knows?"

She climbed into the back seat of the car and waited for the others. Lost in her own thoughts, she did not notice, as Carson did, that Henley pressed a large wad of Jamaican cash into Derrick's hand before climbing into the driver's seat and starting the engine.

"He deserves it," he replied in answer to Carson's questioning look. "I mean, he has nothing and he did me a great favor."

"Oh, I don't know." As they pulled out onto the beach, Carson was again stunned by the pure beauty of this undiscovered piece of paradise. "Personally, I think he has almost everything."

Miss Leola was so overjoyed to see them that she didn't even question why Molly had been held prisoner for a week on a remote peninsula on the eastern end of the island. But as Carson gathered up the belongings he had left behind at Lantana House, he knew that the people back at Mango Grove would not be as easily satisfied as Miss Leola with the mere fact that Molly was alive and well.

It hurt him to think that if he went along with Henley's plan, he would not be able to tell the truth to Gwen and George and Emma, when they had helped him out so much in his search for Molly. And Jazmo, who, just because of what he had gone through, deserved a real answer most of all.

"So what are you planning to tell everyone back at Mango Grove?" he asked Molly, when they finally left Miss Leola and her cooing excitement behind. "I mean, George and Gwen even drove all the way out here with your postcard. Don't you think you owe them an explanation?"

Nervously, Henley glanced up at Molly in the rearview mirror and their eyes met for an instant. Frowning, he brought his attention back to the unpredictable, winding coastal road he was driving and swerved immediately to avoid a nanny goat and her kids who were wandering into his lane.

"Well, I guess we'll just tell them as much of the truth as we can," Molly answered at last. "We'll tell them that after someone tried to murder me, I was kidnapped and held prisoner for seven days by a strange but kindly Jamaican man on the eastern shore of the island." She laughed. "Sounds too fantastic to be true! Nobody'll believe it anyway."

"How will you explain Henley's presence? Or is he just going to drop you off at the gate?" Carson's tone began to take on that old argumentative tone again.

"I suppose he could do that," Molly retorted. "Or I suppose I can say that Henley saved me from someone who was trying to murder me and took me to a friend's house where I recuperated from the trauma and then he came back to bring me home. Only you got there first. Now that's about as true as you can get, Carson. What more do you want?"

They settled into an angry silence, each of them staring out of their respective windows. "I think I'll take a different route home," Henley said in a loud cheerful voice. "I thought I would take this road south from Annotto Bay and meet up with this highway here. I hear it's the best road on the island, flat, straight and fast."

"Fine with me," Carson said in a monotone. "Whatever gets us there quickest."

"Sounds great!" Molly's perky reply was purposely the opposite of Carson's. She leaned over Henley's shoulder and plucked the map out of his hand. "We can see some new parts of the island that way. I'll navigate."

"Anyone mind if we have some tunes?" Henley turned the radio on and cranked it up. They each lapsed into their own thoughts again until the news came on.

"...On the hour, this is Radio RJR news. Police are still looking for a young American girl, missing since last Tuesday when she disappeared from a guesthouse in the Titchfield Hill section of Port Antonio..."

"Shit!" Henley sat up straight. "How did the police get in on this?"

"Well, what the hell would you have done if someone you cared about dropped off the face of the planet? Of course, I went to the police. And the American Embassy. So you better have your story ready for them too." Crossly, Carson slumped down in his seat again. "And if you want to avoid any more problems, you better tell me what it is when you figure it out."

Molly blinked and stared at Carson. His expression hadn't changed. Neither had his attitude. She wasn't sure, but she thought he had just admitted that he was on their side.

"Don't worry, Carson," she quickly assured him. "We've got hours ahead of us. By the time we get to Negril, we'll have it all straight."

After they had passed through Sav-La-Mar, Carson seemed to perk up noticeably. Molly and Henley were both feeling rather hot and irritable, stiff from the long day's drive, so Carson's change in mood was very obvious. The odd, sinking feeling in Molly's stomach indicated that she knew why. Her head was telling her that this was okay, it was better than okay, it was great. But her heart seemed to be saying it would take a little time to fill in the holes, even thought this was what she had been wanting.

"You can drop me off at this road up here," Carson announced to Henley when they were about a mile from Negril.

"Out here?"

"Yeah, this is where I'm staying now. About three or four miles up."

"Well, we can drive you up there." Henley could not conceal his curiosity.

"No, it's really a rough road. It would destroy the suspension of this rental car. Anyway, I don't mind the walk. I've been sitting all day."

Henley went around to the back of the car and took Carson's pack out of the trunk. Not knowing what else to do, Molly also got out as the cloud of dry dust they had raised settled back down onto the shoulder of the road.

"I still have the room at Mango Grove if you guys want to stay there tonight. Miss Faye will give you the key, Molly. You airline ticket is in the top dresser drawer. How soon do you think you'll be going home?"

Molly swallowed hard. "Soon," she managed to say. "Maybe tomorrow or the next day."

Well, I'll come down in the morning and see you then. I guess we have a few more things to talk about." He shouldered his backpack, obviously anxious to be on his way. "Thanks for the ride, Henley. I'll see you tomorrow, Molly."

They stood for a moment and watched him walk towards the hills. "Are you okay?" Henley asked, putting his arm around Molly's shoulder and looking at her closely.

Still watching Carson's retreating figure, her lips tightened and her chin lifted determinedly. "Yes, everything's just how it should be," she answered. Then she turned away quickly and got back into the car.

Henley poked his head in through the window and grinned. "To Oz?"

She grinned back. "To Oz."

They drove on into Negril, Henley laughing and Molly shrieking as he went the wrong direction around the roundabout in the center of town. As they approached Mango Grove, he asked in a carefully casual voice, "Do you mind sharing that room with me tonight?"

She did not answer right away and he pulled up at the gate, waiting for her reply. Two busloads of pale-faced tourists, fresh from the airport, drove by, making the little car fairly vibrate with anticipation.

"Well?"

"No," she replied at last. "I don't mind. In fact," she turned to face him, an impish gleam in her eye, "I'd enjoy spending the evening with you."

Familiar bodies on the other side of the gate had stopped moving from place to place under the mango trees and were peering curiously at the car that was blocking the driveway. They waited patiently, with hands on hips or arms crossed on chests, to see who the new arrivals were who had come to join them for a night, or a week, or a month.

Henley took a deep breath. "Are you ready?"

She nodded, her heart pounding almost visibly. "I'm ready. Let's go." And they drove in through the gate.

57853572R00137

Made in the USA
Charleston, SC
23 June 2016